She gazed at him s
head. "Nathan, what's become of you.

"What do you mean?"

"You've turned cold."

Had he? Well, she didn't know what had been going on with him since they'd parted, either in his life or in his heart.

There was so much he couldn't tell her. About his inn failing, about the fact that his finances were on the ropes, about the feelings he still carried for her...

"I was concerned," he admitted, "when I saw on the news that your cruise ship had hit a reef. In fact, I checked my phone that day to see if you'd called me."

Shoot. He hadn't wanted to admit that.

"I thought of you that day, too," she said softly.

She had?

"Thank you for your thoughts," she continued. "But the best you can do for me is to help us be successful with our show. Come on, Nathan, it's Christmas. Think about the kids."

He *was* thinking about the kids. She had no idea.

Dear Reader,

Welcome to Christmas in New England!

For my first Harlequin Heartwarming novel I wanted to write a holiday story about hope, healing and second chances at love.

Emilie O'Shea is a professional figure skater who's left homeless just before Christmas. Concerned about the young cast of international performers in her care, Emilie takes the only offer of employment she can find: travel to wintry New Hampshire to present their holiday spectacle at a resort in the mountains. The catch? The resort is owned by Nathan Prescott, the man who broke her heart two Christmases ago.

Nathan Prescott has put his unlikely romance with Emilie behind him. Nathan, a consulting accountant, never expected to fall for a free-spirited performer with few family roots. He shouldn't have been surprised when she refused to accompany him home when his life's goal finally came to fruition: he was able to buy back Prescott Inn, the resort founded by his grandfather.

But the hotel has too many empty rooms this holiday season, and finances are tight. Nathan's cost-cutting endeavors have earned him the nickname Mr. Scrooge. Only Emilie seems to be able to lighten his heart, even as her figure-skating troupe upends his staid plans and breathes life into his world again.

Can he prove to her that she's worth more than his business to him? Dare he hope that this time, she'll choose to stay?

Enjoy the show!

All the best,

Cathryn Parry

HEARTWARMING

Christmas at Prescott Inn

——

Cathryn Parry

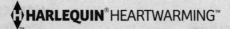

Recycling programs
for this product may
not exist in your area.

ISBN-13: 978-1-335-63391-0

Christmas at Prescott Inn

Copyright © 2018 by Cathryn Parry

Printed in U.S.A.

Cathryn Parry writes contemporary romance from her home in Massachusetts. Her Harlequin Superromance novels have received such honors as a Booksellers' Best Award, HOLT Medallion Awards of Merit and several Readers' Choice Award nominations. In her free time, she loves figure skating, planning as many vacations as possible and pursuing her genealogy hobby. For more information about upcoming releases and to sign up for a new-book-alert email, please visit her website at cathrynparry.com.

Books by Cathryn Parry

Harlequin Superromance

Summer by the Sea
The Undercover Affair
The Good Mom
The Secret Between Them
Secret Garden
Scotland for Christmas
The Sweetest Hours
Out of His League
The Long Way Home
Something to Prove

Visit the Author Profile page
at Harlequin.com for more titles.

To Otis, who sat with me through every book, every late-night session, every sunny afternoon on the back porch.

You were a very special cat, and a true member of our family. You'll be forever missed.

CHAPTER ONE

CHRISTMAS ARRIVED AT Prescott Inn the day after Thanksgiving.

Nathan Prescott stepped into the lobby just in time to see two workers erecting a large blue spruce tree. The sharp smell of pine needles wafted to his nose. The annoyingly upbeat jingle of seasonal music—Bing Crosby singing "White Christmas"—met his ears.

Nathan frowned. He didn't mind if Christmas never came this year.

The inn's rooms weren't filling up. Expenses were excessive. He was worried about his investors' meeting tomorrow and what they would decide. They'd already threatened once to shut down his line of credit.

Nothing could be worse than that.

Gloom descended over his heart.

"A cup of warm spiced cider, Mr. Prescott?" His front desk clerk held out a mug that steamed with the scent of apple and cinnamon. She gave him a tentative smile.

Nathan just shook his head and continued walking toward his office.

As he strode past the stone fireplace, the commotion of tree-decorating and decking-the-halls continued around him unabated. He scowled as a worker brought in a crate of red poinsettia plants.

More money spent—expenses his investors expected him to be cutting. But as he opened his mouth to refuse the delivery, a movement behind the lobby couch caught his eye.

Nathan paused. A dark-haired boy, about six or seven years old, popped up his head. A look of terror appeared in his hazel eyes.

He recognized the boy as one of the kids from the homeless shelter. During the winter months, Nathan housed some families with young children from the shelter. This particular boy had moved in with his mother the week before Thanksgiving. His mother never seemed to be around—working, Nathan supposed. He'd noticed the boy because he always seemed interested in what was happening around the inn.

As I was at his age, Nathan thought.

Nathan should have kept walking. But the small portrait of his grandfather, Philip

Prescott, seemed to wink down at him and ask him to stay.

The boy flushed and pointed to a round, red Christmas ornament. "It fell down," he stammered to Nathan, retrieving the delicate antique and carefully placing its metal hook around a sturdy branch of the spruce tree, cut down from a forest on the mountain. Both Nathan and the boy stared at the partially decorated tree. It still needed lights. And a star for the top, but the decorators would get to that.

Nathan balled his fists in his pocket. The kid seemed so lonely, always hanging around by himself and watching whatever activity was going on in the lobby. "You like Christmas?" Nathan asked gruffly.

The boy dipped his head, but he nodded. There was a short silence between them.

"Well…" Nathan wasn't great with kids. And he was usually so busy doing the best he could for his employees and for the shelter families, which to his mind meant putting a roof over their heads and food on the table.

"Where are the stockings?" the boy suddenly asked. He stared directly at Nathan.

"Ah…"

The boy glanced at the stone fireplace, the

centerpiece of the inn's lobby. "The stockings," he repeated. "For Santa Claus."

Nathan's heart sank. The boy still believed in Santa. He was so young. Nathan couldn't bear to see the kid's heart get crushed with the truth. "Well, those don't go up until Christmas Eve." Nathan coughed, remembering his own childhood here, and added, "That's the tradition at Prescott Inn." He nodded to his grandfather's portrait.

The boy chewed his lip, looking thoughtful. "Is there an extra one I can borrow?" he asked in a small voice. "We didn't bring our Christmas things with us."

Nathan's heart was in his throat. He waited for more from the boy, but he just gazed at Nathan with his huge brown eyes.

The boy's situation reminded Nathan so much of his own childhood—of himself and his sister as children—left alone by their parents and living here in Prescott Inn, which was still owned in those days by their grandfather. Nathan's grandfather had been the person who'd given them stability. A place to set down roots. A refuge amid all the confusion.

"I'll get you a stocking," Nathan promised. "With your name on it."

"Jason," the boy said.

Nathan nodded. "Jason," he repeated.

Jason smiled and then darted over to the crate of multicolored ornaments. Nathan realized that they'd made a deal, the two of them. And now he had to honor it.

More cuts. I can think of more cuts to make. More ways to slash the budget and increase revenue for the holiday season.

Head down, Nathan changed course away from his office and descended the stairs that led to the newly designed breakfast lounge. Yes, they'd paid entirely too much money for this renovation, but that was water under the bridge. Right now, the important thing was to prepare an action plan for tomorrow's meeting.

Nathan pushed through the swinging doors to the kitchen. One of the waitresses jerked her head up and glanced at him with a worried expression.

"Have you seen Nell?" he asked. Nell was his marketing manager. Actually, she was his niece. Just a dozen years his junior—Nathan's sister, his only sibling, was eight years older than Nathan—Nell was fresh out of college. But she was the best he could afford for the inn on a shoestring budget. And he had an important job that he needed Nell to do.

"No, sir. I haven't seen her." The waitress smiled wanly at him and nodded before hurrying off.

Nathan glanced around at the empty dining room and buffet area.

The chef wasn't at his station. Neither was the under-chef.

Nell, who usually met him each morning to sit down and review the front desk reports, wasn't present, either.

"Hello!" he called out. He had a right to be upset. Was he the only one concerned about keeping the inn up and running?

Two years ago, it had been a miracle when he'd managed to assemble a group of investors to buy the sprawling resort complex at auction. The previous owner had bought it from Nathan's father after he'd squandered his inheritance. Between the two of them, they'd run the place into the ground.

Prescott was Nathan's family name. Prescott Inn had been started by his grandfather. Nathan had a lot of work ahead to bring it back to the stable business that it was in his grandfather's day. But first he had to keep it open through Christmas.

"Hello?" he called once more.

No one answered him.

Was something wrong?

Cocking his ear, he pushed open the kitchen door and heard the telltale sound of a television news show coming from the direction of the bar. Following the trail, Nathan headed past the near-empty breakfast lounge and walked into the bar alcove beside the lower-level portion of the great stone fireplace. There was a slight chill in late November, but he'd told the staff to wait before ordering the wood for the fireplace, as the price of wood was astronomical.

There was his kitchen staff, standing around the wall-mounted television set intended for guests. The morning chef, the morning under-chef, and one of his waitresses.

And Nell.

"What's going on?" he asked quietly.

"Oh!" Nell started. The two chefs in their clogs and white uniforms cast their eyes down sheepishly and quickly headed back toward the kitchen.

"Look what's happened, Uncle Nathan,"

Nell said, pointing at the television. "It's a real disaster!"

"No, *this* is the disaster." Nathan crossed his arms. "Our inn. By the way, how is your marketing assignment going? It's almost Christmas and we have to figure out how to fill the rooms for the holiday. The investors are going to ask me tomorrow for specifics, and I want to give them some results from the plan we discussed."

Nell stared at him as if not comprehending. Then she turned back to the television. "Didn't you work on a cruise ship once, Uncle?"

"A… *Why?*" Blinking, Nathan followed her gaze. On the television screen, he saw what appeared to be a bird's-eye view of a large ship lying tilted at an angle—half sunk—in a postcard-perfect, azure-blue sea.

He blinked in disbelief. "Is that a *cruise* ship?"

"Yes, it is. Last night it hit a reef in the Caribbean and flooded. They had to evacuate almost eight thousand people in the darkness. Can you imagine? It's horrible. All those people facing that trauma."

Emilie! Does she still work on a cruise ship?

He swallowed, staring at the television screen.

Nothing seemed to be happening now, from what he could see. "Is everyone safely off?"

Nell tilted her head at him. "They think so, but they're not sure. What was the name of the ship you were on, Uncle? You were on one for several months, right?"

Yes, he'd been a staff accountant on the *Empress Caribbean*. But it had been longer than several months—just over a year. "Doesn't matter," he murmured. He'd left that job two Christmases ago, when he'd bought Prescott Inn. He rarely spoke of his onboard experience to anyone.

"What ship is that?" he asked Nell, gesturing toward the television. He squinted at the screen, but the shot from the news station's helicopter was too far away for him to see the name on the side. But the red-and-blue logo looked awfully familiar.

"Um, they said it's the *Empress Caribbean*. What's wrong?" Nell blinked and then stepped toward him. He must have gone pale. He certainly felt light-headed. "Oh, Uncle. Is *that* where you worked? The *Empress Caribbean*?"

He dragged in a breath, not wanting to answer her.

He swallowed instead, staring at the television screen. *What if Emilie still works on board?* Fear coursed through his blood.

A Coast Guard ship was parked near the vessel. His mind flashed back to the safety drills he'd practiced with the crew and passengers. One per week. Nathan hadn't technically been part of the crew—his job had been to prepare a report on how the company could cut onboard costs. Ironic, considering the situation he found himself in now.

A newscaster in the background droned on about the specifications of the ship. Year launched, tonnage, number of crew, passenger capacity. Nathan could have recited all that himself.

"When will they know if everyone got off all right?" he asked Nell.

"They didn't say." Nell stared at him in curiosity. "Are you all right?"

"I'm fine." His stomach felt as if it was turning inside out as he took out his phone to check his messages.

Nothing. No calls or texts.

Emilie's contact number was still in his phone, but she hadn't called him. She'd never called him in the two years since he'd left the ship. He didn't even know why he kept her name in his phone.

She'd left *him*, and it had been years since he'd last seen her. Ironically, again, she'd accused him of choosing the inn over her.

She'd been wrong. And it had hurt.

He swallowed, not wanting to think about those days. There was no reason to expect she would ever call him again, even in an emergency. He needed to focus on his inn's survival, which should be his top concern.

"Uncle," Nell said gently. "They're reporting that, so far, there are no major casualties."

"That's a relief."

"Are you *sure* you don't have any friends there?"

He stiffened. He'd purposely never spoken of the year he'd spent at sea as an accountant—never mind the show skater he'd fallen in love with and had wanted to marry.

It had been insanity on his part, and he was no longer insane.

Two curious faces stared back at him—Nell's and the waitress's. Nathan just shook his head at them. "No. That wasn't my ship."

Still, he was irritated with himself for opening this can of worms with his staff in the first place. Wishing to deflect any further questions, he asked sharply, "Nell, I'd like that update on the competitive analysis of other resorts I asked for. How far have you progressed?"

"Um…" Nell said. "About that…"

"Please take more initiative," he instructed her, disliking that he was speaking so brusquely. But since Nell had no information for him, he would have to fudge those details at tomorrow's investors' meeting. "You and I will discuss this further tomorrow after my meeting. Clear?"

Nell visibly sighed at him. But she nodded.

A pang went through him. She looked so much like his sister. He wanted to be good to her, but he was helping her the only way he knew how. He'd reopened Prescott Inn and had given her a job when she hadn't any prospects.

That was how he could help people. Through business. Nathan took care of business.

Even if he didn't seem to be doing such a great job of it at the moment.

Without a word, he turned and walked back through the empty dining room and toward his private office, which was on the second floor of the lodge, overlooking the lobby.

Usually, numbers were his friends. But of late, they didn't have anything positive to say to him. He knew before he even checked them what tale they would tell.

His business was in the red. It was bleeding money. And for the first time in his life, he couldn't seem to stanch it.

I can't fail, he reminded himself, the sweat breaking out on his forehead even though the room was still cold.

He put his head in his hands as his mind flashed backed to the kid. Jason.

Nathan might not be able to give him long-term security, but if Nathan could just keep the inn open long enough to provide refuge for the boy through Christmas, then maybe he wouldn't feel like he had failed.

He'd been so proud when Prescott Inn had first reopened. The local newspaper had compared Nathan to his grandfather, Philip Prescott, and touted the renewed hope Nathan was bringing to their depressed mountain town. Nathan had believed he could do that. After all, he'd had a successful career advising companies on how to cut costs and balance their books.

Now Nathan had to live up to the promises he'd given everyone two years ago. He had to figure out a story to sell to his investors to keep the money coming in, and before

tomorrow's meeting, in order to turn this disaster around.

As for Emilie…well, he shouldn't worry
about her. He had no reason to believe that she
still sailed aboard the *Empress Caribbean*. She
could have left that job and gone anywhere.

She wouldn't be thinking of him, that was
for certain. She'd made that much clear the last
time they had spoken.

CHAPTER TWO

Two thousand miles south of Nathan, on a small island in the Caribbean Sea, Emilie O'Shea hurried across the beach, toward the medical station.

Streaks of orange ran across a beautiful azure sky as morning broke over the horizon.

Nature's beauty contrasted sharply with the semiorganized chaos on the tropical island, where ship's officers and crew from the *Empress Caribbean* had led the passengers after the evacuation. The ship was now disabled, lying on its side about a mile offshore.

Emilie had spent ten years living on Empress Cruise Line's ships, and she'd never heard of such a thing happening, to any of the company's vessels. The whole night had felt surreal.

Since they'd landed on the beach ten hours ago, the ship's crew had been herding the passengers, group by group, to boats ferrying them to an adjoining island, which had an airport.

Emilie and her troupe of nine other figure skaters had been part of that process, but thankfully Emilie had been able to send the troupe for a much-needed break to a gym across the island, where they were bedded down in cots.

But Emilie herself couldn't rest yet. Hurrying across the open beach, the morning sand cool on her feet, she found the doctor's tent. Dr. David was on duty. Emilie knew him because there was always a member of the medical staff stationed backstage during their figure skating shows, just as a precaution.

At the moment, Dr. David seemed to be finishing up splinting a child's sprained wrist. Emilie waited until the child and her parents had departed and Dr. David motioned her inside the tent.

"I never thought I'd see the day," he murmured, shaking his head. "We're actually shipwrecked!"

"At least everybody's safe and accounted for." She shivered, thinking of all the passengers who'd been in the skating rink when the alarm had sounded. Luckily, they'd all escaped safely. The skaters in her troupe were safe, too, and that's what Emilie felt most responsible for. She got to the point of her visit and pulled out her phone. "I'm here because I'm worried about Katya. She fell when the ship hit the sandbar, and I want to show you the footage."

"I already checked her shoulder, Emilie," Dr. David said gently. "She'll have a big bruise, but as long as she takes care of it with ice and rest, Katya will be fine in a few days."

Emilie had thought so, too, but… "Now she's complaining about a really bad headache. She said it hurt too much to walk over with me to see you. What if she struck her head when she fell?"

Dr. David gave her a look of concern. "When did the headache start?"

"About an hour ago. I asked her if she hit her head, but she says she can't remember." Emilie took a breath. Katya seemed so fragile and distraught that it was scaring Emilie. "I have a video from last night's performance, but it was so dark inside the ice theater, I can't really tell what happened to Katya. I'd like you to look at it, if you don't mind. And maybe you could come to the gym and check on her again?"

Dr. David held out his hand for the phone. "Let me see the video." He eyed Emilie curiously. "Where did you get the footage, anyway? I thought no one was supposed to tape the shows."

"I got it from a passenger," she admitted.

"And no, they're not supposed to tape our shows. But when the guy showed it to me, I wheedled a copy from him."

Dr. David laughed. "You're always the charmer where the passengers are concerned," he teased. He knew she had a large email list of former audience members who followed her upbeat online blog postings.

Unfortunately, that would have to be curtailed, at least until she got another laptop. Hers was currently underwater, along with all her other things.

Clothes, photos, memorabilia…and a certain gold necklace.

Emilie blinked away the moisture in her eyes. *Stay positive*, she chided herself. She brought up the video on her phone—thankfully *that* had been collected by one of her quick-thinking skaters—and settled beside Dr. David to view the scene once again.

The recording was shaky and also dark because the house lights were down. Taken by an audience member, it showed the tops of people's heads mostly. They'd had a full show last night—every seat on three sides of the rectangular ice stage had been filled. The ice surface, just one third the size of the indoor rink Emilie had skated on during her childhood in

Florida, was lit with colorful spotlights, moving fast over the ice. A theatrical fog machine gave the appearance that the skaters were stepping from a festive holiday dream.

Emilie fast-forwarded the video to the end of the second number of the troupe's new Christmas spectacular. It was a high-energy number involving all the members of her company—five males and five females. The troupe consisted of two pairs teams, an ice dance team, two mixed singles skaters who sometimes paired off for dance numbers, plus two more spotlight soloists.

Watching them perform the familiar choreography, Emilie felt a quick burst of pride. They'd been hitting all their marks in the new show. The transitions had been moving smoothly, and up to that point, the performance had been going off without a hitch.

Gasps of awe went up from the audience as the show segued to a solo from Katya and her partner, Sergei—the star pairs team originally from Russia. They entered the ice with a majestic lift and throw.

At that moment, Emilie had been helping Julie, her champion singles skater, change from her snowflake headdress and into the costume for her next number. But she couldn't help pausing to watch the pairs team, peeking through the curtains to check that all was well with the new number, the first time Katya and Sergei had ever performed it live.

Emilie was the group's ice captain. At twenty-eight, she was the ancient member of the troupe, affectionately nicknamed the "Ice Mom," because she took care of the others. She considered the role a privilege. Along with skating in the shows, she was also the liaison with the ship's production manager and the skaters' production company, who employed them. But Emilie took her duties even further than that. She considered the troupe her own little family, and did whatever she could to make them happy.

Last night, all the skaters had been nervous because it was their first time performing the show in front of an audience. They were the only troupe in the fleet performing this particular number, and Emilie was on the line for its success.

She'd been eager for the opportunity to prove herself. Performers on cruise ships were usually required to retire by their early thirties, so Emilie had to think about her next steps. She hoped to be hired as a choreographer by the production company that put together the shows for the cruise line. And if her troupe succeeded, so would she. If they didn't…well, the business was cutthroat. There were extremely few openings for choreographers.

And until the accident, the audience had been loving the show. There'd been lots of kids present, which was always great. Their enthusiasm fed Emilie. If not for the pleasure she gave to the audience, she probably would never have picked skating as her career. The audience *had* to be happy.

Squinting at the screen, Emilie focused on Katya. The petite pairs skater with the intricate blond braids looked the part of the ice princess she was playing. Delicately, Katya stepped into a spin.

"There! Stop the video!" Emilie said. She jabbed her finger at the screen of her phone, but she wasn't quick enough—Dr. David moved the phone away from her.

"Not yet, I want to see this," he said.

On the video, the ship shuddered and gasps rang out from the audience.

Katya tumbled from her spin, and before Sergei could catch her, she slammed sideways into the boards.

Dr. David paused the video and then backed it up, moving it forward in slow motion. "Katya doesn't hit her head," he murmured.

"See? No part of her head ever touches a hard surface. Maybe she experienced some whiplash, though. Are her pupils dilated?"

"No," Emilie answered, thinking back to her own examination of Katya. Dr. David had taught Emilie the basics of checking for concussions. "She just says she has a headache. I want to be sure it isn't anything serious."

"Once my replacement shows up—hopefully in the next twenty minutes—I'll head over to the gym to take another look at her."

"Thank you," Emilie said quietly.

"I'm sure she's fine, but until I get there, I'll send you back with more ice. First, though, do you mind if I watch the rest of this video?"

Emilie winced. She'd only been able to watch the rest of the video once. It was far too painful for her to see again. "It's just chaos," she murmured. But it was more than that. It was the end of her troupe.

"You guys should be proud," Dr. David remarked. "I heard from the security officer that your team evacuated the ice studio much faster than anyone expected."

Yes, the troupe had done an exceptional job under horrible circumstances.

Dr. David touched her phone to start the video again.

Katya lay on the ice for only a moment. As her troupe had often practiced, Gary, their other male pairs skater, dashed forward and escorted Katya behind the curtain.

At the time, Emilie had checked her natural instinct to run over and check on Katya herself—that was a nasty fall—but she was too well-trained to actually do so. There were other professionals on hand for that. They handled such falls fairly often, unfortunately, due to the rocking of the ship at sea. The show must go on.

But she'd known this wasn't just choppy seas. The ship had shuddered again, and Emilie had grabbed the railing. The overhead lights started flashing. Not a good sign.

"Hey, Emilie," Gary, the big ice dancer, had said in her ear. "Which emergency signal is this one?"

"I don't remember," she'd answered. There were so many to keep track of. She'd had to think for a minute. Different blasts and codes meant different things. There were signals for cardiac arrests and "man overboard" crises and general security warnings. They'd even turned back to port once or twice during her years at sea, but this…

Seven short drones on the ship's horn sounded, followed by one long blast.

"Crew and guests assemble at muster stations," Bill, their cruise ship director spoke over the ship-wide intercom.

"It's the evacuate ship signal!" Emilie realized.

"No way!" Gary said. "That's only for drills!"

"Trust me, this is no drill." Emilie slammed on her plastic skate guards so she could run off to assist passengers.

"Everyone to the muster station!" she shouted to the audience as loud as she could. She leaped over the rink's railing, still in her glittery elf costume, and began to usher the audience out of the auditorium.

Incredibly, the startled passengers paid heed to her.

Emilie gave silent thanks for all the evacuation drills she'd been forced to endure over the years. She and her skaters knew exactly what to do.

"Is everyone cleared from the area?" she asked Gary once the room was nearly empty. He'd nodded, expression tight with the urgency of the situation.

"I scoured the seats one last time—we're clear up top. The security officers are scanning passenger keycards, so they'll know if anyone is missing. The rest of the troupe is already at our muster station. They're starting to launch the boats. It's time to go, Emilie."

The ship had begun to list, so she let Gary grip her wrist and pull her down the hallway, toward the stairwell.

The ship made another jerky pitch, and Emilie bumped into a corner rail. Gary tumbled against her. The two were in a crazy position, tangled as if they were lovers, and for several seconds, they'd been stuck there, suspended in time.

They both laughed nervously.

She'd never had any romantic thoughts about Gary—he was like a brother to her. But her mind shifted to Nathan Prescott in an instant. The only man who'd held her and kissed her on this romantic cruise ship. And for a moment, she felt as if he was right there with her again. But her months with Nathan had been a crazy time of happy infatuation. They'd been in love with each other, and maybe a little bit in love with love itself. Then he'd left.

Gary pulled her to her feet, as the evacuation announcement sounded again. They made it above deck and waded through the crowd to their muster station.

The video ended abruptly, and Emilie shook herself out of her own memories.

They were all safe now. This issue with Katya was hopefully surmountable, with Dr. David's help. She needed to trust in him and be grateful.

Dr. David stared at the still shot for a moment, and then handed her the phone back.

"I hope you and your skaters land on your feet after this, Emilie," Dr. David said.

"We will," she answered, though inwardly she was less certain.

Her troupe's home, possessions and performance venue were now a hundred feet below water. The ship was damaged enough that it wouldn't be repaired anytime soon, if it was repaired at all. Yes, there were ten other ships in the fleet, but all of them were fully staffed with ice-skaters. Emilie and her troupe were homeless. They had no prospects—they were jobless. At best, the cruise line would probably want to send the entertainers back to their far-flung hometowns and terminate their contracts.

Realistically, Emilie's performance career would likely be over. She was nearing retirement age, and was the oldest of her troupe. And with no way to prove herself, she didn't have a hope of advancing to her dream job as an entertainment choreographer.

Dr. David patted her shoulder and handed her an ice pack to give to Katya. "Something will come along. Be thankful it wasn't worse." Another little girl was stumbling across the beach toward the medical tent, crying, accompanied by what looked to be her grandmother. A reporter tried to catch the grandmother for a comment, but the woman waved him off. Emilie had seen a few camera crews on the island trying to get the story. "I'll be along to see Katya as soon as I can," Dr. David promised.

Nodding mechanically, Emilie gathered herself to return to the gym and her troupe. She did her best to put a smile on her face.

"Take care of yourself, Emilie," Dr. David called after her. "If for some reason I don't see you again, enjoy Christmas!"

Yes, she reminded herself. Christmas was a time of hope.

And nothing was more important than hope.

"So, HAVE WE lost our jobs?" Katya asked. She lay beneath a thin blanket on a rickety metal cot, looking distraught and frail.

Emilie passed Katya the ice pack she'd received from Dr. David and sat beside her on an empty cot. "Honestly? Probably, yes. But it's just for the moment until I think of an idea to keep us all together," she said in a soothing tone.

"Do you really believe you can find us something else?"

"I do." Emilie checked Katya's shoulder. Her bruise seemed to be looking angrier.

She gave Katya her brightest smile. Years of practice hid her doubts.

Katya seemed to relax. The lines of her forehead smoothed out, and her breathing seemed less shallow.

On the inside, though, Emilie was worried. She'd heard word on the walk back to their little camp that she and her troupe would have to stay inside this gym for at least another day. Emilie could think of worse places to be marooned, but her troupe was getting restless. They'd want answers soon.

Emilie gazed into her wounded skater's eyes, checking again for dilated pupils, but didn't see anything wrong. "Dr. David said he'll be over as soon as he can."

Katya closed her eyes and sighed.

"The diving performers are being flown home to Australia this afternoon," Gary murmured beside Emilie, his voice matter-of-fact.

"How do you know that?" Emilie whispered, standing to face him so that Katya couldn't see.

Gary shrugged. "Their booking agent called the dive captain and told him," he murmured back.

Emilie nodded and subconsciously patted the pocket of her jacket, where her phone was zipped. She'd already spoken to Lynn, their manager at the production company, just to let her know that everyone on the team was safe and accounted for. Lynn hadn't said a word about the future, though, and Emilie had been too traumatized to think of asking at the time.

At least Curtis, the male half of their ice dance team, had kept his wits and remembered to gather up the skaters' phones, jackets and street shoes. They may not have clothes—indeed, Emilie still wore her Santa's elf costume—but at least they weren't still in skates, and they'd been able to use their phones to contact loved ones.

"Hey, what are you two whispering about?" Katya asked. "If you know something, tell us!"

The other skaters gathered around her, too, pressing for details.

She explained what Gary had said about the divers. "But, guys, the other entertainers are in a different situation. They work for a different production company." She made a mental note to call Lynn again in Colorado Springs, where their production company was located. She didn't want to do it within hearing of her team, though.

"My parents were supposed to visit me on the Christmas sailing," Curtis remarked. The rugged ice dancer was from a small town in Nova Scotia and hadn't seen his family in nearly six months. Curtis sat on a nearby cot, put his elbows on his knees and gazed up at Emilie. "Do you think Empress Cruises will let them change their booking to whatever ship we're on next?"

Emilie doubted they'd be assigned to another ship, but she didn't want Curtis to worry.

"We'll cross that bridge when we come to it," Emilie reassured him. "Wherever we end up, we'll work to get your parents there for Christmas with us, too."

"They're going to dismiss us all and send us home, aren't they?" Lynette turned to Emilie. Lynette was Curtis's dance partner. "There *are* no other ships to put us on. Think of it, guys. Every ship is already staffed for the season."

"I cannot go home!" Katya sat up and looked at Emilie in alarm. "Please! We have to find a place *somewhere*."

Emilie swallowed. Katya had confided to

Emilie that she desperately needed this job to help her family at home. She sent money every month to her mother and grandmother.

Katya's skating partner, Sergei, said something to her in Russian, which Emilie didn't understand. The two held a quiet conversation.

Emilie touched Katya's arm. "What's he saying?"

"That he doesn't want to go home, either. He wants to stay with me. You must do something for us, Emilie. Please."

Sergei was usually the one to keep Katya calm and happy. It had always surprised Emilie that they didn't have more than a platonic relationship.

Katya gave a soft cry and put her hand on her mouth. "All my papers are in the safe in the room!" She stared wildly at Emilie. "All our things are gone—at the bottom of the ocean! What will we do?"

"It's all right. I've kept copies of your paperwork in my computer." Emilie felt Katya's forehead. Thankfully, she didn't seem to have a fever. "You should get some rest. I'll help you work it out once we get off the island."

"But your computer is at the bottom of the ocean, too!"

"Electronic backups for all our files are in

the cloud." Emilie gestured upward. "It's safe." Saved were copies of everyone's information—visas and paperwork and even costume measurements. Skate sizes, too—not that that mattered since they had all evacuated the ship wearing their skates.

"So, you can help us find a new ship?" Katya asked, her face hopeful. "Yes?"

"You're the Ice Mom." Gary rose a brow at her.

"Yes, I certainly am." Emilie smiled. "Don't listen to the gossip from the diving team or the dancers, either. Listen to me. I'll call our production company right now and see what they can do for us."

"Thank you, Emilie." Katya leaned back in her cot. She seemed pale. Emilie made a mental note to be here when Dr. David showed up.

She turned to Gary, her de facto assistant. "Gary, you're in charge while I'm gone. Please make sure that everyone sticks together. I'll be back shortly."

She headed again for the beach, this time to make her call.

She *would* keep them together. Last year had been a depressing Christmas because it had been the anniversary of her breakup with

Nathan. She had vowed that this season would be different.

She *would* keep her skaters together, at least through Christmas. She didn't know how, but she would make it happen.

Then she caught sight of the reporter she'd seen earlier. He was still trying to record eyewitness accounts of the accident.

Maybe he'd like to see an eyewitness video…

"Hello!" She waved to the young man.

Immediately he trotted across the sand to her. "You're a skater!" he remarked.

"Yes." She smoothed the skirt of her elf costume. "We haven't had time to change yet." She held out her hand. "I'm Emilie."

"Joseph." He shook her hand vigorously, then fiddled with his phone screen. "Would you mind if I asked you some questions? I've heard about you all in the troupe. One of the passengers was raving about you—said you were heroes. Her family was at the skating show."

"We just did what we were trained to do," Emilie said.

"Yes, but you made sure everyone was evacuated quickly and safely. And you were calm."

"The passengers were great." Emilie dug out

her phone. "Would you like to see video of it? A passenger shared it with me. He said he planned to put it online when he gets home. I can give you the link once it's up."

"That would be fabulous." Joseph smiled gratefully. "I promise I won't record it."

Ten minutes later, after he'd seen the video for himself, he prodded Emilie to speak to him for a recorded interview.

She talked about her troupe's dilemma. She did the best she could to pitch their need for a home for Christmas. Or at least a job.

It was the best she could think of to do for her skaters. She hoped it was enough.

CHAPTER THREE

THE NEXT MORNING, Nathan met with his investors at his local savings and loan.

Rob, his principal investor and also the bank's director, didn't mince words. "Nathan, unless you can turn the cash flow around in the next two weeks, we'll be putting Prescott Inn on the market at the end of December."

No!

"Take a look at my plans before you discuss that step," Nathan said, gazing from face to face at the four men seated around the table. He wouldn't give up without a fight. "There's no need to make any drastic decisions just yet. Let me walk you through the numbers." He passed out the reports he'd prepared for each investor. "Start with the expenses I've earmarked to cut."

Rob reluctantly reached for his copy and flipped to the table that bulleted the list of Nathan's proposed tactics.

"It's a start," Rob remarked. "But you have

to keep going. And you also need marketing ideas that don't cost money. The rooms don't fill themselves."

"We do have ideas, great ones," Nathan assured him. He thought of Nell and the marketing research he'd assigned her. For now, though, he held up a second bound report, which he'd received from his property consultant this past summer. "This study describes all of our winter facilities and their state of repair as well as future maintenance needs. My team is currently looking into targeted promotion and free publicity for the low-expense venues as appropriate. These efforts will increase bookings for the holiday season."

"Ah. You're talking about the sleigh rides and such." B.G. Richards, one of the minor investors, reached for the report, smiling with nostalgia at the photo on the cover. "My kids are looking forward to using the ice rink this Christmas. Will it be open to the community?"

Finally, Nathan had an ally. He directed his attention on B.G.—a local construction manager and family man who supported the homeless shelter and had a pretty big heart when it came to kids. "As you know, B.G., that's a big part of the reason I led this effort to purchase the inn—to keep the use of the facilities in the community and allow access to the local children."

B.G. nodded, but of the five of them present at the meeting, Rob was the majority investor, and he was scowling at Nathan. Nathan modified his approach. "Of course, we will close the rink if necessary—and any other facility—if it helps the short-term cash flow. At least until we get back on our feet." He stared hard at Rob. "Rest assured, I'm prepared to do whatever is fiscally necessary to turn this crisis around."

Rob nodded with satisfaction. He seemed to like that Nathan had used the word *crisis*.

"That ice rink B.G. mentioned is expensive to keep up," Rob remarked, closing the cover of his report. "As the property consultant noted, there are maintenance costs. Electricity." He crossed his arms and stared at Nathan. "I think you should take a look at that expense first."

"All right," Nathan said. "But I'm asking for your continued patience with my overall plans. Right now, we're performing an analysis of the winter programs our competitors are offering so we can better gauge which facilities Prescott Inn should keep open." He glanced around the table. "My plan for the turnaround is good. It will bear fruit."

"Very well. We'll meet again next week and

review your progress." Rob stood, signaling the end of the discussion. "It goes without saying that any mention of Prescott Inn's financial precariousness will not be discussed outside of this room."

They all nodded. The group of five disbanded.

Nathan raked his hand through his hair as he left the savings and loan and headed to the inn's Jeep, the resort's logo emblazoned on the side of the vehicle.

He felt as if he'd been body-slammed. He tried not to show it outwardly, but this meeting was official notification of his worst nightmare come true. All that Nathan had earned today was a reprieve. And a warning to prepare himself for the worst.

All he'd wanted had been to buy and reopen his grandfather's inn. For two years, he'd managed to hold on to that dream. He still hoped he could keep it going. But time was running out.

As Nathan drove through town, people waved at him from the sidewalk.

I can still stop Rob from closing the inn. I have until Christmas. Like Rob said, I can come up with even more programs to cut.

Nathan pulled his Jeep in front of the inn's entrance and left the engine idling as he reached into his briefcase and again pulled out the report from the property consultant.

Frank, their valet parking attendant who was also their bellhop, came up to the window. "Park the car for you, Mr. Prescott?"

"No, thanks, Frank. Could you please go inside and tell Nell to come out and join me? I'm moving our meeting from the conference room into the Jeep."

He wanted to personally check out the outdoor winter facilities. Maybe a drive into the mountains and fresh air would clear his head.

Should he shut the skating rink or not? That was his biggest outdoor activity expense.

"Sure thing, Mr. Prescott. I'll let Nell know right away."

Frank backed away and then turned sharply before he headed inside. Nathan half expected Frank to give him a smart salute. Frank had been so happy to have his job back from the old days that he'd shaken Nathan's hand every morning since then.

It made Nathan sad to think of it now.

Nathan took the bound property consultant's report and then got out of the Jeep to circle around to the passenger seat. Once there, he flipped through the pages again while he waited for Nell.

Finally, she came running through the inn door and headed toward him, zipping up her winter coat and swinging her purse over her shoulder as if it was the best morning of her life.

He was glad someone was happy.

"What's going on?" she asked, out of breath.

"You drive," he directed. "We're heading up the mountain road. We have to make some cuts, so the skating rink is the first item on the list to consider. If necessary we'll put up a Closed sign in front of the entrance. We can pick it up from the facilities shed."

Her eyes widened at the news. Seeming hesitant, she got inside and then adjusted the driver's seat, pushing it forward. "Um, I thought we were going to have a strategy session about my marketing research?" she asked nervously.

"We are. We'll talk about your findings and your ideas for promotion while we drive. Just make sure they're low-cost." He fidgeted with his report, impatient. He loved his niece, but at such a critical moment for the inn, he wished he could also afford a marketing manager with experience. Still, Nell had energy and enthusiasm, and she was family. She had just graduated with a degree in hotel and hospitality management. So maybe she had some ideas for him. He *needed* good ideas.

He held up the bound report that he'd shown his investor team. "After we visit the skating rink, we'll swing by the base of the cross-country ski trail. I want to assess the current condition of the fencing. Plus, I want to see the sleigh and make sure the barn where it's housed is still in good condition."

Nell wiped her hair from her eyes and pressed her lips together. Without a word, she adjusted her seat belt and flicked on her seat warmer. It was cold in the Jeep. Their breath made steamy puffs in the frigid air.

Still no snow outside, though. Not even a flake.

She turned the Jeep out of the parking lot and toward the main road. "Can we, um, talk about the importance of the outdoor skating rink?" Nell asked, hesitant.

"Why?" he said, cautious. Rob had specifically pointed it out as an item to consider cutting.

"Because…I think we should." She nodded decisively. "You know how the local kids loved the rink last winter."

"Did they?" he said blandly. He didn't want

to remember that. His mind flashed to the boy, Jason. Did he like to skate?

"Yes." She nodded and stepped on the accelerator as the SUV started up the steep mountain road. "The ice rink also sets us apart from our competitors in the hotel market."

That was what he needed to hear about. "How so? Tell me about your research. What did you find out about our competitors' activities? What are their plans for the Christmas season?"

"Well…" Nell smiled enthusiastically, clearing her throat. "I checked our closest competitors, the resorts you suggested I look at." She paused while they waited for a logging truck to go rumbling past. When it was safe to do so, she cautiously turned right. The road wound a short way up the mountainside.

"And?" he murmured, paging through the consultant's report to the end, where all the maintenance numbers were located.

"And…they all provide shuttle-bus access to the local downhill ski resorts. But we don't do that."

"We can't," he said. They had offered the service last year, and the cost hadn't justified the benefit. Besides, in Nathan's experience, their guests didn't ask about skiing until after the New Year.

"Yes, I know." Nell curled a stray lock of hair behind her ear. "We have to cut expenses." She glanced sideways at him. "However, Uncle, while the two top resorts offer sleigh rides for the kids, they also set up portable outdoor skating rinks in the winter."

He remained silent. He would ignore the skating rink reference for now. Rob was right—it was an excellent place for him to cut electricity and insurance costs. "Tell me, do our competitor resorts charge extra fees for the sleigh rides, or is the access inclusive with the room fee?"

Nell's cheeks reddened.

"You didn't check?" he guessed.

"Well…" They drove past a vista with a spectacular view. At the top of the mountain, near the pathway that led to his family's ancient, dilapidated outdoor skating rink, Nell suddenly pulled over.

He sighed. "What *is* it, Nell?"

"I have a confession," she blurted. "Actually, I have something I really need to show you." She turned around and reached for the purse she'd tossed in the back seat.

Surprises were never good. Nathan could feel the muscles in his neck tensing.

She pulled a folder from her gigantic purse, and then turned back around. From the folder, she plucked out a few pieces of paper and handed them to him. "Uncle," she said, taking a deep breath, "As your marketing manager, I suggest you read and then sign this contract."

He stared at her. "What is this?"

"Well…after yesterday morning and the discussion we had, I made an inquiry. I knew that if I didn't act fast, then the opportunity would be gone. You were at the bank all morning, so I made an executive decision."

His temple throbbed. She was his niece—he couldn't get angry at her. "I'm the one who makes the executive decisions," he said in measured tones.

"You told me to take the initiative," she pointed out. "So I did. And it's not going to cost us anything."

What initiative? he thought, irritated. "Nothing is free, Nell."

"Just listen. You know how we were watching that cruise ship accident on TV? Well," she said proudly, "it gave me an idea. So I called Empress Cruises."

"You called Empress Cruises?" he asked incredulously.

She nodded and set her chin. "I want us to hire the show skaters, Uncle."

"The…"

"Yes. The figure skaters who give ice shows on the cruise ship. I told the lady from Empress Cruises that I was interested in hiring them, and she gave me the number of their production company. They're the ones that handle their contracts, you see," she said proudly.

He knew all that. He knew way too much about how the skaters' business worked, in fact. He gritted his teeth. He was dying to ask about Emilie, but he could not.

"Uncle Nathan," Nell said, "please don't get mad at me. Hear me out."

Obviously, she was flustered that he wasn't as enthusiastic as she was, but for the moment, he couldn't even speak. She had no idea of the pressure he was under, or the danger that their inn would be shuttered before the end of the year. She chattered on, pushing her outrageous, unformed idea.

"Those top two resorts you told me to study for competitive analysis? Well, they both have skating rinks, like us. But what they *don't* have are shows or skaters to entertain their guests. It's something we could have that they don't—a competitive advantage, if you will. So I pitched the production company my idea to send the troupe from the sunken ship here to perform. It's a win for us because these skaters have media attention right now. *Huge* media attention. Have you seen the television interviews they've been getting? It's gone national! And we could get publicity by helping them out. Just think of the headlines—'Prescott Inn saves shipwrecked skaters' Christmas!'"

His head was swimming. Assuming all this was true… "But they're cruise ship performers, Nell. The rinks are so much smaller."

"Oh, no, Uncle. You're thinking of this the wrong way. The skaters have a family-friendly Christmas show ready to be performed anywhere, even on land. I checked that part out."

"We can't," he said softly. They couldn't afford to hire them at all. Not in the remotest possibility. Rob had told Nathan to keep the truth of their financial precariousness a secret from everyone outside the circle of investors. And he understood why—if word got out that the inn might be put up for sale, then who in their right mind would call to book a room? And bookings were what they most needed.

He shook his head and thrust the contract

forward. Emilie was an entirely separate issue. She'd been the love of his life, and Nell didn't know about her, either. But that was his private pain.

Nell's face reddened. "Uncle, this is a really good idea."

"Fiscally," he said gently, "it isn't."

"It is! We need to bring in revenue. People will come to the inn to see these skaters perform. We'll fill up rooms for the winter."

"For *Christmas*," he interjected. The investors had made it clear that the holiday season was his immediate concern. The inn wouldn't even last the winter if they didn't have a successful Christmas first.

"Yes." Nell nodded. "And as your marketing manager, I believe this will make us stand out. It will attract people to come and spend money and fill our rooms. Once the skaters are settled, there will be a show every day until Christmas, with the biggest finale on December 24. And as for costs, yes, there will be room-and-board expenses, but they're minimal. There are ten figure skaters in the troupe and they're used to berthing two to a room. Our rooms are bigger than cruise ship rooms, so they should like that. I figured we have the older, un-renovated rooms in the west wing that we rarely rent anyway. We can give them a good cleaning, and they'll be set to go. We can give the skaters a standardized menu to order from in the dining room, so that will streamline costs, plus, we have a gym they can work out in, too, at no cost and—"

"Stop." He held up his hand. He didn't even want to listen to the idea anymore. It was making him remember Emilie and their life together on the ship. They'd worked out together in the ship's gym every morning. He'd lifted weights, and she had worked on her stretches. She'd smile at him in her yoga pants and sports bra, with her hair in a carefree ponytail.

"Uncle, we can't lose with this deal!" Nell insisted.

"What about their salaries?" he asked, forcing himself to think logically. "That's a huge expense right there."

"The cruise line is covering their contracts through Christmas," she said, excited.

"Why would they do that?"

"I told you, there's been attention in the national media. Haven't you seen the video?"

"What video?" Nathan had been too busy preparing for his investors' meeting to watch news or check social media. That was Nell's job.

"A passenger was recording the ice show just

as the ship hit the sandbar," Nell said. "And he kept filming as the skating team evacuated everyone. The skaters were heroes. They kept their cool and got all the passengers out. The ice captain—a skater named Emilie—was interviewed on the chat shows last night and this morning through Skype. She's a really great spokeswoman. So now everybody is super concerned about her troupe—they're calling them 'the homeless figure skaters.' Maybe it's embarrassing for the cruise line. In any case, the cruise line has offered to pay their salaries through Christmas if we agree to cover room and board. Then they won't be homeless for Christmas, will they?" Nell smiled brightly at him.

Nathan's head was spinning. Nell had lost him at the word *Emilie*. Was she really talking about *his* Emilie?

He couldn't stand it anymore—he had to satisfy his curiosity. Ignoring Nell chattering beside him, he scanned through the contract to the end, where the skaters' names were listed…

And there she was. *Emilie O'Shea, Ice Captain.* Nathan's hand shook slightly. She'd been promoted to the job two years ago, just before their breakup. She'd been so proud of her promotion that day—so much so that she'd chosen her job and her skaters over being with him.

He still felt sick over the way it had ended. How could he relive the pain of that day again? He passed the contract back to Nell. "No," he said firmly.

Nell frowned at him and crossed her arms. And then with renewed vigor, she kept pressing. "Did I tell you the skaters will come with their own costumes and props for the show, which has already been choreographed?"

"There are insurance fees and other expenses," he said with tight lips. Whatever Nell could think to throw at him, he would counter. The truth was, he *couldn't* evaluate the opportunity from a neutral perspective because the proposal involved Emilie.

"*Read* the contract, Uncle. It comes with insurance from the production company. Besides, that's a minor detail. Look at the big picture. We need to fill rooms in order to have a financially viable Christmas. Am I right?"

More than she realized.

But Emilie had hurt him. And he had said things he later regretted. He had enough on his plate right now keeping his resort open without having to deal with the pain from his past personal life.

Plus the skating troupe would require him to keep the rink open, adding to his expenses.

On the other hand, Nell believed the troupe could be a solution to their financial woes. If skaters brought in enough income to offset the costs of their room and board, she could be right.

Still, he pushed back. "There are other considerations," he said in a quiet voice. "I've sailed on a cruise ship with entertainment staff. You haven't. Believe me when I tell you that, in my experience, they bring drama. And commotion. Plus, they're used to eating all day long. They bounce in and out of the facilities as they please. They interact with the guests—"

"So, let them! Maybe they could give impromptu skating lessons." Nell's eyes were lit with excitement. "Uncle Nathan, you're always telling me to buckle down and get serious, and I have. This is a *good* idea. Everyone loves outdoor skating at a New England inn at Christmastime."

Maybe so. But bottom line, he couldn't cope with seeing Emilie again.

He looked out over the path that led to the old ice rink. He'd skated here as a boy himself, when his grandparents had been alive and the inn was thriving. Those had been wonderful days...

But he shook his head. There were so many costs associated with this plan. "No, Nell."

"Uncle, I don't have anything else to recommend to you." Nell threw up her hands. "I've been brainstorming ideas for days, and I don't have any other decent ones. But this one's a winner—I *know* it. I understand you're concerned about cutting costs because you're an accountant at heart. Well, I'm a marketing person. We think of unique ways to bring in money. And the show skaters will give us the promotional ability to attract clients. We'll have a unique story to tell about them—"

"The fact that we are a family-owned business, not part of a national chain, *is* our unique story," he said in a harsher voice than he'd intended. "Don't lose sight of what we're really doing here, Nell," he warned.

She crossed her arms. "Then I'm not sure I can help you anymore."

He stared at her. "What do you mean?"

"You don't listen to what other people say. You're too closed off." She gazed steadily at him. "Do you know that some of the staff are afraid of you? There's been talk."

He stiffened. "About what?"

"You're too focused on cost cutting. We're worried that you're turning into Ebenezer Scrooge."

He laughed and shook his head. *Ridiculous.* He couldn't worry *enough* about cost cutting. Not after that meeting with his investors this morning. That was his all-consuming purpose for the next several weeks at least.

"Nell," he said in his most serious voice, "I'm going to be honest with you. But this is strictly confidential. No one else can learn what I'm going to tell you. Can I count on you to keep it secret?"

She bit her lip, but she nodded. "Yes. You know that you can, Uncle Nathan."

He hoped he was doing the right thing in trusting her. She was his family, so she had a right to the facts. "We're having financial problems," he said grimly. "Bad ones. My investors have given me a directive to turn around our cash flow by Christmas. If I don't make the numbers they've given me, they'll shut us down—finished and sold—at the end of the month."

"Shut us down?" The blood drained from her face. "You mean close the inn?"

"Yes, Nell."

Her mouth gaped.

"We have to keep it extremely low-key that we're having these financial problems," he warned. "Because if it becomes public knowledge, it could further damage the business. Can I trust you to support me on this?"

She nodded, swallowing.

He nodded, too. *Case closed. No more talk of bringing in Emilie and her show skaters here, no matter what it would do for us.*

"But that's all the more reason to bring in Emilie and her skaters. I can get us lots of positive publicity if we bring them in," Nell stubbornly repeated. "Look. Here's the interview Emilie did this morning. The recording is from a Miami station, but they played it on the national morning shows, too."

He stared at Nell. It appeared she really didn't understand the seriousness of what they were going through.

"Nell," he said patiently, "As I said, we can't put money into a venture like this, so please stop suggesting it."

"The contract doesn't require us to put in any money. They *have* to find a place for Emilie or it would be bad publicity for them. Just *read* the contract, Uncle. You haven't even looked at it yet. How can you make a blanket statement that we can't afford it if you won't even read it? Don't you trust me? *Me*. I'm your family, Uncle."

Her face was red with passion. And yeah, it killed him when she put it that way. He *would* like to indulge her. Nell was his closest family left in the area. Nathan's sister—Nell's mother—lived out in California. She'd been his sole ally as a kid. Only she really understood what pain their chaotic childhood had been.

Plus, Nell did have some good ideas.

Without a word, he picked up the contract and examined it. He read it line by line, paragraph by paragraph, because that was prudent business sense. It was practical.

It read exactly as Nell said it would.

Interestingly, he noted a paragraph that gave him an out if he was in any way dissatisfied with the troupe's performance. He could cancel the agreement at any time, for any reason, and they would have to leave.

"How did this get in there?" he asked Nell, tapping the paragraph. From the production company's perspective, it made terrible business sense.

"I asked for it," she said proudly.

"You?"

"I knew you'd be a tough sell. I knew that clause would help to convince you."

"They really, really want those skaters to find a home, don't they?"

She smiled at him. But she hadn't won yet.

He leaned his head back on the seat.

Nell waited patiently.

He sat up and scratched some figures, in pencil, on the side of the contract. If the inn's maintenance manager, Guy, took care of the physical upkeep of the rink, and if they didn't spend money on outside vendors, and if the publicity Nell was talking about came through…

"The skaters can have the rink," he murmured. "But only half of it. The front half, where the floodlights still work."

"All right," Nell said cautiously. "Yes, I suppose they're used to skating on smaller surfaces."

"Guy will run the Zamboni once a day only, in the early morning, before work."

She nodded. "Okay."

"And put it in the contract that they're definitely to bring their own music, props, costumes, equipment and stage curtains. They have to be prepared to use our facilities as is. We're not responsible for any big improvements or outlays of investment. I mean it, Nell."

"Of course! Oh, yes! I'm sure they'll agree to all that!"

He nodded, thinking grimly of Emilie. If this project went forward, he would have to face her again.

He didn't relish that confrontation.

Then again, Emilie might not want to deal with him, either. They hadn't parted ways on the best of terms. It had been abrupt, really.

"You would be the point person in dealing with this project," he said.

"Great! Thank you for the opportunity, Uncle."

The inn was a big place. He and Emilie might not even cross paths with one another. They could each pretend that the other didn't exist, as they had been doing for the past two years.

Yes, Nell was capable of doing her job, and so was Emilie. The two of them could handle the shows without his input or interference.

And maybe Emilie wouldn't want to come to Prescott Inn. She was the one who'd rejected him, after all. He would just have to see…

"So will you sign it, Uncle?" Nell said eagerly.

He gazed into his niece's anxious brown eyes. "*Please*, Uncle?"

EMILIE PAUSED AT the end of the hallway, phone glued to her ear, on hold with her boss, Lynn Bladewell.

Three days had passed since the *Empress Caribbean* had sunk. The production company had finally moved them off the island and into a hotel in Miami. It was still early in the day. The other skaters were in their rooms, exhausted from the ordeal.

After two days of living on cots in the school gym and assisting the cruise line with evacuating the last of the passengers from the tiny island and back to the mainland, they were now officially in limbo. Below Emilie, the Florida sun shone brightly on the Atlantic Ocean. Blue skies spread across the horizon as far as the eye could see. Gentle, perfect waves rolled in along the sparkling water.

Home. Or at least where her family lived. But Emilie hadn't truly called Florida home since she started working for the cruise line.

Emilie's mom, older sister and niece had met her at the hotel yesterday, when she'd first arrived with her troupe. They'd all cried and hugged each other. The ship's sinking had scared everyone, but it was okay, Emilie had told them they were all safe. She kept reassuring them of that over and over.

"Stay with us for Christmas, honey?" her mom had asked.

"I *have* to stay with my team, Mom." And she did. That's where her heart and her purpose was. The team needed her, and she felt responsible for them. Besides, she *liked* helping them. "Sergei and Katya are from Russia, and we have Gary and Rosie from Canada. Then there's Lars from Norway. I can't just abandon my people, who are so far from home, and at Christmastime."

"Well…they can certainly spend Christmas with us," her mom offered.

Emilie had smiled sadly at them. "Thanks for offering. I really do appreciate it." But the thought of ten more people crammed into Mom's tiny Fort Myers condo just didn't make sense.

"So, what are you going to do, honey?"

"Well, the production company told me they're working on a deal to get us into a land-based resort for the holiday season at least. If the deal goes through, the cruise ship has promised to honor our salary arrangement at least through Christmas, even though they don't have to." Emilie had been well aware that the media coverage she'd received had given her leverage with her bosses.

"So, where will you be working?" her sister had asked.

"I don't know. I'll find out tomorrow."

And now here she was, waiting on the phone with Lynn. Still on hold. Nervous, she paced the hotel corridor. She was just *so* hoping that whatever Lynn arranged would enable them to stay together for Christmas. *And* keep their paychecks coming in. Frankly, she was still worried about Katya. She was rooming with Julie in the hotel, and Julie had confided to Emilie that she'd heard Katya tossing and turning in her sleep last night.

"Emilie?"

She jumped to attention. "Yes!" she said to Lynn. "I'm here!" She turned away from the window with the sand and the sun and the beach outside. After two days on a hot, sandy island she was just a little bit sick of the heat. "Do you have something for us?" she asked, praying with all her heart that they did.

"Yes, actually. The contract is being processed."

"For all of us? We can *all* stay together? Because that's really important to me."

"Well…I'm not sure we can do that."

"What do you mean?"

"Emilie, I'm not sure all of the skaters have visas to work in the States," Lynn said gently.

That would mean Katya. And Sergei. Possibly half Emilie's team, if she counted all her international skaters.

"Well, can you check, please?" Emilie said firmly. "I don't want to leave anyone behind."

"Emilie, we may have to."

"In all my interviews, I talked about how the troupe sticks together. How would it look if that only meant the skaters with paperwork?"

Lynn sighed. Emilie knew Lynn was worried about bad publicity.

"Let me call you back," Lynn said. "I need to speak with Donnie."

Donnie. The president of their production company.

"Thank you." Emilie hung up the phone and sat down to wait at the end of the quiet corridor, arms curled around her knees. She didn't have to wait long—just ten minutes until her phone buzzed.

"Yes, Lynn?"

"Emilie. Congratulations. We're fortunate that all your skaters are covered. Your team has a contract."

"That's fantastic!" Emilie leaped to her feet.

"Don't celebrate quite yet. Because here's

the thing—this job is going to be a lot more responsibility for you personally. We don't have any support teams to send you. You might have to reconfigure the show choreography somewhat depending upon the size of the local facilities."

"But that's perfect for me! You know that I want to be a choreographer with the company someday!"

"Yes, we know. But you're aware we don't often have openings. That said, if you can make a really great show that a lot of people are excited to come see, then I'll keep you in mind for further opportunities. Donnie would prefer two separate shows, if you can swing it. It could be a big deal for us if you're successful. Donnie's eyes are on this project."

Emilie swallowed. The phone was actually shaking in her hand, Lynn's promise was so exciting to her. She would get to keep her team's jobs for Christmas *and* have the opportunity to audition for her own dream job.

"Don't worry," Emilie promised. "I'll make it a success. What's the next step?"

"We'll arrange for a van to take you to the airport. I'll email you your tickets and itinerary shortly, so keep checking your inbox. From Miami International, I imagine you'll be flying to Boston's Logan Airport and then driving up to New Hampshire by shuttle bus."

"Wait? We're going to New Hampshire?" Emilie suddenly felt nervous. *Nathan Prescott* lived in New Hampshire.

But he would never… She shook her head.

"Yes," Lynn was saying, "New Hampshire. Is that a problem?"

"No, no," Emilie said quickly. "Sorry. I just assumed we were going to a rink someplace sunny. With artificial ice."

"I'm told it's a seasonal rink with natural ice. Rather old-school."

"Okay." She could adapt to that.

Scratch that, she *had* to adapt to that. Whatever it took to keep the team together and to secure their new jobs.

"Emilie, are you still on board with us?"

"Oh, yes!"

"Then the van will meet you at the arrival gate and take you all to the resort in the mountains. The place is called Prescott Inn."

Prescott Inn! It *was* Nathan who'd hired them.

Emilie felt as if the wind had been knocked from her. She slid down the wall until she was sitting on the carpet. It was suddenly hard to breathe. Or maybe she was hyperventilating.

"Are you there, Emilie? I heard a strange noise."

Emilie nodded. "I'm here," she managed to croak, hand over her chest.

Her mind was whirling. She was going to Nathan Prescott's inn!

But why? Thoughts of him made tears spring to her eyes. He'd chosen his *inn* over her. Why would he want to see her now? And at the same inn that he'd shown her was more important to him than she was.

Did this mean he was second-guessing his decision? Did it mean he still cared about her?

They really had been in love, she thought wistfully.

Or maybe she was jumping to conclusions. His contract with them could just mean that Nathan simply wanted to help them out. He'd been on the cruise ship once, too, so he understood their predicament. Even if he'd only been a consulting accountant for the cruise line, he knew what the cruising life entailed. He *got* how serious a ship sinking was. It was a terrible, frightening experience, and even though they'd been lucky enough that no one had been seriously hurt—

"Hello? Emilie? Can you hear me? I think I've lost you."

Emilie cleared her throat. "I'm still here."

Sort of. She was having trouble processing her own scrambled and upset reactions. Honestly, though, what did it matter where the opportunity came from? Her team was being kept together and employed, if only for the short term. She was grateful for that. It was what she'd wanted. They would all feel better when they heard the news.

And the chance to prove herself to Lynn was just icing on the cake.

"So," Lynn continued. "That's it, then. I'll process your contracts from our end and take care of the final details."

"Okay…" If she could think of any other terms, now was the time to state them.

"Um. Lynn," Emilie said, "what about a clothing allowance? We've lost everything in the sinking. Our rooms are underwater, and nothing is salvageable." She assumed that to be true, anyway. "And none of us have warm coats or boots to wear in New Hampshire."

"You're right," Lynn agreed. "Since this will be such good PR for us, I'll see if I can authorize an advance for you. Let me get back to you on the amount, okay?"

"That would be great." Emilie would organize a shopping expedition to a local mall here in Miami. That would lift everyone's spirits. "I can't think of anything else right now, but if I do, I'll let you know."

"Please don't ask for anything else! I'm out on a limb for you as it is."

"We'll make you look good, I promise!"

Lynn sighed. "Just make a great new show and reconfigure the ship's Christmas show for the new ice. I'll talk with you soon." She ended the call.

Emilie stood from her position on the carpet and dusted herself off.

Things were looking up.

And as for Nathan, well…

She checked her phone. He hadn't called her. But somehow, she had hope in her heart. He'd reached out and offered them this life-line, hadn't he?

She would show him her honest appreciation for that when she saw him. He had broken her heart once, but in the spirit of Christmas, maybe it was time for forgiveness.

CHAPTER FOUR

WHEN EMILIE WALKED inside Prescott Inn, she found a lobby decorated for Christmas, with a fully trimmed tree, pine wreaths that smelled of the north woods and garlands atop every doorway.

She took a deep breath and appreciated the Christmas spirit.

This boded well.

But as she waited for someone to come out and greet them, she wondered why the inn felt so empty. And where was Nathan?

"Oh! Here you are!" A young woman with a big smile and dark hair came out from an office behind the front desk. She helped Emilie load her bags—meager as they were—onto a rolling brass luggage cart.

"Did you have a pleasant flight?" the woman asked sweetly.

"Yes." Emilie touched her hand to her throat. "May I speak with Nathan Prescott, please?"

A blush crept over the woman's cheeks. "I

can answer any questions you might have. My name is Nell Lewis. I'm his marketing manager."

"Oh! Well, does Nathan still work in this building?" She already knew the answer—the night before, she'd done an internet search. It had pained her, but in his official photos, Nathan Prescott was as handsome as ever. He looked just as he had the day he'd walked off the *Empress Caribbean*.

Reluctantly, Nell nodded. "Yes, and I am sorry, but Mr. Prescott is occupied at the moment. He's put me in charge of helping you settle in." She smiled brightly at Emilie. "How are your skaters? You're Emilie O'Shea, right? I saw your interviews on TV."

"Yes, I'm Emilie, thank you. And my skaters are outside, in the van." Emilie forced a smile at Nell, still wondering if Nathan's marketing manager knew about Emilie and Nathan's romance.

From the blank way Nell looked back at her, though, Emilie was willing to bet that she knew nothing at all.

"Well, will Nathan be down later, then?" Emilie asked.

"He…would rather I handle all the details, simply because he's so busy." Nell shifted her feet, clearly uncomfortable with the message she was meant to deliver. "He's given me instructions for managing the ice-skating project, as we've taken to calling it, so tomorrow, once you're settled, you and I will take a drive up to the ice rink, yes?"

"You mean the ice rink isn't part of this building?"

"Oh, no." Nell shook her head, still smiling. "It's an off-site facility."

"So…Mr. Prescott isn't going to be involved with us *at all*?"

"I'm afraid not," Nell said apologetically. "No."

Emilie got the message—Nathan didn't want to see her. She quickly blinked away the moisture in her eyes. She could handle working with Nell—the young marketing manager seemed kind enough—but Nathan's outright rejection of her?

It hurt. More than she'd realized it would. She'd never expected that he wouldn't want to see her at all.

Her heart heavy, she retreated across the room to the stone fireplace and faced it, determined to compose herself while Nell went outside to greet Emilie's team.

The cold fireplace she stared into seemed like

a metaphor for her life—for the next month, at least.

Couldn't Nathan even *pretend* to greet her kindly, even for old times' sake?

They'd *loved* each other once.

Her gaze followed the long track of the chimney. Up, up, up. Near the top, just to the right, she noticed a picture window covered with wooden blinds. An office or a conference room on the second level. Shielding her eyes and squinting to guard from the glare of the sun, Emilie peered inside that window as best she could through the slats of blinds where *someone*—a man—watched them gathering below.

It was Nathan. She recognized his dark hair and the outline of his familiar broad shoulders. And besides, she *sensed* his presence by the grim stillness of his large form. Even from all this distance away, she could feel the coolness in his eyes as he gazed down at her.

She put her hand to her mouth, swallowing a gasp.

Nathan stepped away. Slowly, the window shuttered.

Quickly, Emilie headed for the lobby restroom. She couldn't face anyone just now.

She'd cried over Nathan Prescott for a long time after they'd broken up. She'd huddled in her cruise ship cabin at the end of the working day, trying to forget him. She'd attempted instead to focus on the mundane rhythms of her schedule. Discussions of the new choreography. The challenges of learning to be a good ice captain, and the dreams of how one day she might graduate into becoming a professional choreographer.

It had been hard to put the broken relationship with Nathan behind her, but each week, it got a little easier. The reality of a show performer meant that one got used to people— important people—coming and going in one's life like a never-ending parade. There wasn't time for pain or longing, because the routine moved fast. New friends came. Old friends returned.

But now, as Emilie huddled—hiding, really— in the public washroom of the country inn that he'd thrown her over for, Emilie couldn't stop the wave of grief that overwhelmed her. She was no longer Emilie O'Shea, seasoned performer and ice captain. She was Emilie O'Shea, jilted lover.

She *had* loved him. Nathan Prescott had snuck into her heart, bit by bit, until she'd embraced him wholeheartedly.

She'd first met him during a public skating session at the ice studio. Nathan had been hanging around behind the counter. He'd been holding a clipboard, and he'd looked so handsomely official. Bored with her own task of checking in passengers, she'd set about trying to get him to crack a smile. He'd been a challenge, but she'd persisted.

"What's a nice boy like you doing in a place like this?" she'd asked lightly, teasing him because his green eyes appeared so serious.

He'd given her a half smile. But then he'd ignored her again, instead frowning at the papers on his clipboard.

Everyone had flirted with her in those days. Even Bart, the Zamboni driver. He called her Emmy-em. And gave her M&M'S that he scooped from the cafeteria up on deck.

But Nathan was different. He was always serious, and always working.

"What are you doing?" she'd asked him seriously, giving up on flirtation.

"I'm cutting costs."

She'd laughed, thinking that he was joking.

"What's so funny?" he'd asked her.

"There are no costs here," she'd said. The skaters never dealt with money or even shipboard charges. That was the province of bartenders, or the workers in the retail shops and onboard spa. She loved their huge, happy cruise ship—with fun things to do and music always playing somewhere. She loved that the delicious smell of food—burgers sizzling or fresh-baked bread—and the fresh salty breeze of the sea were never far from her nose. The warm Caribbean sun shone nearly every day. And hundreds of joyous people, all on vacation, were always up for happiness.

So how could this guy be so grim?

Just then, a passenger had shown up before her desk, requesting two pairs of skates for himself and his girlfriend to take a twirl around the on-ship ice rink.

"Oh, I'm sorry," Emilie had informed him in her sympathetic tone. "Before I can lend you the skates, you'll need to change into long pants and a pair of socks." She'd pointed to the sign before the desk. "It's Captain's rules for skating. But I'll make sure to hold your skates aside for you when you return." She'd smiled at them, making it seem as if the ship might possibly run out of skates if she didn't set theirs aside—it wouldn't, but making it seem like a special favor to the guests usually appeased their irritation of having to go back to their rooms.

As the couple left, Nathan had asked her,

"Why isn't there a shop here in the ice studio where they can buy pants and socks?"

"I don't know. You'll have to ask the captain that question."

"Right." Nathan had nodded. His face had lit up as he scribbled a note on his clipboard. That was the secret to what made Nathan tick—he enjoyed business. All aspects of it were interesting to him. She'd never met anyone quite like him.

But one of her specialties was shopping, so she had given him her honest opinion. "You know, if I *was* to put a store here, I would also stock it with yoga pants and cute tops that give the skating logo for the ship's rink."

"Or the cruise line logo," Nathan had suggested.

"Better yet, the ship's logo intertwined with a skate. Something you could only buy here, on ship."

Nathan had cocked his head. "That's a good idea." He'd glanced around her studio as if with new eyes. And she did consider it hers; she'd been here so long, she'd had a hand in designing it. The walls were jazzy and exciting, with blown-up photos of the skaters performing. Throughout the day, she changed the soundtracks, alternating between pop, classical and rock music, depending upon her mood. "This is a really appealing place you have here," he'd said.

"Thank you." She'd grinned at him, but Nathan hadn't reacted other than to continue assessing her.

Then the old classic "I'll Be Home for Christmas" had come over the speakers, and Emilie could only sigh. The yearning, crooning voice of Perry Como always put her in the Christmas spirit. Como was way before Emilie's time, but she enjoyed this soundtrack because her Italian grandmother had adored the singer. Her grandmother had played his Christmas album over and over in Emilie's youth.

Thinking of her grandmother, Emilie had suddenly felt very sad. And a disquieting feeling— nostalgia mingled with guilt.

Stay hopeful, Emilie, she'd chided herself. It was always important to keep hope up, both in herself and in others.

But Nathan had peered at her, as if seeing into her heart. As if needing an answer into what bothered her.

"My grandmother used to play that album," she'd said softly. "She lived with us when I was young. When she passed away, I…" She swallowed. *Let's just skip that part.* She took a deep breath. "I really miss her."

Nathan had looked directly into her eyes. "The song makes me sad, too," he'd said softly. "My grandfather played that album. He owned an inn in the mountains when I was a kid. I miss him." He gave her a sad smile.

At the time, she hadn't picked up on his mention of the inn. In fact, he'd never talked to her about it again.

Instead, after that first beginning, he'd included her in his shipboard life and routine. And more and more, with each passing day, she'd found herself looking forward to seeing Nathan Prescott. He'd let her bring his mood "up," so he was as smiling and relaxed as she was. He'd let her infuse her enthusiasm into him so he wasn't so stoic and serious.

In turn, he'd hung around during her practices. During all her performances. And on their days off, they'd explored islands together. They'd taken advantage of the cruise ship adventure, both on ship and in port. It had been magical. The past had fallen away. There was only the perpetual present. For almost a glorious year...

And then, on the anniversary of the first day that they'd met, he'd arranged a dinner for them at the fancy French restaurant on the ship. She'd dressed in her best formal gown and strappy sandals. Her roommate had helped her put up her hair. Like Cinderella, the members of her troupe had helped with her makeup. A borrowed shawl. A festive purse…

Nathan was going to ask her to marry him. Everyone said so.

Dinner had been lovely. A bottle of champagne had been popped open. Nathan's eyes had been so bright. His smile was infectious. A lock of dark hair had curled over his forehead, and he'd smiled with that dimple in his cheek. She was head over heels in love with him. Not the kind of love that burned out quickly, but a love that really felt like it could last a lifetime.

He *did* have an engagement ring for her—a gorgeous one-carat solitaire. She had never held a more beautiful piece of jewelry. But the commitment and the happiness it symbolized was the most important thing.

And then, he'd ruined everything.

Instead of bending to one knee and expressing his undying love for her, promising to be with her always, Nathan Prescott had suddenly started talking about an inn in New Hampshire.

"I'm buying it, Emilie," he'd said with excitement in his voice. "I've been waiting to tell you because I wanted it to be a surprise. We can move up there as soon as your contract is finished next month."

Her mouth had dropped open in shock. *New Hampshire? An inn? Where had this come from?*

But Nathan hadn't seemed to notice her distress. "You and I can work to bring back my grandfather's inn to what it once was. I know you'll love it up there."

"But I'm a show skater, Nathan," she'd tried to explain. "I work here, out of Florida, on cruise ships. And I just got promoted."

"Wait, what are you saying?"

"That I'm renewing my contract in a month," she said patiently. "You know this."

Frankly, she'd felt blindsided by this inn thing, and she was fighting tears. Just weeks ago, they'd talked about maybe finding a condo together locally. "What about us renting a place down here and me skating and you working for the cruise line? Like we discussed?"

"Emilie," he'd said, his voice taking on a tone as if he was trying to be patient with her, "this is a once-in-a-lifetime opportunity. It just came up, and I had to act fast. It's what I've always wanted. What I've *really* wanted." He'd looked at her quizzically. "I thought I told you about my dreams for the inn."

"No, you didn't." Her throat felt raw, and it was becoming difficult to speak. "Not at all."

"But I've talked to you about Prescott Inn. About my grandfather. And when I was a boy."

But beyond the basics, he hadn't told her much about his past. Not really.

In his defense, she hadn't opened up about her childhood, either. She hadn't wanted to. She'd preferred to live in their never-ending cruise ship present. It had seemed happier that way.

With sadness in his eyes, he'd nodded to the ring he'd bought her, resplendent in its jewel box. "Will you come with me to New Hampshire to build a life with me? Please, Emilie." His voice had caught. "I love you."

She loved him, too. But no—she couldn't move to an inn in New Hampshire. "I need to stay here, Nathan," she'd said helplessly. "I'm an ice captain now. I have responsibilities."

His face had clouded over. "Is that what's important to you?" he'd said shortly, in a tone that indicated he was dismissing the importance of the role to her.

She'd suddenly been angry. He wasn't thinking of her point of view at all. "Nathan, it *is* important to me." Her voice had cracked, embarrassingly, with the emotion that she'd felt.

He'd shaken his head. "But you can skate and choreograph in New Hampshire, Em. I can't move the inn to the cruise ship—don't you see our problem?"

That wasn't their problem. "It's not the *fact* of the position for me, Nathan. It's the *people* that I'm helping here. I'm important to them."

"On the cruise ship?" He'd outright laughed at her.

He'd shaken his head again. "Em, it's a fantasy life out here on the ocean. I mean, it's fun for the short term, but it's like living in Neverland. We're not building anything of lasting value that will provide for people in the future."

"Of course we are!" she'd said. "My team is an all-new cast. We have an all-new show to implement." And she was responsible for them. That was crucial to her.

That he didn't see it as she did hurt. "This *isn't* a fantasy," she said. "This is us being real. How can you feel that way about the life we've been living together?" She'd dug her nails into her palms, trying so hard not to get too upset in the middle of the fancy restaurant.

He'd set his chin stubbornly. "The inn is important to me, and to a lot of other people, too. It's a chance to build something in my community. To get back what my grandfather made. To grow *roots*."

"Why haven't I heard this before now?"

He shook his head sadly. "Maybe I was under your spell."

That had hurt her cruelly.

There had been pain in his eyes, too. "I'm trying to say, Emilie—not very well, I realize—but please try to understand what I mean. Working at sea isn't *permanent*, at least not to me. I need to go back home and make something concrete of my life."

"I don't agree with you that our life here can't be permanent," she'd said, equally stubborn. "After I finish performing, I hope to choreograph. That *is* a concrete goal. You've made a huge, wrong assumption about me. It's as if you've never even met me before."

"So, that's what you want to do in your future?" he'd asked, looking miserable. "Choreograph cruise ship shows?"

"Yes, Nathan."

"Can you at least come and spend a year with me and see how you like it?"

"I can't." Wasn't he hearing her? "I just got

promoted. People are counting on me. I can't leave them."

"They'll be fine without you."

"No, they won't." Her voice was rising.

"So, when does it end?"

"When everyone is happy and taken care of."

His jaw had hardened. A subtle movement, but it was there. He was impatient with her.

And it had *hurt*. Because he was belittling her and discounting her needs.

"You care more about your inn than you care about us," she realized.

He'd stared at her, but Emilie knew that it was true.

And suddenly, the bubble had popped. There was such a fundamental difference in what they each wanted, and there was no talking this out.

She'd gotten up from the table. She hadn't been able to stop the tears then. Still, she felt that as much as it hurt, she was doing the right thing, that she was saving them both from making a terrible mistake.

"I'm staying here, Nathan," she'd said softly. "If you realize that our relationship is as important as your inn is, then you know where to find me."

She'd turned and walked away.

He hadn't followed her. At first she'd felt numb, maybe from shock. But the next day, he'd packed his things and left the ship for good. She'd never heard from him again. He'd never called her. She'd never seen him again.

Until just minutes ago, when she'd stood in this cold, unfeeling inn and gazed up at him in his remote conference room so far removed from them all.

Emilie stood in the lobby bathroom and ran hot water in the sink. The creaky, groaning pipes and the antique faucet handles reminded her that she was in the country—his country— so far from her old life on the cruise ship.

But that ship had sunk, and now she was forced to deal with Nathan again.

She took a long breath, detecting the orange-and-clove-scented Christmas potpourri placed on the side of the sink. The orange scent did remind her of Florida…

Without glancing at herself in the mirror, she moistened a paper towel and pressed it to her cheeks. With the warmth on her skin, she felt a little comforted.

It wasn't wise to cry over him anymore. It wasn't good to constantly revisit the past. Home was far away now. She was at his inn, in his element, at least until Christmas. She needed to put the past hurts behind her and move forward with her own agenda, staying out of his way as he hopefully stayed out of hers.

She had to think of her troupe and their well-being. *They* were her responsibility. And surely they were as uncertain and unsure of themselves in this new element as she was.

With that strategy, she could make the great shows that Lynn expected of her.

Resolved, Emilie strode back to the lobby.

The members of her troupe milled about. Rosie, Julie and Lynette wore tight, fashionable, brightly colored clothing that they'd bought in Miami. They looked like exotic birds who'd flown into a foreign country.

Katya wore a fur-trimmed hood. Somehow, she'd also made a new friend—a large gray tabby who dozed atop Katya's lap in a spot in the sun, atop the finest of the lobby chairs. Beside Katya was a decorated Christmas tree with a star on top. At least there was a bit of Christmas spirit to cling to.

Gary finished bringing in all their bags, along with the bellhop—Frank—who'd loaded the cases atop his rolling brass cart. Her troupe's mood was festive, surprisingly, but then again, from their point of view, why wouldn't they be excited?

They were employed. They all had a future now, and she was happy for them. They seemed upbeat. Tired of traveling, maybe, but curious about the new surroundings.

Out the window, Emilie noticed the beautiful view of the mountains in the distance. She should reassess her view of the inn as "cold." It was really a *happy* winter wonderland.

Though there was no snow at the inn. Not quite yet.

But it would come. Her first white Christmas. She gazed at the Christmas tree and swallowed. She could only pray that Nathan didn't make this holiday too hard for her.

Why *had* he offered them this contract? Perhaps he felt guilt or regret for the way he'd treated her, and this was his way of helping her out after seeing the news about the ship.

Or, perhaps he'd come to appreciate her point of view.

If she chose the hopeful way of looking at things, this is what she would believe.

But she couldn't be his. Her future was with her skating company. She would advocate for her troupe's well-being in this new assignment, as she always did.

Whatever was to come with Nathan down the road, she would handle. With her chin up. Without drama.

"There you are, Emilie!" Nell bustled over, smiling, holding a stack of room keys. "You've been traveling so long—you must be tired. Would you like to see your rooms now?"

"Yes, please." Emilie focused her mind on the tasks at hand. First, she would get her team settled and make sure they had some lunch. Next, she would inspect the ice surface. She planned to take about ten days to rework the show and practice with the troupe. Then they would perform a formal dress rehearsal, followed by an opening night. After that, they would skate one performance per day—alternating between two shows—for a successful run until Christmas.

"Great. I've arranged six rooms for you and your team." Nell motioned for Frank to follow them with his cart piled high with their luggage. "Some of your skaters will be doubled up, so I'll leave you to decide the specific room assignments."

"That's fine." Emilie would keep roughly the same room assignments they'd had on the ship.

As ice captain, she would receive her own room. She'd double up eight of the skaters by sex and give the sixth room to Gary since he had seniority among the male skaters and often served as her assistant.

Emilie told the team she'd be back for them in a moment, and then she, Nell and Frank set off down a hallway that led behind the stone fireplace.

"Your rooms are in the west hallway, all in a line," Nell continued as she fell into step beside Emilie. Frank and the cart with its squeaky wheels fell to the rear. "I have ten keys, one for each of you, but I'll give them to you to dole out."

"Perfect."

Nell turned down another short hallway and then opened the first door. The room was spacious, if a bit drafty and cold. But that might just be Emilie, used to tropical weather.

"I'll bring you an extra blanket," Nell apologized, shivering herself.

"Thank you." Emilie looked on the bright side. "It's nice to have windows."

There were no windows in her ship's cabin, not even a porthole, and it had been very dark, indeed.

But before Emilie signed off on the arrangement, she checked that there were enough towels and toiletries in the bathrooms. The offering of shampoo, conditioner and soap products was a nice touch for the skaters, as many had lost most of their personal items in the shipwreck.

"Lynn—my boss—mentioned that there's also a gym on-site we can use?" Emilie asked.

"Yes. It's here in the west wing, but down one floor. The inn is situated on a slope, you see, so even though your rooms are at lobby level, there's a ground floor below us."

"And the dining room—where is that?"

Nell hesitated. "On the ground floor, too."

"Is there a problem?" Emilie asked, coming to understand Nell's hesitations as an indication of discomfort.

"No," Nell confessed. "It's just that I thought it was a bit early for lunch. But never mind—we'll get that straightened out with the staff."

"We have some special dietary requirements," Emilie said. "Two of my skaters are gluten-free. We have one paleo eater and one vegan. I take it that can be arranged?"

"Um…" Nell's face went pink. "I'll have to ask…"

"Surely you have guests with such dietary restrictions? We should talk to the chef about it."

"Yes. Of course." Nell nodded swiftly. She

swallowed. "Our kitchen is modern, and our staff trained to handle all types of food allergies."

"Great. Then I'll send my team downstairs now."

Nell hesitated again. "I'll go with you."

"Actually, I'd like you to take me to see the ice surface." Emilie wanted to check the size of the rink to see how much she needed to rework the Christmas show. Then, there would be calls to Lynn to arrange for any new scenery or props or reconfigured music.

"Um," Nell stammered, "Actually, I thought we could do that tomorrow."

"Oh, no," Emilie said sweetly. "Tomorrow we have to start practicing, first thing. We only have eleven days until opening night. The team will be practicing daily—it's my top priority."

Nell's face blanched and Emilie started getting concerned.

"If you're busy right now," Emilie hastened to say, "I'll take the walk over by myself."

"That isn't possible," Nell blurted.

"Why? Just set me on the path, and I'll head on over."

"No." Nell shook her head. "I'd rather drive you. It's a half mile away, uphill. And it's cold outside." She eyed Emilie's thin jacket.

A half mile uphill *was* longer to walk than she'd expected. "Is there a shuttle bus available?" Emilie asked. "I don't have a car at my disposal."

Nell shook her head again, sheepishly. "I'm sorry. We had a mini-bus last winter, but my—but Mr. Prescott had to cut it." She blanched again and put her hand briefly to her mouth. "I mean, Mr. Prescott decided to discontinue the shuttle because it didn't get much use, frankly. Guests seem to prefer to walk. It's quite pleasant most of the time."

Nell was sugarcoating things for her boss. Nathan was *cost cutting*. Emilie knew all about that from their time on the cruise ship. She clenched her jaw.

"Well," Emilie said, willing herself to stay calm, "how exactly does Mr. Prescott plan for us to get ten people back and forth from the skating rink to the inn every day with all our bags of equipment?"

Nell looked frightened.

"He didn't think about that, did he?" Emilie remarked.

Nell shook her head.

"Could you arrange to rent us a van?"

"Um…"

Emilie sighed. "I really would like to speak

with Mr. Prescott, please." There was no circumventing it. She clearly needed to advocate for her troupe directly with Nathan.

"But he'd rather I be your point person," Nell admitted.

"Because he's avoiding me?"

"Oh, no," Nell said quickly. "It's just that it was *my* idea for you to come here, and as such, it's my project to manage."

Confirming that Nathan had told Nell nothing about his past with Emilie. And now Emilie also knew that Nathan hadn't, in fact, lured her here because he had lingering feelings for her. That Emilie and her troupe were here at all was a quirk of Christmas fate, as it were.

And apparently she'd had no lasting effect on his values. He was taking the side of money, "the concrete and tangible." The human factor—emotional relationships—just didn't seem to be as important to him.

Well, Emilie had news for him, he was about to find out how important those things were to *her*. The comfort and safety of her performers were her top concern.

Emilie stood. "Let's take a drive to see the ice rink, please. Just you and I." She saw Nell's reluctant expression and added, "I really must insist."

"Okay," Nell said, worrying her lip. "Um, we'll take my car. Just let me go to my office to pick up my coat and keys, okay?"

Back in the lobby, Emilie quickly passed out the room keys to her team. A front desk clerk—Martha, whom Emilie immediately liked—gave the skaters directions to the on-site restaurant, with instructions to ask the waitress to charge their meals to their rooms.

"The food here is top rated. Tell your server about your dietary requirements, and they'll handle everything with the chef," Martha said.

That was great to know. Feeling better now that the skaters would be set for the after-noon, Emilie waved the skaters off. Honestly, she was hungry, too, but that would wait. She wanted to go to the ice rink without her team so she could assess the situation privately. She didn't want to alarm anyone. Nell had said the ice rink was outdoors. Presumably, it would be cold. They weren't used to cold rinks, not anymore. Their beautiful shipboard ice stu-dio had been quite comfortable. Emilie truly hoped that Nathan's facility at least had heat-ers inside…

Nell came out of her office, which was be-hind the front desk. "Are you ready?" she asked Emilie.

"Absolutely."

Outside, in the parking lot, they climbed into Nell's ancient little Honda and then chugged up the steep mountain road.

Sunlight sparkled on the ice-frosted pine trees. It was a beautiful day, but freezing. Emilie shivered, rubbing her hands under the dashboard heater vent that was taking too long to warm up. Luckily, the drive took barely three or four minutes.

"Here we are!" Nell cheerfully parked the Honda in a small dirt parking lot—more of an outcropping, really, with a spectacular view of the pine-covered valley below.

As Emilie got out of the car and stretched her legs, she saw that off to the side was a charming rustic sign labeled Prescott Inn Skating Rink set over a pretty pathway lined with crushed granite. Emilie couldn't see the rink because the trail dipped downward into a glen and out of sight.

"I'm going to warn you," Nell said, ducking her chin and averting her eyes from Emilie as she undid her seat belt and then exited the car. "Don't get too nervous about the location. I know it's more primitive than you're used to."

"I think the location is adorable. Very Christmas-y." At least, it would be if they decorated it with holiday lights and holly garlands. Maybe Emilie would suggest that to Nathan as an improvement once she decided upon their signage.

Emilie shut the car door and then tucked her hands into her jacket pocket, bracing herself as she followed Nell and picked her way across the frozen parking area, toward the pathway.

"Is the rink heated?" Emilie asked. In her competitive days, she'd skated in cold Northeastern rinks, though as a Florida girl, she hadn't relished the experience.

"Heated?" Nell gaped at Emilie for a moment before vigorously shaking her head. "Oh, no. That isn't possible."

"Not at *all*?"

"Emilie, this is a traditional New England ice-skating experience. It's quaint. Generations of people have enjoyed this location in winter." Nell smiled at Emilie as if willing her to see the potential, like a perky real estate salesperson selling her a fixer-upper. "Darling little rinks in the forest don't exist like this anymore. Well, you'll see," Nell finished, shrugging her shoulders and reverting back to the hesitant young marketing manager.

The path to the venue certainly was *rustic*, all right. Once Nell opened the gateway and they proceeded down a short hill, Emilie stumbled over a protruding root in the path and nearly pitched headfirst into a wooden railing.

"Watch your step there, please," Nell chirped.

Emilie would have to prepare her team for this. As she righted herself, she gazed into the clearing ahead.

And there, in a depression in the forest was the saddest "ice-skating rink" Emilie had ever seen.

It was completely open-air. With no roof whatsoever. It barely had *boards*.

And heaters? If they wanted warmth, they would need to install firepits! But that might be dangerous, because the railings surrounding the rink were wooden. Beyond the boards, the viewing stands were bench-style and aluminum. The size of the ice surface would have been large and adequate—Emilie judged it to be close to NHL-regulation size—but half of the oval was completely unfinished. And the "finished" half looked like it had been prepared by an amateur who had no idea what they were doing. The ice was rough, with bumps on the edges.

Emilie's jaw dropped. She was appalled by these conditions.

"So…what do you think?" Nell said cheerfully. "It's so cute, isn't it? The rink was built by Philip Prescott as a gift for his young bride, Ava, because she loved to skate. Isn't that romantic? Guests just love this place, especially children." Nell attempted a perky smile that just came out desperate.

Emilie sank onto a bleacher seat. Yes, the romantic story was nice in theory, but this was a real-life disaster.

How were they supposed to *skate* here? The circumstances weren't even close to what she'd been led to believe that they were.

"Now, don't get nervous…" Nell began, sitting beside her on the bench.

"What happened here, Nell? Who did this!"

"Um, well…" Nell bit her nails. "Our maintenance manager, Guy—he fixed it up yesterday. Uncle Nathan said that you guys were used to a small rink for your shows, so just the front half of the ice would be sufficient for you and—"

"*Uncle* Nathan?"

"Um, yes." Nell looked miserable. "I'm sorry I didn't tell you that before."

Nathan had a niece? He'd never mentioned that to her when they'd been dating on the cruise ship.

Emilie tamped down her bitterness and

glanced at Nell. She was at most a decade younger than Nathan—her parent must have been significantly older than Nathan. Now that Emilie studied her, she could see the family resemblance in the color of their hair and the oval shape of their faces.

Nell blushed furiously. "I didn't mention it to you because I was trying to be professional." She gave Emilie a pleading look. "Uncle Nathan is actually my mom's younger brother."

An older sister. Yet another thing Nathan had neglected to discuss with her two years ago. Emilie shook her head. She'd seen enough of this so-called ice surface he'd arranged for her. It was time for a talk with *Uncle* Nathan.

"Are you mad at me, Emilie?" Nell asked.

"No, I'm not mad at you at all, Nell. You're just doing your job." Emilie turned toward the parking lot. "I'd like to go back to the inn, please. It's important that I speak with Mr. Prescott about the ice surface. And there's no need to show me to his office—I know where it is."

"Please don't get me in trouble," Nell whispered. Her lips were trembling, and Emilie took pity on her.

"Don't worry," she soothed the younger woman. "I'll only have positive things to say about how you've helped us settle in. But Mr. Prescott can't delegate everything to you. He's hiding from his responsibilities. And there are some things about me that he needs to understand before we proceed any further."

Nell nodded miserably.

Emilie clasped her hand. "Honestly, don't worry. It will work out all right for you. You'll see." She smiled at Nell. "Now, it's time to face Mr. Scrooge."

CHAPTER FIVE

NATHAN COULD FIND no more expenses to cut.

He sat in his office, staring at a spreadsheet on his laptop. He'd been through each department with a fine-tooth comb.

Tired, he leaned back in his chair and closed his eyes. Emilie's troupe would have to stick to a shoestring budget. He'd instructed Nell to make that clear to them.

He figured he just had to stay in his office until Christmas was over. Then the skaters—and Emilie—would go home.

But when he'd actually heard her arriving through the front entrance—and every cell in his body had seemed to be aware of her presence—he'd had to force himself not to get up and look for her. He'd turned up the sound on the television so that he wouldn't hear her voice.

Instead, he'd found himself straining to hear it.

He'd finally overridden his reason and moved

to the window, flicking a finger between the blinds to peek down...

Emilie had stood in the room below him, looking like an angel. She was dressed in a short jacket and a hat with a pom-pom on top. She hadn't changed a day since he'd last seen her.

She'd gazed up at him. Their eyes had locked.

Nathan had sucked in his breath and dropped the blinds back into place, stepping away from the window. He hadn't realized how much it would jolt him to see her...

Now he shook his head and rose from his desk chair—he needed a break. He left his office, headed down the back stairs and went outside to the veranda to clear his head.

The cold hit him mercilessly—he'd forgotten his jacket. He stood alone, slowly filling and then emptying his lungs in the fresh winter air. A few solitary flakes sifted down from the heavens. Beyond the outdoor pool, now closed for the winter, the mountains rose in the distance.

Forget her. A few weeks and she'll be gone. We'll either increase our room reservations due to her troupe's presence, or we won't.

There really wasn't any reason for him to

interact with her. Nell was more than capable of taking care of Emilie and the other skaters.

A child's laughter interrupted his thoughts. The boy whom Nathan had spoken with the day after Thanksgiving in the lobby, Jason—the little one who lived in his inn with his mother—came scampering out the door, struggling with a large gray tabby cat who didn't seem intent on being held.

Unaware of Nathan's presence, Jason knelt and released the cat, who dashed off, disappearing into the brush.

"Is that your cat?" Nathan asked.

Startled, Jason lowered his gaze. "No, I'm not sure whose cat he is," he mumbled.

"He seems to like you. He lets you pick him up."

The boy brightened. "I found him last week. I've been taking care of him every day."

Nathan nodded. He'd seen the cat around. He suspected it might be staying inside his inn, in the boy's room. He wished he didn't have to determine that question, or if the rules were broken, because he liked the boy and didn't want to hurt him.

Jason sat on the back stoop and clasped his arms over his knees. He wore a coat that had seen better days and jeans that looked too big.

"Have you named the cat yet?" Nathan asked gently.

Jason shook his head. "I feed him and take care of him. My mom said if we can't find his real owner, then I get to keep him because the inn allows cats."

They did. In certain rooms—that had been one of Nell's marketing ideas, and since it seemed to be popular, Nathan hadn't stopped the program. But there were very strict rules. After the guest checked in, the cat had to remain in the owner's room at all times.

Nathan glanced at the time on his phone. It was just after noon. "Don't you have school today?" he asked.

"I already went and came home."

Jason might be in the half-day morning program. Nathan wanted to ask whether someone was taking care of him, but he didn't want to get the boy or his mother in trouble.

"You should name the cat," Nathan decided. "After all, he's yours now, and you're responsible for him. Give him a name that you think fits. I only ask that when you're not with the cat, you keep him in your room. Do you think you can do that?"

Jason stared at him. All of a sudden, he looked frightened. "Are you the boss here?"

Nathan nodded. For now he was.

The boy relaxed when he saw that Nathan wasn't going to take his cat away. "His name is Prescott," the boy decided.

"After the inn?"

"Uh-huh." The boy picked up a rock and threw it.

"Where do you usually live?" Nathan couldn't help asking.

The boy shrugged.

"Do you like it here?"

"Yes." But he glanced down at his sneakers, and Nathan could tell that he missed wherever it was that he came from, and that he was lonely.

Nathan blew out a breath in the frigid air. If he had to guess, they'd probably moved a few times during these past months. Gayle—the lady in charge of the shelter program—had told him once that some of these kids had very little stability in their young lives. It gutted Nathan to think of Jason feeling homeless. He understood how difficult that could be for a child.

Jason was the youngest child Nathan had housed. He would do everything in his power to protect him—at least while he still had any power left.

Nathan cleared his throat. "There are some

skaters moving into the rooms beside you. If they bother you or Prescott in any way, just go to the front desk and ask for me. I'm Nathan."

The boy tilted his head. "Why would they bother us?"

"They probably won't." Maybe it was a dumb thing for him to have said, never mind to have thought. Honestly, the only person whose presence the skaters would bother was *him*.

Nathan rubbed his arms. It was too cold to be outside for long without a jacket and gloves. Besides, he needed to get back to work. He turned, just as Prescott the cat came running out of the brush toward Jason, who whistled softly to him.

"Does Prescott have a litter box?"

Jason shook his head. "He lets me know when he wants to go outside. He's smart like that."

"What does he usually do when you're in school?"

Jason flushed and then hung his head.

Nathan had an inkling that maybe the boy hadn't gone to school today after all. But he couldn't be sure, and honestly, it wasn't Nathan's business. Unless the cat destroyed inn property or bothered a guest, then Nathan wouldn't intervene.

Another manager might have evicted the boy and his mother already. From a business sense, it was crazy that Nathan was so concerned about helping them.

He waved goodbye to Jason and then trudged back inside, making a mental note to look up Christmas stockings that he could order online. One for Jason. Maybe one for Prescott, too. He would pay for them himself, of course, and—

Wow, I'm losing my mind.

Sighing, he headed up the back stairs to his office.

And then his afternoon got worse, because outside his closed door was Emilie, knocking softly.

Nathan slowly exhaled, willing himself to be calm—to overlook the fact that he still obviously was hung up on her.

She still wore her hat and the thin red jacket that looked new but not really warm enough for New Hampshire.

He smiled to himself. This weather would be an adjustment for her. He leaned closer. She smelled like…an unfamiliar shampoo, not her usual ship's brand. Jarred by her presence, he waited.

She rapped with her knuckles again, her back to him. This time, she pounded on the door, louder and more insistent. "Nathan!" she called.

He cleared his throat. "I'm right here."

She whirled to face him, her eyes huge.

Don't show that you care, he told himself.

"How long have you been standing there, watching me?" she demanded.

"Only a moment." He walked past her and opened the door. With his free hand, he motioned for her to precede him. "Please," he said, trying to be polite and formal. On his best behavior, but not familiar.

Her lips pursed, Emilie marched ahead of him.

She was angry with him, and he should expect nothing less. She'd been angry with him when they'd last spoken, too. She'd left him sitting alone in the ship's fancy French restaurant, the engagement ring he'd bought her left behind on the white tablecloth, in its lavender velvet case.

He'd been deeply hurt when she'd walked away. Rejected, though he would never admit what he'd felt to anyone.

Adopting the mild, neutral expression he used when dealing with bankers, real estate agents and lawyers—the banes of his existence—he motioned her to a seat in front of his desk.

"No, I think I'll stand," she said stiffly, crossing her arms.

"That's fine." He sat in his own comfortable leather desk chair and leaned back. "What can I do for you, Emilie?"

She took a deep breath before answering, as if deliberately calming herself. Then she looked him in the eye. "You can explain something for me, Nathan, because I'm a little bit confused." She gave him a small smile and a shrug, as if they were back on the ship and she was flirting with him.

He simply gazed at her, not changing his expression a millimeter. He would not be charmed, and as soon as she realized that, the better off they would be.

A crease appeared over her brow, and she frowned at him. "Why did you invite me here, anyway?"

"I didn't invite you. Nell did. She saw your plight on television and felt sorry for you."

"Nell." She stared at him with reproach. "Your *niece*."

Then he understood why she was upset. He hadn't told her about Nell.

"She was young and away in college on the West Coast while you and I were dating."

"Dating?"

He nodded silently. What did Emilie want to call it? They never had officially become engaged to be married.

"So…" Emilie sat in the chair. "Nell doesn't know about…our past history, then?"

He shook his head. "No."

"Why not? Why not tell her before I showed up here to live and work on your property?"

He didn't answer. He couldn't answer. *Because it's painful for me to think about it, let alone say it out loud, that's why.*

Emilie sighed. "Nathan, we should talk about this."

"There's really no point."

"There is. I don't want any awkwardness between us." She gave him a charming, rueful smile. He knew Emilie—this was one of her "show smiles." She was *on*. Performing for him as if he was a guest in her audience.

He would have none of it.

Folding his hands, he leaned toward her over his desk blotter. "You're here to do a job. You have a show scheduled, I believe, in just about two weeks. I've left the details to Nell to coordinate. Anything you need, please see her."

Emilie's lips thinned and her chin set. "I need the ice fixed, Nathan. It's unacceptable."

Only being able to open half the rink was

unfortunate, but it was the compromise with the expenses he'd had to make with Rob, his principal investor, to keep it open at all.

"Sorry," he said. "It's as fixed as it can be. What you see is what I have to offer."

She gaped at him. "We can't skate on that so-called ice!"

"I saw what you skated on aboard the ship. That surface was quite small."

"It's not the size—it's the unevenness. I need a smoother and more functional ice surface. Anything less just won't work for my skaters."

Maybe he should've checked Guy's work. Nathan would consult with him tonight. "Very well. I'll look into it."

"That's not good enough!"

He stared at Emilie. She was bristling with anger. She could be a very protective mama bear when it came to her people. He had loved that about her. He willed himself to stay resolute in the face of her anger. "It will have to be, Emilie."

"Why are you doing this, Nathan?" she asked between her teeth. "You *know* we need a dedicated Zamboni driver to work with us." She shook her head. "Come on, you remember how we operate—an ice technician, more lighting…" She ticked off her requirements on her fingers. "And external heaters—firepits, I'm thinking, at least for the audience."

"A Zamboni driver *is* working with you. I'll supervise him myself when he clears the ice again to make sure it's smooth enough," he conceded. "But that's all. And you'll have to wait until I can talk to him later tonight, when I'm not busy. Beyond that, I'll instruct Guy to prepare the ice each morning before you arrive. But that's all he can do for you, Emilie. That's the agreement I made with your production company."

"*You're* going to judge the quality of the ice, Nathan?"

"I know about preparing ice surfaces. I even drove the Zamboni when I was young. I was trained by the best."

She threw up her hands. "You never told me any of this!"

"What does it matter?" he asked, suddenly tired. "It will be prepared for you each morning to the proper specifications. That's all you need to know. Didn't Nell tell you all of this?"

"No, but I didn't specifically ask her." Emilie took in a breath. "She's doing a great job, by the way, so don't blame her. She tried to protect you, but I insisted I had to talk to you one-on-one. And why not—because you're keeping secrets from her." Emilie took another breath and then shook her head. "You're making things difficult for no reason. You could have told Nell the truth. You also could have informed me of your plans yourself, rather than keeping me in the dark. Do you think I enjoy being confrontational and causing bad feelings? Because I really don't. I don't enjoy it at all."

True. Emilie preferred pleasing people. And yes, he *was* keeping secrets, all around.

He closed his eyes and leaned back. Nell didn't know that he had a past with Emilie. Emilie didn't know that his inn was inches away from going under.

He wished he could give her everything she wanted, or at least explain why he couldn't. But his investors had made it clear the information was confidential. He'd taken a risk telling Nell.

"Please, Nathan," Emilie appealed nakedly to him. "I concede that you have an agreement with my production company, but at least can't you see about getting us transportation to and from the rink? With all of our gear, it's too far for us to walk."

She was right—it wasn't practical for them to walk. There were ten skaters, plus all of their equipment bags and props. He hadn't thought about that detail.

But how to address it? He'd stopped the shuttle bus service because of the inn's money troubles. He could rent her a car, but to balance that expense, he would have to cut something else. And the last thing left to cut was the family shelter program.

He thought of Jason. *No.* He wasn't putting that little boy into the cold—not under any circumstances.

There was only one solution.

He squared his shoulders. "You're right. I forgot to prepare transportation for you. I'm sorry." He reached into his pocket and took the key off the chain. "You can use my Jeep. I realize you'll have to take a few trips to get everyone back and forth up the mountain, and I apologize for that, but it's all I can offer you at this point."

"Your Jeep? Your *personal* vehicle?"

"I'm not heartless, Emilie," he said quietly. "I'm simply practical."

And as she took the keys from him, looking befuddled, he realized another blunder he'd made. He'd been so intent on protecting himself from being affected by her that he'd forgotten what *she* had just gone through.

"I'm sorry about what happened on the *Empress Caribbean*," he said quietly. "I hope you're okay after that ordeal." Really, this should have been the first thing he'd said to her.

She gazed at him softly, shaking her head. "Nathan, what's become of you?"

"What do you mean?"

"You've turned cold."

Had he? Well, she had no idea what had been going on with him since they'd parted, either in his life or in his heart.

There was so much he couldn't tell her. About his inn failing, about the fact that his finances were on the ropes, about the feelings he still carried for her...

Don't think about that.

"I was concerned," he admitted, "when I saw on the news that the *Empress Caribbean* had hit a reef. In fact, I checked my phone that day to see if you'd called me."

Shoot. He hadn't intended to admit that.

"I thought of you that day, too," she said softly.

She had?

"The evacuation was traumatic for me, and also for the troupe." Emilie paused. "I'm ice captain now. Did you remember that?"

"Of course I did." How could he forget?

"Well." She exhaled. He could tell she was trying to keep her dignity, too. "Thank you for the sympathy. But the best you can do for me is to help us be successful with our show."

"Well, as long as your definition of success doesn't affect my overall costs or my running of the inn, then you and I will be fine."

"That means we're in trouble, doesn't it?" She raised one brow and shook her head lightly at him, gently poking fun. Then she turned serious. "Come on, Nathan, it's Christmas. Think about the kids in town that we can perform for. Surely they need a nice rink?"

He *was* thinking about the kids. She had no idea.

"As I said, Emilie, I can host you here as long as it doesn't add to my costs. That's what I can offer you in the way of sanctuary. That's my bottom line."

"Grinch," she murmured.

"Call Santa Claus and ask him for help."

She snorted at him.

But their conversation was at an end.

And honestly, the situation made him sick. He'd love to give her a big beautiful rink with fantastic lighting and a dedicated ice technician like she'd had on the ship.

And he was tired of failing. So tired of feeling low and without hope.

He couldn't give Emilie what she wanted from him. And what he wanted from her wasn't even on her radar.

She might see it as him turning cold, but now all he could do was focus on the inn's cash flow and revenues for this month. Try to meet the demands of his investors. Keep the inn open as long as possible, for those kids' sakes.

And *that* didn't involve Emilie or her troupe. They were just a means to an end. They were part of his *marketing without cost* campaign.

She stood, sensing the meeting was over, as well. He held the door for her. At least now she wouldn't want to see him again.

Why did that make him feel even lower?

EMILIE STOOD IN the hallway, feeling dazed. What had just happened? She'd lost that round—that was for certain. She'd gone up to Nathan's office to ask for a nicer rink, and instead he'd stonewalled any of her attempts at improvement, anything that would cost him money.

They actually had an adversarial relationship now! He had no intention of supporting her troupe at all.

Hiring them hadn't even been his idea.

She shook her head. He'd certainly turned hard where she was concerned. Once upon a time, they'd worked well together, but those days were over.

She headed downstairs to their rooms again. If she was going to impress Lynn and Donnie with her shows, it was clear she couldn't count on Nathan to help her.

But what if she started her *own* campaign to promote the troupe?

She paused. Yes, it was genius! If people signed up to see their performances and hear their remarkable story, then Nathan wouldn't be able to deny her request to fix up the facility. He would have no choice but to support them in the way that her plans required.

And Nathan? She'd need a campaign for him, too. To win him over, she was going to be in-your-face kind to him. Or maybe just in-your-face. Deal with him only through Nell? Nope. He was going to face *her*. Emilie wouldn't take his not-so-subtle hint that he didn't want to see her. She would wave to him, bring him coffee, roam his property to her heart's content. She would encourage her skaters to treat him the same way, too.

The doors were open to three of the six rooms that her troupe occupied. Music played from the speakers on someone's iPhone. Curtis and Lynette tossed a mini foam football back and forth in the corridor. Rosie was dressed as if she was still in Florida, showing off her dance moves as she tried to intercept the football away from Curtis.

"Team meeting!" Emilie called cheerfully. "Everyone into my room!"

Gary fell in beside her. "Let's take the day off."

"We've already had too many days off." Emilie opened up her room with her keycard and then propped the door open with the wastebasket. Gary followed her inside, with Rosie close behind.

Emilie took off her coat and hat and tossed them onto one of the two double beds. "Rosie, will you go and get the others, please?"

"Julie is downstairs in the lounge." Rosie grinned at Emilie. "There's a really cute chef that works here. His name's Claude. He's from Paris originally."

Interesting—a French chef. Julie had hung out with an Australian diver on the cruise ship. She'd told Emilie she liked men with accents.

"Okay, would you please go get her? And also knock on Katya's door. Gary and Curtis, will you round up Lars, Sergei and Drew, please?"

"Sure thing, Ice Mom," Gary said.

"It's time to get serious! Our first performance is in less than two weeks, and we still need to adapt our show to the constraints of the new venue. And Lynn has also asked for a second show, separate from the Christmas one."

Gary saluted her, winked and then headed off with Curtis. Lynette skipped off to tag along, too.

While Emilie waited for them all to return, she went out and grabbed her suitcase and bag from where they'd been left in the corridor, and then wheeled the case into her room to begin unpacking.

From the corner of her eye, something streaked past her on the floor. Something furry and gray, and scurrying on four legs.

Emilie shrieked and ran back into the hall.

A small boy crouched on the floor, looking frightened. He gazed up at her with big eyes.

"Oh," Emilie said, light dawning. "That was the cat I saw earlier, wasn't it? The inn cat that was up on the lobby couch." In Katya's lap.

The boy straightened. "He's *my* cat. I'm responsible for him. Can I go get him, please?"

"Of course." Then Emilie shuddered. "I

hope he's not chasing mice. I really don't want to see any dead mice."

"They're better than live mice."

"Hmm. Maybe you're right." But she certainly hoped that Nathan spent enough money to take care of any rodent problems. Knowing him, he figured the cat took care of that item on the expenses list. She shuddered again, not wanting to think about pest control.

But before the boy could go looking for his pet, the tabby cat crept back to the doorway of Emilie's room, poking his sweet little head around the corner. The boy scurried over and lifted him into his arms.

"May I touch him?" Emilie asked, scooting down to the boy's height.

"Yes. He likes people. He likes to play, too."

She brushed the thick soft coat of the tabby cat's fur. "What's his name?"

"Prescott."

"Oh! You named him after the inn."

"Uh-huh." The boy nodded.

"And who are you?" she asked.

"Jason."

"Are you staying here with your parents, Jason?"

With a flushed face, he lowered his head and shook it.

"With who, then?" she asked gently.

"My mom," he mumbled. "We live over here." He pointed to the room directly across the hall.

"Ah. So you and I are to be neighbors. My name is Emilie. I'm in this room by myself, but my friends are in the five other rooms all down the hall on this side."

Just then, a maid rounded the corner of the corridor, pushing a housekeeping cart.

"Hello, Greta," Emilie said, reading the maid's name tag.

Greta paused. To Jason, she chided, "You were supposed to wait upstairs in the break room with me."

Jason hung his head further. "Prescott ran downstairs. I had to go get him."

Emilie intervened on his behalf. "It's quite all right. He and Prescott aren't bothering any-one."

"Still, his mother would like him to wait up-stairs in the maids' break room until she gets home from work."

Jason sighed and pulled Prescott closer to his scrawny chest. Emilie could tell that Jason didn't want to go back to the break room. "He's welcome to sit with us. It's no trouble."

Greta leaned toward Emilie and murmured in a low voice, "He lives here. He and some other families live in this hallway. Full-time, I mean."

"Oh." From the tone of Greta's voice, Emilie wondered if they were part of a social services program that the State or private aid subsidized. It wasn't her business to ask, though. "Well, Greta, I hope those families are okay with us moving in. There are ten figure skaters staying in these six rooms, and we can be rowdy sometimes."

Greta brightened. "I've heard of you all. You're the cruise ship skaters. I saw you on the news. You helped all those people get off the ship safely. You're famous!"

"We just did the job we were trained to do," Emilie murmured. She cleared her throat. "Where are the other kids now? I assume they're in school."

"Yes," Greta replied. "They'll be home at three o'clock. The bus drops them off at the front entrance."

"I'm Emilie, by the way." Emilie stuck out her hand, giving Greta a wide smile.

Just then, Lynette came trotting down the hallway with Rosie and Julie, their loud voices bouncing off the walls.

"And this…" Emilie explained to Greta, "is

Rosie, Julie and Lynette. Katya is… Where i
Katya?" she asked them.

"She's napping," Julie replied. Julie was stil
Katya's roommate.

"Is she feeling okay?"

"Bad news from home, I think," Julie whis
pered. "She Skyped with her mom earlier."

"I'm sorry to hear that," Emilie murmured

Lars showed up, flanked by Gary. "Did yo
know the Wi-Fi here is free? And fast. An
unlimited."

"So everybody's been on social media an
messaging apps while I've been gone?" Emi
lie asked.

"Oh, yeah. Except Julie. She's been makin
new *friends*." Lars smirked at Julie, but Juli
just good-naturedly nudged him in the ribs.

They were all like siblings with one an
other. Even Sergei, who kept quietly to him
self.

"Well," Emilie said to Greta, "this is most o
us. Please don't feel like you have to clean ou
rooms every day. Just dropping off clean tow
els and toiletries is basically all we require."

"It's not a problem." Greta paused. "Wha
was it like to survive the shipwreck?" sh
asked in a low voice.

"It was…difficult. But we're all happy it led us here."

"Prescott Inn is a beautiful place. Well, I'd best get on with things." She smiled gratefully at Emilie. "Thank you for indulging Jason."

"We'll look out for him. Don't worry!" Emilie waved to Greta and motioned Jason and the cat inside her room. He sat in a chair and quietly petted his cat.

"I can't wait to see the new costumes," Julie said as she followed Emilie inside the room. "I wonder if they'll send us warmer ones than the costumes we used on the ship?"

"Interesting idea." Emilie could think of a new design to make use of the outdoor arena…

"All right, let's start our meeting." Emilie prepared seats for her team as they all piled inside. "Where's Sergei?"

"He's comforting Katya."

That worried Emilie. She would have to keep the meeting short so she could check on Katya as soon as possible. "All right, we'll leave them be for now. Everybody, please take a seat." There was plenty of room for the eight of them—plus Jason and Prescott—to spread out across the two double beds, a small couch and a pair of chairs.

It was also nice to be in a room with a window. She now had a huge closet, too—more than enough space for Emilie's few clothes. And the floor wasn't rocking beneath them. Emilie wasn't prone to motion sickness, but it was a nice change to be on land. Just for now, though.

"So, we have to drive in a Jeep to get to work to the outdoor rink every day," Emilie informed her skaters first. "That'll be different for us."

"What will be the same?" Lynette asked. She was the youngest of the troupe, at eighteen. "Will we interact with guests in the morning? I loved the parades we had on the ship. It really promoted a nice spirit, particularly during the holidays."

Parades. An interesting idea. On board the ship, the skaters, along with the musicians and dancers, had been responsible for leading a parade down "Main Street," which was really the main shopping concourse, three times per week. Kids loved it. Vacationers of all ages joined in, too.

"Sure, of course we'll have parades," Emilie said, eying Jason, who'd seemed to perk up at the mention of parades. "We're going to do everything fun that we did on the ship. We're going to act just like cruise ship show skaters, because that's who we are."

"And the sooner we'll be back on board when they have another opening for us," Rosie chimed in.

"Sure," Emilie agreed.

"I've called my parents," Curtis announced. "They said they're going to book a stay at the inn during the week of Christmas."

"That's great," Emilie said. Nathan should be happy to hear of another room being booked.

"There don't seem to be too many guests staying here, Emilie," Gary remarked.

"Well, we're going to try and change that. I'll talk with Nell. Maybe we can get a local reporter in here, drum up some more excitement."

"We should perform something for the reporter. And try to get a big audience to make a good impression on the media." Julie shifted on the bed, crossing her stockinged feet beneath her.

"Good idea." Emilie nodded. They were all professionals. And she could use her contacts with the media she'd talked to down in Miami. A few of the national-based and New York–based shows had picked her interview up, too. Maybe she could leverage that into someone from the Boston stations driving up here?

Curtis cut into her thoughts. "So…we're doing the same show as we performed on the ship, right?" he asked.

"Yes, plus one other that the production company has requested."

"Another original show?"

"It won't be completely original, don't worry. Pieces of it will come from our old performances, just because of the time constraint. I'll wait and find out what costumes get delivered. And the sets, too. But we'll lay out some ideas and get oriented to the new rink and see how it goes."

"How big is the rink?" Gary asked.

Emilie hesitated. If her plan worked and she drummed up interest for the shows—sold lots of tickets and hopefully rooms—then Nathan would *have* to give her what she wanted. She definitely would insist on the improved, professionally groomed ice surface, but what about the size? Half a rink seemed so lame. If she used the entire ice surface, she could make a really spectacular program. Something to impress Lynn and Donnie.

"That might change, too, depending on how big an audience we can attract."

Yes, with the whole rink, she could choreograph something truly special. Without the dips and waves of the cruise ship as it sailed, the program could be utterly fantastic.

"I can help you," Jason piped up. "The other kids here and my friends at school are all excited about your show. I can get them to come."

"That would be great, Jason! How many other kids live here?"

"Um." Jason counted on his fingers. "Five, besides me."

"How old are they?"

"Big kids."

"Teens?"

Jason shook his head.

Middle schoolers, she assumed. A good age for her type of show. Maybe she could set aside some tickets to give away; she didn't think the families here had much money. Audiences weren't always about selling tickets.

"Well, Jason, welcome to the team! You can help me talk to the other kids when they get home from school, okay? And Nell, too. Now, who has my phone? I need Nell's number." Nell should be down here with them to help plan their caper.

"What are we going to do?" Gary asked.

"We," Emilie replied, "are going to start by spreading Christmas cheer among the patrons of Prescott Inn."

Just wait until Nathan found out.

CHAPTER SIX

On Monday afternoon, Nathan headed into town to run some errands.

He dropped off a copy of the skaters' contract with Rob, and then showed him the progress he'd been able to make with the inn's weekly expenses. To Nathan's surprise, Rob was optimistic about the skaters. But Nathan sensed that the results from next week's expense report would tell the tale. Between now and then, Nell needed a big push on publicity to raise the inn's bookings—and therefore revenues—for the Christmas season, or else they were all in trouble.

The rattletrap car that Nathan drove back to Prescott Inn belched smoke as he pulled into the parking lot, making him think longingly of his Jeep. Emilie had that, of course.

Put her out of your mind, he told himself. *Continue with the plan.*

He pulled into a space by the valet parking stand and waited for Frank.

Frank rushed over, poking his head inside the rattletrap's open window.

"Oh! It's you, Mr. Prescott!" Frank looked confused. "Where is your Jeep?"

"The skaters are using it this month, Frank."

"Okay." The other man nodded. He eyed Nathan's ride. "That's a sweet twenty-year-old Monte Carlo you're driving, isn't it, sir?"

Sweet? The battered sedan had once belonged to his late father. "Yes," Nathan answered curtly, and then handed Frank the keys.

The only reason Nathan hadn't sold the car two years earlier was that Nell had been using it. When she'd bought her own car last month—a used Honda—he'd tried to sell the Monte Carlo, but maybe because it needed extensive body work, he hadn't found a buyer yet. "Please park this for me, Frank."

"In your regular spot in the front?"

"No." Though the car was inspected by the State and deemed road worthy, it didn't exactly give the appearance of "country luxury" he hoped to convey. "Put it far in the back, where customers can't see it."

"Right, Mr. Prescott." Frank nodded solemnly.

Nathan got out of the car and stretched. He

couldn't help asking, "Are the skaters practicing up at the ice rink?"

"No, sir."

Nathan's neck tightened. He hoped that Emilie and her troupe weren't hanging around the lobby. Or worse, congregated in a loud group, laughing at a table in the restaurant.

"Nell is with them today," Frank added. Then he stepped inside the car, shut the door and backed out the Monte Carlo.

Thoughtful, Nathan strode toward the curb. The Christmas lights over the entranceway twinkled brightly.

He frowned. It was still daylight. He'd thought he'd asked Guy to keep the lights off during the daytime. The electrical costs added up…

But before Nathan could head inside to find Guy, an SUV zoomed in front of him, cutting him off and making it impossible to take another step.

Irritated, he brushed his sleeve and glanced up. It was his own Jeep that had nearly run him over.

He walked over to the driver's side, censorious words on his lips for Emilie.

But it was Nell who was driving. His niece opened the door and hopped out. "Hi, Uncle Nathan," she chirped.

On tiptoe, she peered over him and called to Frank, who had stopped the Monte Carlo to see what she wanted.

"Frank! Could you please help me bring the props inside? They're in the back! This is a last-minute thing, and we're really rushed!"

"Sure thing, Ms. Lewis!" Frank shouted back. Abruptly, he parked the Monte Carlo and left it in the front loading lane beside the hotel. He hopped from the car and then rushed over to where Nathan and Nell stood beside Nathan's Jeep.

"Thank you, Frank," Nell said, breathless. Her cheeks were pink. Nathan noticed that she'd put on red lipstick and smoky eye makeup that made her look like she was going someplace special.

"What's going on?" Nathan asked.

"Like I said, it's a last-minute initiative, otherwise I would've explained everything to you."

"I know I said you should take the initiative, but—"

"Don't worry, Uncle, it's not costing you a penny." With a mischievous twinkle, Nell went over to the rear of the Jeep and pulled out a bag from the back, and then tucked it under her arm and hurried after Frank, who was teetering under the awkward load of a yard-size plastic snowman.

What the…?

Before Nathan could decide what to think, a shiny black town car pulled into the unloading lane beside Nathan's abandoned Monte Carlo. From the driver's side of the sleek conveyance stepped Paul, the town's limo driver and a friend of Nathan's since high school.

Paul tipped his cap to Nathan. He wore a black livery suit and his best professional demeanor. Paul often taxied travelers both to and from the regional airport in Manchester and the international airport hours away in Boston. There was also an Amtrak station in the state capital that he sometimes served.

"Got two guests for you today, Nathan." With a flourish, Paul opened the passenger door and held forth his arm to assist a woman out of the car. "This is Vera. She has a reservation at the inn."

Vera looked to be in her early eighties. Her hair was gathered in a distinguished silver bun, and she moved slowly with the aid of a cane. As she got out, she stood to her full height, sniffed the air and smiled at the gentleman who alighted onto the lane beside her.

Paul hastened to the trunk of the town car to

remove two large suitcases and then set them on the walkway beside the brass cart Frank used to bellhop.

Except, Frank was inside the inn somewhere, helping Nell. Nathan cleared his throat. He wasn't too big to do any task required of him at the inn. It was just that he was a little rusty. He hoped he did a good job…

Paul ducked inside the car again and came out holding a plastic pet carrier, which he placed on the curb.

"Fluffy!" Vera exclaimed. She smiled up at Nathan. "Young man, will you assist me with my cat, please."

"Ah, certainly." Nathan silently blessed the decision they'd made to set aside a number of rooms as "pet rooms." It seemed this strategy was paying off. None of their major competitors allowed pets.

"Will you be checking in today?" he asked the couple, as Paul got back inside his black town car and zoomed out of the parking lot.

"Yes. We are booked for three nights," Vera told Nathan. "We're looking forward to a quiet stay in the country."

Nathan nodded as he stacked their luggage onto Frank's brass cart. Neither Vera nor her husband made a move to pick up Fluffy, so

Nathan gingerly picked up the cat in its plastic crate.

Oof. Fluffy was heavier than he looked.

Vera inched her way forward up the ramp with short steps while her husband courteously held her elbow.

"Will the sleigh ride be operational this week?" Vera asked Nathan, as Nathan put down Fluffy's crate and tried to figure out how best to get the feline guest inside safely. He didn't fit on the cart, not with the couple's large pieces of luggage.

"Ah…we need snow for the sleigh ride to be operational. But once it snows, yes, there will be rides later in the season," Nathan answered. He figured that Guy would drive the sleigh. The horses came from the farm next door, as they always had.

Vera and her husband had reached the double doors that led to the inn's entrance. Frank still hadn't returned to open them for the guests, so Nathan hefted up Fluffy's crate and left the loaded baggage cart where it sat. He strode over and opened the lobby door for them.

Loud noise drifted from inside the building—music and singing. Festive chaos, led by the skaters.

Nathan's heart sank. *So much for Vera's quiet week in the country*, he thought.

He cleared his throat again, deciding to stall the couple outside for a few moments. Maybe Emilie and her troupe would finish up and go away if he waited. "So, yes, as I was saying," he repeated to Vera, covering for his delay, "as soon as there is a snowfall, then we will have sleigh rides. You can be sure of that."

"With jingle bells?" Vera asked.

Nathan had seen the old bells on the hook in the barn. They still had them. "Yes, jingle bells will be present."

"And hot chocolate?"

He smiled broadly. "We have a fully staffed kitchen, with hot chocolate and marshmallows."

"And a shuttle bus so we can shop in the craft shops in town?"

His smile died. No, no shuttle bus. Vera and her husband were customers, though, who would presumably be purchasing meals in the restaurant each day, adding to his revenue. Nathan pasted a smile on his face and nodded to Vera. "We'll arrange something so you can shop locally, yes." Maybe he would ask Nell to offer space in the lobby to artisans and organize a crafts fair on the weekend.

"Wonderful! We used to come up every year during this week in order to celebrate our wedding anniversary," Vera confided in him. "But then the inn changed hands and the quality of service went down."

"We stopped coming altogether," the husband interjected.

"I assure you, the inn is under new management and our quality of service is excellent," Nathan replied politely. "May I ask how you heard about us again?"

Marketing research was always good. He wished Nell was here. Was she inside with the skaters?

Whatever they were doing, they hadn't stopped making a racket. Even standing outside the building, he clearly heard even louder music coming from the lobby. Then loud, enthusiastic clapping.

"Why, we saw the ad, of course," the lady remarked.

Ad? Nathan hadn't approved any expenditures for an ad. Newspaper ads could be quite expensive.

"Which ad was this?" he asked nervously.

"The great big billboard by the highway." Vera rubbed her arms. "My, it's getting cold. May we go inside, please?"

"Yes. Certainly." Nathan would deal with the question of the billboard later.

Just then Frank came outside. Nathan had never been happier to see him. Being a bellhop was harder than it looked.

"Mr. Prescott! Let me assist you with that!"

"Oh, you're a *Prescott*!" Vera exclaimed to Nathan.

"One and the same." Nathan tucked Fluffy under his arm like a football and then waved the couple through the doors ahead of him.

The din of music was overpowering inside the lobby. Nathan cringed. Maybe the couple was hard of hearing. It appeared so, because neither of them seemed bothered by the commotion in the least.

But then they rounded the corner and the surreal scene by the fireplace couldn't be denied. Vera stopped in her tracks and put her gloved hand to her lips. "My goodness!" she exclaimed. "What is this?"

Nathan had no choice but to stand by helplessly with them and watch the show in progress.

And what a show.

The ten cruise ship skaters were decked out in what Nathan remembered as their "shipboard" uniforms. Formfitting black pants on the women, the men in jeans. They all wore long-sleeved shirts with the skating logo on the front. Must be their Christmas outfits, Nathan thought, because the T-shirts had a red background with a sprig of holly worked into the logo design.

Though the troupe wore sneakers instead of their usual skates, they danced and twirled and jumped in a carefully coordinated routine. The snowman that Frank had carried in earlier was paraded between them as they danced around the tree. In the front, in a position of prominence, a petite skater was being lifted and twirled aloft by a big, muscular guy who looked to be her dance partner. A male freestyle skater stepped out and, with two powerful introductory steps, leaped into the air.

Yeah, it was a quadruple toe loop jump. Nathan had learned enough about skating from Emilie to know what that was. It was also a skill that not too many guys in the world possessed.

A flashing blur in the air, and then the man solidly landed on one foot.

Cheers broke out from a group of assembled children.

Nathan had no idea the skaters had such an audience. But there they were. A whole crowd of kids, more than lived in the inn. Nathan supposed they were local schoolchildren.

Jason waved at Nathan, so he waved back. Jason's gray tabby cat was perched in his lap. Nathan didn't have the heart to do anything about that. Jason looked like he needed a friend, and if Prescott made him happy, then Nathan wouldn't evict the little fur ball.

Five other young kids were squeezed beside Jason on the same couch—two boys and three girls. These kids definitely lived in Nathan's inn, though they seemed to be a few years older than Nathan's little friend.

And then Emilie walked past, doling out candy canes to the children in her audience, which they all too eagerly accepted from her.

His heart lurched in his chest. Emilie had always been good with children. Back on the ship, the performers had danced in a parade down "Main Street." Before Christmas, they'd happily passed out candy canes.

Nathan swallowed the lump in his throat. Those had been good times.

Don't think about those days. Don't think about Emilie. Tend to your customers.

He turned back to the couple he'd helped inside. Luckily, they were smiling while they watched the skaters, who were now exiting the "stage," taking their bows.

"It's not usually as noisy as this." Nathan apologized to Vera and her husband in a low murmur. "I'll have a talk with the skaters and make sure it settles down for the rest of your stay."

"Oh, that's quite all right." To her husband, she said, "Jaspar, these are the cruise ship skaters we saw on TV last week. Remember, they were looking for a place to stay? I think it's nice they've found a place to perform." She turned to Nathan. "We're very impressed. It's why we followed the ad on the billboard."

"Look, darling, we're on TV, too," Jaspar remarked, pointing behind Nathan.

His head swimming, Nathan followed Jaspar's gaze and spotted a camera crew. Nathan hadn't even noticed them. A man with a professional-looking camera on a tripod was crouched beside the Christmas tree, filming a female newscaster Nathan vaguely recognized from a regional television station. The newscaster stood before Emilie and Nell and was holding a microphone out to them. An interview.

Nathan groaned. "I apologize for the cameras," he murmured to Vera. How was this possibly the quiet week in the country she'd signed on for?

The newscaster signaled to her cameraman for a break. She was a stately woman who wore a modern wool suit and expensive gold jewelry. She looked like she had money—frankly, the kind of clientele Nathan hoped to attract to his inn, to spend lots of cash to help him move his business out of the red and into the black.

Nell zipped over to Nathan, glowing. He didn't have the heart to reprimand her. He couldn't be "Uncle Scrooge" to her when she seemed so pleased with herself.

"Uncle, the woman from the news wants to interview you next. Let's go get you ready." Without waiting for an answer, Nell straightened his tie and used her fingers to comb his hair.

He stepped back from Nell's "fixing." He had no intention of being part of their news story.

"We'll talk in my office later." For now, though, he eyed Vera and her husband. Frank had led them to the registration desk to check in. As Nathan observed them, Vera suddenly stopped and bent over, opening up the cat carrier that Frank carried, and retrieving Fluffy from his confinement.

Oh, no! Prescott was seated only twenty feet away, in Jason's lap. Nathan could just imagine the catastrophe if the pampered prince and scrappy Tom got into it in the lobby.

In an attempt to prevent a potential cat fight, Nathan dashed toward the pet carrier, ready to intercept Fluffy if need be.

But Vera scooped Fluffy into her arms, cooing at him, where the persnickety white Persian contentedly sat and blinked slowly at Nathan with his smug blue eyes. Fluffy seemed to prefer to ignore that there was another male cat anywhere near him.

As Vera noticed Nathan, who was perspiring heavily, she smiled sweetly at him. "I enjoyed the show, Mr. Prescott. It reminded me of days gone past at Prescott Inn. The early days, before you were born."

Nell had wandered over, too, just to add to Nathan's discomfort.

"You were here in the old days?" Nell asked Vera, while Nathan winced for what might come out of this little exchange.

"Oh, yes," Vera answered Nell. "Jaspar and I came every year at this time for years, while it was still named Prescott Inn. That's where we celebrated our wedding anniversary. But when the inn was sold, the quality went downhill, so we stopped our yearly visits. As I was telling this nice young man, we took a chance when we saw the advertisement for the skaters. We watched them on TV. They were so brave for helping all those passengers disembark from the sinking cruise ship."

The wheels seemed to be moving behind Nell's eyes. "Well, the official debut of their Christmas show is coming up soon. Will you return for it?" she asked Vera. "Please."

"Why, yes, that would be lovely! I hope that means the ice rink is open this year. We came for the sleigh rides, too, of course."

Nell gave Nathan a pointed, triumphant look. Then she asked Vera, "Did you ever skate on the rink, in the old days?"

"Of course we did," Vera said. "In fact, Jaspar asked me to marry him on your little gated skating pond on the mountainside. I would so dearly love to see it again."

Nell smiled more broadly. Nathan could guess where this conversation was heading. And he couldn't disapprove. He stood by, shocked, watching his niece in action.

"I can certainly arrange that for you," Nell was telling Vera. "My name is Nell Lewis, by the way. I'm the great-granddaughter of the original owner."

"Oh, you're Phil Prescott's great-grand-daughter?" Vera clasped her hands to her lips. "Jaspar, did you hear that?"

"Phil Prescott became a dear friend of ours. He was our youngest daughter's godfather." Jaspar nodded, his eyes clouding over as if remembering happy times.

"Such a great honor you gave him." Nell touched Jaspar's arm. "Sadly, I never met my great-grandfather. He passed before I was born. And I grew up on the West Coast, so I don't have memories of the inn as it was in the past. But I do feel a kinship with those days now that I work here."

And while Nathan stood, mouth agape at Nell, his niece gently led Vera over to the newscaster.

Nathan followed from a safe distance. The last thing he wanted was to be roped into an unscripted television interview. The reporter would no doubt dig into his reasons for reopening the resort, which would only lead to painful parts of his past that he did not want to revisit.

An interview with Vera and Jaspar, on the other hand, was good publicity for them. Nell was a genius.

He listened as Nell convinced the newscaster—Janet, Nell called her—to interview Vera and Jaspar.

Janet nodded enthusiastically. Nell jumped up and down, not hiding her youthful enthusiasm.

He felt a moment of pride for his niece. Yes, he would discuss the cost of the billboard with her later, but for now, he would let her enjoy her victory. She seemed to be hitting her stride.

Where he hadn't connected with a guest personally, Nell had. Where he had avoided an opportunity to promote their inn because of his own reluctance to talk about the past, she had righted his error and was making the best of it.

He glanced once again at the skaters, disciplined performers that they were, circulating and speaking with other guests who'd gathered in the lobby. They handed out flyers for their upcoming shows. Despite the ordeal of the ship sinking, there they were, enthusiastically forging ahead.

"Uncle?" Nell waved at him from across the room and then came skipping over. "Isn't this exciting?" she whispered in his ear.

Nathan watched as the camera turned on and Janet began conducting her interview with the Christmas tree as a backdrop. Vera and Jaspar were evidently reenacting the details of Jaspar's proposal of marriage, because the gentleman had bent to one creaky knee and was lifting his hands, palms up, in a beseeching gesture.

Beside him, Nell sighed. "It is *so* romantic. And do you see how successful our efforts have been? I want you to note that it's all free. It cost us nothing to bring in the news team."

"What about the billboard?" He couldn't help asking.

"Oh, the ice-skaters' production company funded that." She waved her hand dismissively. "Emilie O'Shea arranged it." Nell grinned. "I like her, Uncle. I can't tell you how much she's been helping me every day."

Yes, he could see Emilie's influence in his niece's positivity and unflagging cheer. He'd always been attracted to Emilie's knack for lifting people's spirits.

But she was also helping get business for his inn. This he appreciated even more.

"What are you thinking, Uncle?"

"That you did a good job, and I'm proud of you."

"You *are*? I'm glad you said that."

He supposed he should say it more often. He just wasn't naturally as expressive as Emilie.

"When will the newscast run?" he asked,

changing the subject. "I assume they're going to take the footage back to the studio to edit the segment?"

"Yes. The producer—" Nell gestured to a young woman holding a clipboard in the corner and talking on her phone "—is guiding the cameraman to take lots of action shots here at the inn. Then they're going to piece together a general interest update on the plight of the shipwrecked skaters, who are heroes because they rescued so many others. We're part of their story now, so that will be positive publicity for us all."

"You did well, Nell," he repeated.

"It was Emilie's work, too. We did it together."

He nodded. He ached to ask further what Emilie had been doing, but he didn't want to divulge his interest.

"Janet told us they're going to run the story tomorrow night," Nell remarked. "Sometime during the dinner hour. Then, over the next several days, they'll run it again at different points. She's excited about the attention this will bring locally. Did you know that Emilie might be able to get the segment picked up by one of the evening news shows? She made connections with them when they interviewed her after the cruise ship sank. That *would* be a coup for us, wouldn't it?"

"Yes." Emilie *was* amazing. There was no doubt about that.

"It's exactly the audience we need. Wealthy people with money to spend, who want an authentic winter-lodge Christmas experience."

He nodded at her. "I'm sorry I ever doubted you."

Nell beamed. "The candy canes were free, too. The village craft fair gave them to me in exchange for a plug on the show. The snowmen we're displaying are part of the deal."

"That's great, Nell. I'm leaving the promotion in your capable hands. And now, I'm heading upstairs to do some—"

"Wait!" Nell clutched his arm, effectively halting his escape. "I have *another* idea! We should do a screening in the downstairs lounge on the big TV tomorrow night. Can't you just see it? I'll have Claude whip up some snacks, and we'll let the locals know via a poster in the coffee shop in town. We can have the skaters come, and then we can…"

"Sure," he said absently, his mind drifting off. Nell wasn't even taking a breath in between her sentences, she was so excited by her plans. But his attention had wandered to Emilie.

She was sitting beside Jason now. She'd scooped her hair behind her ears and had bent over to look at what the boy was doing. Maybe admiring a drawing he'd made, or helping him with his homework.

"Emilie's interview made me cry," Nell was saying.

Nathan jerked up his head and stared at his niece. "I thought Janet interviewed you together. Did Emilie give a separate interview?"

"She sure did. She talked about landing on her feet and how our inn saved the skaters. Janet asked her lots of questions about their odyssey, and Emilie talked about the special show they're going to design for us. Uncle, I think you should go over there and thank her for saving our butts."

They weren't saved *yet*.

"Uncle, do it." Nell gave him a little push.

"Did…she say anything about me?"

Nell looked at him blankly. "Why should she?"

"Right. Never mind." Part of him was relieved that Emilie hadn't let on to anyone about her past relationship with him. If she had, Nell would have said so.

Still, his pride took a bit of a hit.

He hadn't *meant* to be harsh with Emilie earlier. Just as he hadn't meant to be harsh with Nell. It was just his way sometimes. He was no good with words; he preferred his actions to tell people how much they meant to him.

"So, will you thank her, Uncle?" Nell nudged him. "Come on, I'll walk over with you."

"No, I'm fine." It was best that he keep away from her. That hadn't changed.

"I think you should say something to her," Nell continued, not letting up. "Compliment her like you complimented me. And just so you know, we filmed some great skating footage at the ice rink today. I had to work like a maniac shuttling everyone up and back, taking turns ferrying people and ice skates and cameras inside your Jeep. It needs an oil change, by the way. The red light is on in the dash."

He groaned. "Right." One more item to add to his to-do list. But more disturbing than realizing that Nell seemed to be taking Emilie's side on all things Prescott Inn was the news of their small rink being shown on film. He hadn't expected that.

Even he knew the facility looked old and run-down.

Seeming to read his mind, Nell said, "Just wait until you see the way Emilie transformed our rink in the woods. That's all that I'm saying." Nell gave him an enigmatic smile.

"What do you mean by *transformed*?"

But Nell had already glided away.

There was no avoiding it now. He'd have to talk to Emilie.

CHAPTER SEVEN

OPERATION "PROMOTE THE PERFORMANCE" appeared to be working.

Emilie smiled inwardly as Nathan approached her. Arranging for the reporter to come in today had been her first step in her plan to sell more tickets to her shows and get Nathan to see her side of things.

But it was best to take it slowly. Though the expression on Nathan's face wasn't sunny—he looked a bit green, in fact—she believed in time that would change. Through her efforts, she could win him over.

She just needed patience with him. And persistence.

"Hello, Nathan!" she greeted him cheerfully. "You look festive today." He was dressed in his business suit, complete with jacket, white shirt and red tie. "Red is truly your color."

He gave her a skeptical frown.

He did look good to her. Tall, handsome, with his hair adorably windblown. She liked him better when he was ruffled enough that he wasn't so uptight and perfect.

"Here, let me straighten your tie for you. You're going to be on camera, after all." She reached over and smoothed out the knot. This close, she smelled the clean scent of the soap he'd showered with this morning. The same smell she remembered from the ship. *Nice.*

"I'm not going on camera. And tell me something, Emilie," he said, drawing back. "What exactly did you do to my ice-skating rink?"

"Why?" she asked innocently. "Are you interested in coming up and watching us skate?"

He gritted his teeth and gave her a warning look.

"I see. You're busy, of course. As are we," she said cheerfully again.

He frowned at her. Nell must have dropped a hint to him about the improvements they'd made—probably to tease him—because both Emilie and Nell had been gently poking fun at Nathan for being a "Scrooge" with one another all morning. Emilie really liked his young niece. She was spirited and smart, and also loyal to Nathan, which Emilie approved of. It hadn't taken much to draw the young woman out of her shell. With her enthusiasm and fresh ideas, she reminded Emilie of some of her own young skaters. If Nell was a skater, then Emilie would adore having her on her team.

"I need to be told when major changes are made," Nathan said. His green eyes focused on hers intently.

Now was a good time to advance her agenda.

"Speaking of changes to your skating rink…" She opened her jacket and pulled out a folded slip of paper, which she then tucked into his pocket.

"What's this?" he asked, removing the small piece of note paper.

"A list of further things we need to complete before we can officially open the first show next weekend."

"Emilie—"

"Oh, wait, but as of this morning, one item is already ticked off. Let me show you." She tapped the list to indicate the item. "The most important thing—the ice surface is now professionally graded and suitable for figure skating."

"How did you do that?" He squinted at her warily. "I didn't authorize any funds."

"Yes, I know." She grinned at him. "I didn't spend any 'funds.'"

He sighed aloud. "Please explain."

"I found a man in the village with ice technician skills, and we negotiated a barter. He does the work with his own tools, and I give him comped show tickets. He has young kids."

Nathan stood blinking at her for a moment. She'd clearly surprised him with her resourcefulness.

"Does Nell know?" he asked.

"She planned to tell you this evening."

"I see." He took her to-do list and pressed it back into her hand.

For a moment, their hands brushed.

Emilie's heart beat faster. The spark of the unexpected contact seemed to jolt her to her core.

It certainly shook her off her game with him. She gripped the slip of paper and swallowed.

"Thank you, Emilie," he said, not seeming to notice how he affected her. "You're eminently capable, and I'm appreciative for your help in promoting the inn."

"It's not just your inn, it's our project," she said, recovering.

"Pardon?"

"You and I are promoting our joint project together."

"Right." He nodded. "It is a joint project. And I thank you for attracting the positive publicity. Nell told me you did a lot of the important work. I appreciate that."

Was she hearing him correctly—after all of his resistance to her, grumbling about her expensive demands, he was giving her credit?

He never ceased to surprise her. Emilie swallowed again. "Well, Nell assumed you wouldn't like the disruption," she admitted. "That's why we timed the bulk of the segment to be filmed while you were out."

"I was…concerned about the filming, yes, I'll admit that. You know I'm not a big parade person." He flashed a rueful smile.

She'd always liked it when Nathan smiled. Now more than ever, it made her feel good in her heart to see him with some of his old lightness.

"I thought you enjoyed my parades," she said. *On the ship*, she'd meant.

A dimple formed in his cheek. A sign of honest-to-goodness pleasure.

And just like that, she was strolling down memory lane.

By his smile, he wasn't backing away from the good memories, either. "You have new uniforms," he remarked, glancing down at her T-shirt.

"My production company sent them." She

felt self-conscious all of a sudden. "Our clothes are…on the bottom of the sea."

"I really am sorry about that, Emilie." He gazed softly at her, his eyes so green. "Did you lose anything special to you—I hope not." He cleared his throat. "I was thinking about your photos. I remember you always liked to keep photos."

She was a sentimental person, that was true. "I have my phone with me, and most of my pictures are backed up on the cloud, so I'm okay with losing most of the hard copies."

She took a breath, attempting to ease the flutters in her stomach. Nobody was within hearing distance, so she was safe in that respect, at least, to talk about the past with him.

In a low voice, she said, "There was that… pendant you gave me. Remember, Nathan?"

It was heart-shaped, with the tiniest of rubies in the middle of a gold setting. Rubies were her birthstone, and one lazy hot afternoon, she'd mentioned to Nathan that it wasn't fair that her birthstone was a ruby because the gem was so dear and out of her budget. She was getting some relief from the heat inside the ship's air-conditioned jewelry store, and he was doing inventory. She was on a break and had just been babbling, really. She'd honestly had no ulterior motive. But Nathan being Nathan—or at least how he'd been back then—had surprised her with the gift later that day. Shocked her, really.

"It was for our two-month anniversary," Nathan said huskily. "Yeah, I remember that day."

Emilie bit her lip, suddenly realizing how dangerous this talk had become. And *she* had led them down this path.

"Well, I should go." She shouldn't feel regret that they hadn't been able to make the relationship work. That was in the past, even though those had been the happiest times of her life.

She shook her head fiercely, pushing away those sad thoughts. "You and I will talk about the rink later," she said firmly. "I really do have other requests that I expect you to take care of. I won't let them go, Nathan."

Nathan's mouth tightened, but then he sighed and lifted up his hands in a gesture of capitulation. "We'll discuss it another day."

"Soon," she informed him. "Tomorrow."

Prescott, Jason's gray cat, interrupted them by running into their path. Prescott braced his little legs on the floor and stared up at Nathan, meowing as if he had a complaint to lodge, too.

Emilie laughed at the cat's adorable expression. Prescott seemed to be on her side.

Nathan chuckled softly. "Go find your owner," he told Prescott.

To Emilie, he said, "I need to get back to work. But I'll let you go first to make sure this great gray hunter won't attack you. I've got you covered."

Yes, he was making a joke. But it just made her feel sadder.

"You like cats," she said. "I never knew that, either."

"We had no cats on the ship," he pointed out.

"Actually, what surprises me most is that you allow children to keep their pets in your inn."

"Why would that surprise you?" He stepped silently aside while Jason bent to pick up his cat. The boy scurried off with him, tucked under his arm.

Nathan frowned at the boy. Had she said something wrong? She wasn't sure what Nathan's relationship was with Jason.

"Well." Nathan nodded formally at her. "Have a good skating practice, Emilie, and thank you again for your help with 'our project.'"

She nodded silently and watched him leave. She'd accepted two years ago, after their relationship had ended, that there were just some things she would never understand about Nathan Prescott.

He ran hot and he ran cold. Mainly, he seemed to wear a shield that kept his true thoughts hidden away from her. That had probably been true on the ship, as well, but she hadn't recognized it back then as she was beginning to now.

Her next step—starting tomorrow—was to get his permission to use the whole ice surface for her program. The ice itself was now prepared, but the remaining problem was the lighting and the rotted boards at one end of the rink. She'd been thinking of ways around those issues—using a curtain to block the boards off, and bartering for labor with a local electrician to fix the lighting—but those were details Nathan had to sign off on. So she had to continue to try to convince him to be on her side.

At least he'd smiled at her today. But in order to truly get him on board, she'd need to understand him better. That would be the secret. Then she'd be able to put on a great show that would impress her bosses and help all the skaters on the team.

Sighing, she turned back to her troupe, wondering what she should focus on next. She still had to come up with a theme for the second show. Emilie wanted to use some of the skaters' old routines, but how could she piece those numbers together into what was most entertaining and emotional for her audience?

This was something for her to mull over.

Vera and Jaspar were strolling past her, so Emilie lifted her hand and waved. Their story would make a nice spotlight feature for the inn. Emilie had something special in mind for the couple's sixtieth anniversary—a touching tribute during one of her ice shows. She and Nell would have to develop the idea further, but until then…

"I'll talk to you tomorrow, Nathan Prescott," she murmured.

"*Nathan* Prescott?" Jaspar stopped in his tracks. He swiveled and gazed at Nathan, who was heading with purpose toward his back staircase. Probably to disappear inside his office again.

"*That* was little Nathan?" Jaspar asked Emilie. "Philip Prescott's grandson?"

"Oh, did you know Nathan when he was young?" Emilie asked.

"Why, yes, we did. Nathan Prescott always used to sit right here." Vera pointed to the couch where Jason had been sitting by the Christmas tree. "He lived in the inn with his grandparents. He and his sister. Nathan always seemed sad to me. I used to feel sorry for him, but he kept busy. His grandfather—Phil Prescott—was a hardworking man, and he expected Nathan to work hard, too, even though he was just a boy." Vera lowered her voice. "His parents were traveling show people, you see. Always gone on tour, especially during the Christmas season. What did I say? You've gone pale, dear."

"Excuse me just a minute." Emilie held up a finger. This conversation with Nathan could not wait. "Hold that thought, Vera—I will be back later."

Without waiting for the older couple's reaction, Emilie ran to catch up with Nathan.

"Nathan!" she called.

In the stairwell, he turned to gaze down at her. "Is everything all right?" he asked, looking concerned.

"No, everything is not all right."

He stilled. "What happened?"

"Your parents were show people? How come you never told me this?"

"Did Nell say something to you?" he asked cautiously.

"No. She's tight-lipped where your personal life is concerned. She's either very loyal, or a little scared of you. Maybe both."

He smiled tightly. "Vera and Jaspar recognized my name, did they?"

"Yes."

He crossed his arms. "I don't see how it makes a difference."

"I want to know why you never told me!"

"You didn't ask." Since she was blocking the stairs, Nathan headed back toward the front desk. As he leaned over to pick up a stack of mail, she followed him.

Yes, she was probably making a mistake in terms of her ulterior agenda, but she just couldn't help it. She'd thought she'd known Nathan better that this!

"Show people," she hissed in Nathan's ear. "Is that like actors, dancers, singers—what?"

"It *really* doesn't make a difference," he said coldly, brushing past her. It was as if their progress of a few minutes ago was now ancient history, and they were back to where they'd stood when she'd first arrived here. *Two steps forward, one step back.*

"You're not going to tell me, are you?" she said, following him. He was headed upstairs again, to his lair, evidently. Washing his hands of her. Well, she wouldn't let that happen.

She hopped in front of his path.

"Emilie, please, I need to get to work," he said in that maddening, calm voice of his.

"Don't get too comfortable. Once Janet is finished with the skaters, she's expecting to interview you. You have to go on camera, too."

"No, I don't."

"If you want to represent the inn and our project, then yes, you do, it's required."

"Nell represented us just fine," he said stubbornly.

"Nell didn't know your grandfather. Janet asked her for some personal anecdotes about the history of the inn, but Nell wasn't born then. You were."

"Janet is getting personal in the interviews?"

"It's a human-interest story. It's supposed to be emotional."

"I thought it was more of an advertisement." He looked cornered.

"No, it's not an advertisement," she explained. "That's not how free promotion works. It's a feature. Advertisements have to be paid for."

Nathan nodded. "Right," he muttered. "I knew that." But he still looked troubled.

"What's the matter?" she asked him gently. Evidently, Nathan's fear was more than just shyness of the camera. "Why don't you want to talk about your grandfather?"

He shook his head. "My grandfather was great. It's an honor to talk about him. Really."

But Nathan raked his hand through his hair and frowned at the nook Emilie had helped Nell decorate for the on-camera interviews.

In front of the Christmas tree, they'd angled a chair so that the gorgeous mountain backdrop was in view. Currently, Janet was interviewing Katya, who was openly sobbing, tears streaming down her cheeks. Emilie would go to her in a moment to see how she could help the younger woman, but for now, Sergei hovered protectively nearby. His presence made Emilie less worried for Katya.

Nathan's stare seemed far away and haunted. He appeared not to even be seeing Katya—he appeared to be gazing out at the mountains instead.

Something was bothering him. Something he wasn't sharing with her.

"Don't worry about the interview, Nathan. I'll help you. Like Sergei stands by Katya."

"That's not necessary," he said coldly. "I know what's required of me, Emilie."

Then he turned away and went over to stand by the Christmas tree.

Emilie felt rebuked. And it put an unsettled

feeling in her stomach. She honestly didn't like being at odds with him.

She didn't like being pushed away. Or arguing with him.

She and Nathan had never had a fight on the ship. Before they'd broken up, everything had always been so free and easy with him. Her whole life on the ship had been that way. She'd been all smiles and happiness, never being a problem for other people. But since the ship had sunk and she'd ended up at Nathan's inn, all of that was changing.

She'd been forced out of her comfort zone, and Nathan wasn't making it easy for her. He was a much more complicated man than she'd ever realized.

Ironically, she'd been attracted to his protective nature right from the start. Nathan was a solid rock of a guy. She'd fallen in love with him the day he'd first attended one of her shows. She'd sprained her ankle while coming out of a backspin at the same time as the ship had lurched. She'd been forced to sit out the next matinee, with her ankle up, necessitating that the troupe work late into the night reblocking the show to make up for her absence. She couldn't even work the stage lights or help with costume changes backstage. Instead, she'd been told to sit with her feet up and rest, and that had made her feel like a drag and a burden, and therefore, guilty, as if she'd done something wrong.

Nathan had sensed that, and so he'd sat with her. He'd held her hand in his and asked her to explain the show and what was going on behind the scenes, making her realize that her worth extended beyond her ability to perform. He liked her just the way she was.

She'd been a goner for him after that day. It was the only show she hadn't really paid attention to, because she couldn't concentrate on anything but Nathan and how sitting close to him, holding his hand, had made her feel.

Later that night, under a glorious moon and a clear night at sea, Nathan had asked her up on deck to look for shooting stars because they were sailing beneath an asteroid belt.

They had shared their first kiss that night—the most perfect first kiss she'd ever enjoyed, romantic and sweet.

Now she stared over at Nathan as he gazed stoically out the windows over the towering mountain peaks. Nathan was the same rock-solid man, just two years older, but their relationship might as well have been a lifetime away from those days.

NATHAN TRIED TO squelch the panic rising within him.

Janet's production assistant combed his hair and then posed him on the stool. Both Janet and her assistant were skilled in prepping victims for the camera—that was certain. But Nathan couldn't relax. He had to be on guard against Janet. He had to protect the inn, at all costs.

He felt exhausted carrying this burden. But it was necessary.

"There. I'm just going to ask you a question or two," Janet crooned before him. She blocked the photographer with her body, but still, Nathan was acutely aware of the camera behind her.

He coughed, and the production assistant magically appeared with a bottle of water. He waved it away. He also waved away her makeup brush.

Let's just get this over with.

Janet was regarding him, tapping her finger on her lip as she assessed him. "On second thought, I'm going to pull up a stool beside you and we'll have a casual conversation together."

He stiffened his spine. "That's not necessary."

"I'm trying to get you to relax."

"Let me tell you about my inn. That will relax me."

"Okay." Janet nodded to the cameraman. A red light flashed on.

Nathan swallowed. A crowd had gathered behind Janet and her cameraman, but that wasn't who Nathan focused on.

Jason was behind them all. Kneeling on the floor beside the couch, taking it all in silently. Like Nathan had as a boy.

Nathan focused on Jason and began to talk. He ad-libbed from the beginning of his canned spiel. His "emotional pitch" for "the story" of Prescott Inn, the one that he gave to developers and investors and guests and employees. Just a few short sentences and words from his guarded heart.

"My late grandfather built Prescott Inn as a home in the mountains for everyone who enjoys the outdoors and a sense of community. The ice rink in the pine forest is a center for our winter family, and we're especially privileged to invite the performers from the *Empress Caribbean* as guests to our family."

Here Nathan paused. The skaters gathered before him in their matching T-shirts, their elf and Santa hats. The petite skater with the blond braids had stopped crying and was listening to him thoughtfully. Most of the others smiled at him. He didn't know where Emilie was, but he was sure she was watching from somewhere.

"We were touched by their plight," he said, continuing. "We watched the news coverage of the ship's accident, and we felt the despair of the passengers and crew, particularly the skaters. My niece, Nell, suggested we do something to help. We've offered up our home to them, and they're offering up to us the joy of their skating this Christmas season."

He swallowed, looking directly into the camera. This was his appeal, his "close," his begging—and yes, he was begging—because he desperately needed people to come out to their inn.

"I'm inviting everyone to come and join us in this family vacation. The skaters will be performing for us each afternoon in the rink in the woods. Please join us this holiday season."

Nathan stopped. He found Jason again in the back of the crowd. The boy smiled and gave him a thumbs-up. Relieved, Nathan stood. If he didn't escape now, Janet would pounce on him with follow-up questions.

Nathan would never be comfortable in front of a camera. Emilie was the performer between the two of them, but he'd realized during this exercise that, in fact, he'd been mistaken.

He was a performer, too. Wasn't he giving the show of his life? He had a mask that he wore most of the day, and as he turned away from Jason, it made him feel sad and tired and ashamed.

CHAPTER EIGHT

EMILIE ENTERED THE LOUNGE, hoping that Nathan had come down from his office to watch the screening of their news segment.

Her gaze scanned the crowded tables before the large-screen television.

There he was, in a far corner, at a table by himself. It was interesting to her that Nathan had spoken of "community" in his short camera segment, and yet he didn't participate with his people.

For all his talk of "family," he wasn't part of a team. He was separate. Even Nell sat with Emilie's skaters. Claude and Frank and Martha gravitated to them, too, even though the inn's staff were off shift at the moment.

Nathan had removed himself from it all, however. She was beginning to realize that he felt it was necessary as their boss to appear separate.

Well, Emilie needed him to be part of the

group. He had something very valuable to contribute.

A collective gasp rang out in the darkened lounge, and cheers began to ring out. Janet had appeared on screen, sitting in a studio with a background graphic showing—of all things—Emilie's face.

It didn't faze her in the least—she was used to seeing her image publicly projected. That was part of show business. Emilie took a seat at Gary's table and prepared to watch the news segment.

As Emilie had expected, two hours of footage and interviews had been pared to a fast-paced and emotional two-minute feature.

What hadn't been snipped away were Emilie's descriptions of life on the ship and an honest portrayal by Katya about the terror of evacuating a sinking ship, and then, with Gary, the following realization of being homeless, with personal items lost forever.

The segment also worked as a fantastic commercial for Prescott Inn. Nell had done a wonderful job bringing the inn's history to life and emphasizing the caring attitude of the Prescott family and the unique attributes of their mountain inn.

And then there were artistically shot snippets

of the cast dancing in the parade, as well as some quick shots of jumps and spins and tricks that they'd done on the ice, all filmed on the workable half of the rink, but filmed in such a way that it didn't show off the rink's flaws.

Nathan's interview had been reduced to two or three short sentences, one of them narrated by Janet rather than spoken by him. It was an effective ending to the piece, though. Nathan's deep voice and comforting, stoic presence gave the whole piece gravitas and thus a comforting ending and call to action.

The show cut to commercial. Cheers broke out from the inn kids, who'd been excited each time a glimpse of their faces had appeared in the piece, mostly during the shots of the parade in the lobby. Even Prescott, the inn cat, had made a short appearance.

The lights went on. The dining room waitress approached Emilie.

"Would you like some fresh gingerbread and whipped cream, Emilie?"

It looked and smelled delicious. Emilie remembered how Nathan had loved gingerbread, especially in the weeks before Christmas. "No, thank you. Perhaps you should offer some to Mr. Prescott?"

"Oh, he's already left."

Emilie jumped to her feet. She'd planned to stop him on his way out. "Nathan!" She strode after him, but with his long legs pumping, she didn't catch up to him until he was almost at the front door.

"Nathan, wait!"

He finally stopped. He wore a heavy black wool overcoat over his suit. On his feet, he wore wet-weather boots, rubber and leather, which made him look like he was a true New Englander. He was pulling on his gloves as he turned to her. A mask of wariness showed in his tired green eyes.

"What's wrong, Emilie?"

She put her hand to her chest, catching her breath. She'd been hurt yesterday afternoon at the way he'd treated her. He'd brusquely sent her away. He'd deliberately kept facts about himself from her. He'd delegated and deflected her issues back to Nell.

Now he was trying to do it again. She wouldn't let him get away with it anymore.

"Yes?" he asked.

She shifted on her feet, suddenly not sure how to proceed. She wasn't used to confronting people.

"The segment came out well," he said, in that exasperatingly formal voice. "You did a good job. Thank you." He turned again for the door.

She touched his arm. "Wait!" She had to put aside her hurt. This wasn't about their past. It was about her and her skaters' futures. The rink *still* wasn't ready.

"Nathan, we only have four days until the dress rehearsal." She swallowed, because his eyes had glazed over. He wasn't interested in a personal appeal.

She would try to be formal, then, like him. "I'd like to schedule a meeting with you," she announced.

"A meeting with me?" He blinked. "Shouldn't you be discussing this with Nell?"

"I have been meeting regularly with Nell, but…she doesn't have the clearance to make certain decisions."

A muscle twitched in his jaw. "And what decisions would those be?"

Don't get upset. Be professional, but proceed with firmness…

She took a breath and smiled courteously. "The team needs help sectioning off the far end of the rink. My production company is sending us curtains and some standard props. But we need to assign two strong workers with ladders to hook everything up."

"You have five fit young men," Nathan remarked. "If you want to borrow our ladders, then have Nell show you to the maintenance hut."

"I can't risk injuring the skaters," she said as calmly as she could. "Nell mentioned that you have maintenance workers who could be temporarily reassigned."

"My maintenance workers are Guy and Frank. Guy is the full-time maintenance manager. You can have Guy—unless, of course, we have a guest emergency and need him back at the inn."

"Well, okay." Emilie put her hair behind her ear. This was a start. "May we have Frank, too? We need two people, and he's been accommodating to us." *Unlike you.*

"No, I can't spare Frank." Nathan crossed his arms. "He's our sole remaining bellhop. He greets everyone who comes to the door. I need him at his post."

"It should only take an hour or two if we do it off-hours."

He thought for a moment. "Okay. That will work."

"So we're agreed?" She hid her shock.

"Yes." He gazed down at her with those

veiled green eyes. "Are we set now, Emilie? Because I have to go."

"Wait!"

He rose his brows as if to say, *There's more?*

And there was. She did need more from him. And she was finding it was more important to her than a functioning ice rink.

She needed Nathan's support. This really was a joint project, and there were many details to oversee. Yes, Nell was a fine partner, but Nathan... Well, she couldn't stand that he had isolated himself from them—from her. It was hard that they had once loved each other, but she could live with that. What she couldn't stand was that he was so remote from her.

How to reach him?

She thought back to the interview last night. Something she'd noticed that had stood out for her and she hadn't been sure why...

"I'd like to schedule time with you to talk about Jason," she said.

"Jason?" He turned to her suddenly. She'd hit the jackpot. He was immediately alert and concerned. "Is everything okay with him?"

"I'm not sure," she said honestly. "He hangs around the rink with us every day, and that's what I'd like to discuss with you." She blew on her hands. It was blasted chilly in this vestibule.

"Yes." Nathan nodded. "I'll have Martha call you and schedule something tomorrow morning."

"I'm sorry, Nathan. I skate during the day. Dinner is more convenient for me."

His brows rose. "You want to have dinner with me? Why?"

"Well, it isn't your scintillating conversation, trust me."

He didn't find her humor amusing. "Is there something I should be worried about? Is Jason okay?"

"For now, yes. But I have concerns." She did her best to smile. "Shall we meet at your place, or mine?" She turned and gestured toward the dining room, her feeble attempt at humor again.

But the dining room had all her troupe inside. And Nell. And a whole bunch of kids and parents and guests who were full of curiosity about who Nathan was, given the mini documentary they'd just watched about him. From Nathan's expression, she guessed that the attention didn't appeal to him.

"We'll meet at the diner in town," Nathan decided.

"That place beside the post office?" Emilie nodded. "I know where that is. It's where I found the technician to fix our ice surface."

NATHAN DID SOME fast thinking. If he and Emilie met at the diner, then all eyes would be upon them. And though he rarely patronized the diner anymore—not since the inn's restaurant was up and running—it had apparently become more Emilie's turf than his these days.

"We'll eat at my place," he said reluctantly. "Tomorrow night."

"That sounds wonderful." She nodded at him. "Pick me up at seven, please."

That sounded intimate to him, like a date. It wasn't the vibe he wanted to give Emilie, at all. He was trying to remain disassociated from her.

"I no longer have transportation to come pick you up," he reminded her, going on the offensive again. "I've loaned it out to you, remember?"

"But I thought you had access to a second car?"

"A junker. It finally died. I gave it to Frank for the parts."

"Oh," Emilie said with a small voice. "Then how are you getting to work?"

"Frank picks me up on his way in. Or Nell does."

"Hmm. Well, in that case, why don't you drive us both in your Jeep? I'll loan it back to you for one night."

"That's very generous of you, Emilie," he said, sarcasm intended. "But no need, I'll have Frank drive me home after work, and I'll cook."

"Well, I tried to please." She shot a smile at him. "As for my part, Nathan, I'll bring dessert over from the inn. Something you like. Gingerbread, or chocolate torte, maybe? Claude promised me he'd make me his special chocolate torte whenever I wanted it."

Claude—*Nathan's* chef. But he seemed to be getting awfully close to the skaters.

Nathan groaned. "You're going to bankrupt me, Emilie, do you know that? And then where will we both be?"

But she just laughed it off as a joke. She didn't really believe him. She had no idea that he *was* that close to losing everything he'd sacrificed so much for.

He absolutely couldn't get close to her. It had ended badly once before, and it would be even worse this time.

But he did want to find out what was going on with Jason. And if she had information he needed, then he had to risk an intimate meal with her.

But he definitely would stay on his guard. Saving the inn was his first priority.

THE NEXT DAY, Nathan tortured himself by looking out of his office window, into the lobby below, watching Emilie as she ran back and forth, opening up special-delivery packages that contained Christmas-themed skating costumes—Elf, Mrs. Claus and Ice Princess.

She wore her formfitting practice clothes—black ballet leggings with a light gauzy skirt tied at the waist to give her the look of a slim ballerina. She was beautiful. Her hair was tied up in a casual bun, showing her long, slender neck and the tight scoop-necked top she wore.

He swallowed. She was always in motion, gracefully busy, it seemed. Her cheeks were flushed and wisps of hair floated around her pretty face.

She was like a butterfly who drew people closer. He noticed that Frank didn't immediately leave after he'd given her the packages. Then he'd started carting all the boxes away—clearly, she'd convinced him to help her load the boxes into the Jeep.

And just how long had he himself been standing here watching her?

Nathan stood and drew the blinds.

How was he going to survive dinner with her tonight? In his *home*. He never should have let himself be maneuvered into hosting her. Nathan rarely had meals with other people anymore. He usually ate at the inn, alone in his office while he did paperwork. He'd left the inn early last night, but only because he'd needed to get away from Emilie. Just being in the same room with her was torture.

But the meeting was set now. *Just keep it focused on Jason.* He agreed with Emilie; something was obviously wrong there...

Nathan shook off his worry. It was more productive to focus on the details of the meal.

He knew exactly what she liked to eat. He'd shared three meals per day with her on ship for a year. He remembered Emilie's tastes. She'd remembered his—gingerbread and chocolate torte. Those kinds of details, to him, had been more important than whether or not she knew he had a niece named Nell and a sister who lived in California and a rotten childhood where the only good thing had been living at his grandfather's inn.

He wondered what she *really* wanted to talk

about. Was Jason just an excuse? Probably she wanted him to invest money in the rink, he guessed. Well, he would be on his guard—there would be no charming him. Not like she was charming poor Frank right now.

From his back window, Nathan could see the Jeep wind up the slope, driven by Emilie. A few minutes later, Guy's truck followed, chugging uphill.

He told himself he was watching only to make sure that Frank hadn't hopped into the passenger seat, ostensibly to help her.

Putting his hands to his head, Nathan slumped at his desk. But he perked up at a text message from Martha:

FYI—our phones have been ringing all day! So many reservations coming in after last night's news segment! Didn't want to interrupt you with a phone call, but knew you'd be excited by the news...

Wow. Nathan sat up. This was excellent news.

He left his office and trotted downstairs to check the numbers in real time.

When he got to the lobby desk, Martha put

her hand over the phone receiver and waved him over, an urgent look on her face.

"What is it?" he asked.

"Nell called just a moment ago. There's been an incident up at the skating rink and she needs you to call her when you get the chance."

"What kind of incident?"

"One of the skaters fell and was taken to the medical clinic."

His heart beat erratically. "Is it Emilie?"

"No." Martha gave him a strange look. "It's Gary." She sighed. "The cute one. He's so nice. Apparently he's not seriously injured, except, well, he got two huge splinters in the palm of his hand from when he fell against the old wooden railing. Emilie and Nell are handling it. They took him to the medical clinic for treatment."

"Wait. They took him to the medical clinic for *splinters*?"

"They're large, sir. And since he is a pairs skater, he needs his hands to lift his partner and skate with her in tandem."

Right. He knew that. Nathan supposed he could concede splinters would be an issue for a skater, and that medical treatment was warranted.

This is more stress for Emilie, he thought.

He remembered when he'd sat with her once after she'd twisted her ankle. He remembered how upset she'd been. His heart had gone out to her, and he'd fallen a little more in love with her that day.

That night, he'd kissed her. Up on the top deck by the hot tubs, when the sky had been filled with stars and the only sounds had been the tranquil sea and the whispering conversation that he and Emilie had shared.

He'd sacrificed a lot to bring back Prescott Inn. He'd sacrificed *her*.

So he'd best keep on his toes tonight. Or he'd lose Emilie…and the inn.

CHAPTER NINE

EXHAUSTED, EMILIE KEYED open her hotel room
door after a long afternoon at the local medical center, and then flung herself on her bed.

"Emilie?" Julie knocked on the door and
then poked her head inside. "How's Gary?"

"He says he's okay," Emilie said, rolling over
on the mattress. "But honestly, we'll need to
change the routines so he's not partnering with
anyone for a while."

"Okay," Julie said, "we'll figure it out." Without asking, she headed inside Emilie's bathroom. "Where's the community hair iron?
Rosie said she doesn't have it."

"It's on the counter. But take it with you,
because I have a call to make."

"I don't want to go back to the room because
Katya is in there crying again. I'll use your
bathroom." She shut the door behind her.

Emilie sighed and dialed her boss's number. She wanted to update Lynn about Gary's

accident. She would have to go see Katya, it seemed, when she was finished with that call.

Lynn Bladewell picked up on the second ring. "Emilie! I was just going to ring you. It's important."

"Okay." Emilie lowered her voice to keep it confidential.

"First, how are things?" Lynn asked.

"Good! We're preparing for the dress rehearsal this weekend. We've modified the ship's Christmas show to fit a bigger rink, and it's looking great. We did have a slight accident today, however. Gary injured his hand, so he won't be able to partner. But I've already started reblocking the choreography, and it'll be fine."

"Oh. Well, seems like you've got it handled. Is Gary all right?"

"Yes, and we took him to a local medical center just to be sure." Emilie paused. "I'm having dinner with Nathan Prescott tonight. The professional appearance of the rink is one of my agenda items."

"That's related to why I was going to call you. We have news, Emilie."

"Oh?"

"Donnie has been reviewing the Prescott Inn project, and he has concerns about its short-term nature. I'm under a lot of pressure on my end to get Mr. Prescott to extend your contract."

Emilie felt a chill pass through her.

"Donnie says that without Mr. Prescott picking up the option to purchase more shows through January and possibly February, he'll have to consider the venture a failure. As such, I'm counting on you to do a fantastic job for us this weekend. It's critical for us. And for you."

Emilie swallowed. Pressure, much?

"So yes," Lynn continued, "please do expand your Christmas program to cover the full ice surface. And for the second program we discussed? Plan on something…spectacular."

Spectacular? She hadn't even gotten a solid idea for the theme yet!

"Really pull out the stops," Lynn said.

"Do I get a budget?" Emilie asked.

Lynn laughed.

Of course. Nobody was willing to give her a budget, it seemed.

"Emilie, I'm planning to visit the inn next week, and Donnie has indicated he wants to join me to see your work, too. This is a big opportunity for you, Emilie."

"Donnie is coming to Prescott Inn? To see us?"

"To see you, Emilie. I suggest showing him the new program you're preparing."

This could be really great for them! But she had to get moving.

"Emilie," Lynn said in a cautious tone. "The fly in the ointment is Nathan. So far he's been dodging my calls. Do you think he would be open to hiring more shows?"

"Well, I stopped by the front desk on the way in just now, and a lot of people have booked rooms for our opening week. So we've definitely been helping his business, yes."

"Significantly?"

"I believe so."

"Could you feel him out as to whether he intends to extend your contract? Add it to your agenda items tonight." She paused. "This is important, Emilie."

"Okay. Yes," Emilie promised. "I'll ask him."

"Could you please call me back after the meeting?"

Emilie swallowed. "All right. I'll do that."

Lynn ended the call, and Emilie lay down on her bed again. She felt like the weight of the world was on her shoulders. Everything seemed much more stressful than it had been.

Julie opened the bathroom door and popped her head out. The hair-straightening appliance was in one hand, Emilie's comb in the other. "Is it safe for me to come out now?"

Emilie rolled over on the bed. "Yes. And please don't stay out too late tonight. We have a lot of work to do tomorrow. And I mean *a lot*."

"No problem." Julie left the appliance and comb on the counter and then plopped on the mattress beside Emilie. "You know I'm always ready to work."

"Where are you going tonight?" Emilie asked, curious.

Julie gave her a secret smile. "Not gonna tell you, Ice Mom."

Emilie tossed a pillow at her. "We're not on the ship anymore. Our situation is more serious now than just having parties in the crew's quarters after work."

"Hmm. This corridor *is* the crew's quarters, in case you haven't noticed."

"Little kids and their moms live across the hall from us!" Emilie chided.

"Yes, and what's the deal with that, anyway?" Julie murmured, scooching closer on the bed. "Are they guests or residents?"

Emilie wasn't entirely sure. Greta, their house-keeping maid, had said that the families were living here "full-time," whatever that meant, but

Emilie hadn't seen the housekeeping maid of late to ask her for more details. Their schedules were simply too busy.

But she did have questions about Jason's situation that she wanted to discuss with Nathan. She hadn't made that up. She should talk to him about her concerns regarding the boy. Jason found his way to the rink every afternoon after school to watch them practice. Emilie wasn't entirely comfortable that they hadn't cleared that first with his mom, but he didn't seem to have anywhere else to go. She felt sorry for the lonely boy and didn't have the heart to bar him from the rink. He was younger than the other kids who were staying at the inn, so he got home from school earlier. He seemed to have lots of time to kill before his mother came home from work, and he enjoyed being with the skaters. But was that appropriate?

Those were questions best asked of Jason's mom, but Emilie hadn't managed to catch the woman. Emilie presumed his mother had already been through a lot, and the last thing she wanted to do was complicate the other woman's life further.

"In your travels, have you met Jason's mom yet?" Emilie asked.

Julie pursed her lips, thinking. "No."

"Will you please watch out for her tonight? You stay up later than I do. And if you see her, will you knock on my door and wake me up? It's important. I really do need to talk with her."

"Okay. I feel sorry for the kid, truthfully. The only thing that seems to make him happy is his cat."

"That cat followed him up to the skating rink today. Did you see him there?"

"Yeah. The two of them were so cute, sitting on the boards and watching us skate." Julie smiled. "You know, skating outside in the woods is growing on me. I mean, it's cold, but I'm getting used to that. And it's nice in the sun. It was a beautiful day today."

It was. Emilie lay back on the pillow and threaded her hands through her hair. Lynn had mentioned her intention to get Nathan to extend the skaters' contract. How would she feel about staying here for the winter? That could be nice. She'd been so desperate for a home at Christmas for them, she hadn't dared to think of the future beyond that.

But to get to that future, well…she still needed an idea for the second show. And she had so many issues to address, especially where Nathan was concerned.

But the bookings *were* up—she'd talked with Martha on the way in, and Martha had said that Nathan was in a great mood because of it.

So Emilie had hope. She really did have hope.

Emilie stood. "Julie, I have to leave for a meeting. If anyone is looking for me, I'll be back by nine at the latest."

"Well, I won't be back until after midnight."

Midnight was when the restaurant downstairs closed. Suddenly Emilie knew exactly where Julie was going: to pursue her interest in Nathan's French chef. "Please don't lead Claude on unless you really mean it," she begged. "This is a small community here, and they're our hosts. We're trying to please them."

Julie zipped up the knee-length suede boots she'd bought with her Miami money. Julie loved those boots. "Don't worry about me—I aim to please. And if you happen to see Nathan Prescott tonight, please put in a request for firepits, okay? A hot chocolate stand by the rink would be good, too."

Yeah, right. Emilie was a miracle worker, was she?

She snorted to herself.

Actually, if she *did* get Nathan to help her

fix the falling-apart railings so that nobody else on her team got splinters, then she *would* be a miracle worker.

Lynn and Donnie's arrival was only a week away. Much too soon for Emilie's liking.

BEFORE EMILIE HEADED to Nathan's house with Claude's dessert, she stopped by Katya's room and knocked.

Sergei answered the door.

"Is Katya here?" Emilie asked.

He nodded silently and then stepped back for her to enter.

Katya was curled up on one of the double beds.

"I'm going to be out of the hotel for a couple of hours for a meeting. But I wanted to check up on you before I leave," Emilie said softly. She sat on the bed beside her. "Katya, when I was at the town clinic today, I saw that they have a counselor on staff. If you'd like me to bring you to meet with the counselor for any reason, then just let me know."

"I'm fine."

Emilie leaned closer. "You can talk to me. I'll help you how I can."

"I'm most worried about sending money

home to my mother. Our contract here is so tentative. Everything is fine, yes?"

Emilie swallowed. "Yes."

"Will we be ready on time for our show?"

They *had* to be ready. As far as Katya was concerned, her costumes seemed to have all come in too small, but with some quick seamstress work on Emilie's part, that could be easily rectified.

"We *will be* ready," Emilie said firmly. "Are *you* okay with the choreography so far?"

"I am glad to have no spotlights on me. Or to be on a moving ship."

"Do you mind the cold here?"

Katya shrugged. "It's nothing."

Katya and Sergei had been smart. They'd used their company money to purchase warm practice clothing, unlike some of the other skaters.

"Well," Emilie said, straightening, "I'm going into town for my meeting. Is there anything I can bring you?" It concerned her that Katya and Sergei had been keeping themselves apart from everyone else. This wasn't how they'd acted on the ship. Then again, on the ship, they'd been part of a vibrant community of crew members who also came from their home country.

"I'm fine," Katya repeated. Emilie was at a loss for how to help her.

Emilie glanced up at Sergei, who was quietly studying Katya.

"Um, Sergei," Emilie asked, "would you mind letting me talk privately with Katya for a moment? I would appreciate that." She smiled brightly at him, and though she got a distinct inkling that he understood what she'd said, he didn't move until Katya translated Emilie's words for him.

When they were alone, Emilie whispered to Katya. "What is really going on to make you so sad? You can tell me. It's safe now. It does have something to do with Sergei, doesn't it?"

Katya closed her eyes and leaned back on the pillow. "Yes."

"You're not upset about your mother?"

"Oh, that is true, I am always worried for my mother. But at the moment, it's Sergei."

"Has he done something?" Emilie asked cautiously.

"No. It's just that I don't love him. He is merely a friend. When we were on the ship, we had our friends. Now, he only has me."

"Does he know how you feel?"

"Yes." Katya nodded. "I tell him."

That was why he'd looked so miserable in

practice. "Katya, how can I help you with this problem? It's important to me that you're happy."

"Happy?" Katya pressed her lips together. "Emilie, I am going down to dinner. You go to your meeting, yes?"

It appeared Emilie was just not making the connection with her. After Katya had flounced off, Emilie knew she had to come up with *some* way to help her team member. Sergei, too. And what that was, Emilie had no idea.

She would just have to add it to her ever-growing list of problems to conquer.

NATHAN PACED. What had he gotten himself into? It was ridiculous, but he was sweating like a teenage boy.

He looked around his home, imagining it through her eyes. It was a solid log-cabin-styled house, on the private edges of town. Nothing flashy or fancy. Two bedrooms upstairs. Downstairs, an open floor plan with a kitchen, dining area and TV room. Standard fare, except for the small size. At least it was warm, with a woodstove that he kept fired up when he was home. Lately, it didn't seem like he was home much. He was giving his job his all, 110 percent, just to keep the business alive.

He opened the kitchen oven and took out the lasagna he'd made for the two of them. Emilie had liked Italian food.

He'd made a salad, too, with the special blue cheese dressing that she'd always ordered when they were on board the ship. Plus a big, hot loaf of crusty bread, with extra butter and garlic.

The garlic wouldn't be an issue; it wasn't as if they would be kissing. As much as he might want to, it was a terrible idea.

There was a soft knock at the door. His heart jumping in his chest, he let her in.

She'd let her hair down and put on pink lip gloss. He noticed as soon as she entered. She smelled good, too. It wasn't the perfume she'd worn before, but this was nice. A warm vanilla scent.

She smiled brightly when she saw him— too brightly, which threw him for a loop, because after Gary and the trip to the emergency room, he'd expected anger from her. Yes, he'd spoken with Nell and received an update on the medical center report, but he really should have called Emilie, too.

She held out a cardboard cakebox. "Merry Christmas, Nathan. I decided to bring you the gingerbread."

He'd always loved gingerbread best. She *had* to remember that.

"Thanks." He set the box—still warm—on the edge of the dining table.

His mouth watered. Claude had never made this dessert specifically for him, so Emilie must have asked the chef to make it because she remembered what he liked.

Emilie is thoughtful to everyone, he told himself. *Not just you—it isn't personal.*

"I'll take your coat," he said politely.

She slipped out of her parka and he hung it on a hook in his kitchen. She bent over and unlaced the hooks on her tall snow boots.

Don't let her warmth weaken your resolve, he reminded himself. He couldn't spend any more money on the rink. If she had demands, his job was either to talk her out of it or to come up with alternatives, such as call her production company and ask for *their* assistance.

She sniffed the air. "Is that lasagna we're having?"

He felt pride in his cooking. "Yes, it is."

"It smells delicious. I remember lots of lasagna dinners with you at the ship's pasta bar. I never knew you could cook yourself." She chuckled, but from the genuine smile on her face, she didn't appear to have an ulterior motive for bringing that up.

He relaxed somewhat.

"This is a nice house," she remarked, walking over to the center of the living area and gazing up at the timber beams and the wide airy space. "Do you mind if I have a tour?"

"Well, it's your basic log cabin home. Downstairs, you can see. Upstairs, just a loft area with bedrooms." He forced a smile at her.

She smiled back, not catching his tension. "Did you build the home yourself?"

"No."

"It looks new," she said, returning to the dining table.

"It's renovated," he admitted.

"That cost a lot of money, I bet."

Where was she going with this? "The house came as a parcel deal with the inn," he explained tersely. "The previous owner lived here. I just moved in."

"Well, it's a very nice house." She smiled brightly at him again. "And you're doing financially well, I assume?"

"Emilie, what's going on? Why are you asking me this?"

Her cheeks flushed. "Sorry, Nathan, I'm not too subtle, am I?" She gave him a sheepish look. "My boss called me right before I left the inn tonight. She said she sent you something about option papers but you've been dodging her calls. I'm not up on business and contracts and things like that, but she asked me to find out if you're...*financially viable*. Those were the words she used."

Uh-huh. Nathan had seen the email from Lynn Bladewell in his inbox and hadn't wanted to deal with it until he could assuage his investors. There was nothing he could tell Ms. Bladewell, anyway—at least nothing truthful. But he couldn't avoid the issue now. He should have known there was an ulterior motive to this dinner.

"Emilie, you can tell your boss that Prescott Inn has never been better financially." There was anger in his tone, and from the flash of alarm that crossed Emilie's face, he knew she'd heard it.

"I'm sorry, Nathan," she said, chastened. "I wouldn't have brought this up if Lynn hadn't asked me to. That's the truth. I really am here to talk with you about Jason."

The difficult thing was, Nathan believed her. And he also wanted to talk about the quiet young boy who troubled Nathan, too.

Nathan swept his hand before him. "Please,

take a seat. I'll bring out the lasagna and the bread and the salad. I'm out of wine, so I hope you're okay with sparkling water."

"That would be great." She gazed at him with a look of genuine relief.

"So…" EMILIE BEGAN, licking her lips to get the last taste of the delicious basil tomato sauce that Nathan had made, and then settling back in her chair. "I told you that Jason has been fascinated by us skating up at the rink in the woods. Well, we caught him walking up the hill by himself, and then hiding behind the trees with his cat."

Nathan gave a slight smile.

"He does love that cat," Emilie continued, "but still, I was worried about him walking on the road alone, so I started giving him rides in the Jeep. And I know that I really shouldn't do that unless I talk with you and his mother. Then again, I was worried about leaving him alone, too."

Nathan nodded, listening intently. His eyes showed pain and compassion. "Jason is often alone. Maybe watching you is his way of… trying to find a family."

"Do you think so?"

Nathan nodded. "I haven't personally met

his mother, but her name is Maria. She and Jason came from the homeless shelter."

"I've wondered about that." Emilie put down her fork and regarded Nathan. "That's kind of you to host those families."

Nathan studied his hands. "It's important to me," he said softly. "The shelter is fine, but it's overcrowded and…not really a place for kids."

"No," Emilie agreed.

Nathan smiled sadly. "I've only talked with Jason a couple of times. But I first met him on the day we were putting up the Christmas tree in the lobby." His face turned cloudy. "Jason asked to borrow a Christmas stocking. He was worried that Santa Claus won't be able to find him."

"That's so sad!"

"I know." Nathan nodded. He gave Emilie a guilty look. "I ordered him one, of course. With his name embroidered on it."

She reached over and touched Nathan's hand. "I'm glad."

She let her hand linger. He didn't move it away.

"So, what do we do now?" she murmured.

His Adam's apple moved up and down. "I'll talk with his mother, and then we'll make sure he has a happy Christmas morning."

Emilie blinked moisture from her eyes.

Nathan smiled at her. "I'm not the Scrooge they say I am."

"You have them all fooled."

He chuckled softly, and she removed her hand.

"Tell me about Gary, Emilie. I talked briefly with Nell about it, but from your point of view, what happened up there today?"

"Well, ironically, Jason was leaning against the railing with his cat, and Gary leaned over to help Jason. We were doing some off-ice practice, and Gary thought it would be dangerous for Jason."

"Oh, no. Nell didn't mention that. But I see where this story is going."

"Yeah. The railing was rough, and Gary tripped over the cat and got splinters in his palms."

"Ouch."

"Gary will be okay," Emilie said. "We brought him to the medical center as soon as it happened."

Nathan dragged in a breath. "I'm glad to hear that, but still, I think we need to inspect and sand the railings."

"If you'll give me the name of a local carpenter, I'll call and ask them to swap work in exchange for show tickets," she offered.

"No, this is my issue. I'll fix it."

"Thank you." She gave him a grateful smile. "Just let us know when the carpenter is due to come, please."

Nathan straightened his shoulders. "I'm the carpenter, Emilie."

"You are?"

"Well, I'm an amateur carpenter, not a professional." He smiled faintly. "My grandfather made sure I was able to do all the major repairs around the place. He wouldn't be happy that I've neglected my duty." He looked at her clearly. "I'm sorry. I'll fix it tomorrow."

"That's... Thank you, Nathan." She thought of the portrait of Philip Prescott that was in the lobby by the fireplace. "Your grandfather sounds like a great guy to have taught you those things."

"He was. I miss him every day."

"I bet he would like what we're doing with his rink." She glanced at Nathan. "It was his rink, right?"

"Yes. He built it for my grandmother, Ava, shortly after he married her. She liked to skate. He loved watching her glide over the ice."

"That's so romantic! I can imagine what

the scene must have looked like back in those days." Emilie got up and set out the dessert for him. "Martha was showing me old photos, but now I have a fuller understanding." She set out the plates and forks, and cut Nathan a piece of gingerbread. "And I have to say, I loved the old-fashioned Zamboni they used."

"Thank you." He eyed the dessert gratefully. "And the Zamboni was more of an ice sweeper, as I remember."

"Yes. It's in the barn, actually." She sat down and cut her own piece.

"You've been in the barn?" Nathan asked, curious.

"We were looking for the old spotlights." She smiled sheepishly at him. "My production company considers my work here a test of my abilities. They've told me that my future hinges upon it. That's why I'm taking so much care to put on a great show."

"I didn't know that," he said softly.

"I'm under a lot of pressure," she murmured. "This ice show has to be top quality. I feel like I need to keep my troupe working. You haven't met them all individually yet, but most of them are young and they rely on me. And the kids— I've incorporated them into the show, too."

"Emilie, your dreams are important to me. I want you to believe that."

"They are?"

He gazed at her so steadily, nodding.

She put down her fork, suddenly touched. She felt as if they'd made a huge breakthrough in their relationship tonight. And it had all started over their shared concern for a little boy who needed a Christmas.

She glanced at the time on her phone. It was after nine o'clock. She should get back. She stood and helped Nathan clear the dirty dishes from the table and then place them in the dishwasher.

"When should I expect you tomorrow?" she asked Nathan.

"Sometime during the lunch hour. But there's one more thing I need from you." His eyes were twinkling.

"Me? What can I give you?"

"Every carpenter requires an assistant to carry his tools and help with the sanding. Jason might normally be an ideal candidate to help, but under the circumstances, you'll do." He gave her a wink.

She couldn't help smiling back. This night had turned into a complete surprise. And an inspiration.

Little did he know, but she now had a surprise for Nathan, too.

When Emilie returned to the hotel, the first thing she did was to phone Lynn as she'd asked. She was so excited with her plans that she couldn't sleep anyway. She knew Lynn was a night owl and wouldn't mind the late call.

"First, Lynn," she reported to her boss, "to answer your question, Prescott Inn is financially viable. They've been quite successful with bookings and reservations because of our promotion."

"Thank you, Emilie. That's helpful for us to know."

"And second—I want you to know this especially—I have a great idea for the theme of our special show!"

A *spectacular* idea.

Emilie couldn't wait to get started.

CHAPTER TEN

NATHAN STEPPED OUT of the inn, into the cold air, and rubbed his hands. The temperatures had dropped the night before, and a thin layer of frost covered the ground and the trees.

Still no snow yet, though.

He'd bundled up into a warm parka, scarf and hat. He'd brought his insulated leather work gloves and boots, plus a layer of long underwear under his corduroy pants.

He'd woken up looking forward to seeing Emilie. Last night had been, well, a revelation. He was actually looking forward to the task of fixing the rink's boards with her. It seemed more appealing today than sitting inside, staring at a laptop spreadsheet whose numbers never seemed to line up correctly.

Tomorrow, he owed Rob a numbers report. But for now, he was giving himself a few hours' reprieve with Emilie before he got back to business.

In the parking lot of Prescott Inn, Nell opened

up the hatchback trunk of her Honda, and whistling, he dropped his toolbox inside, beside a pair of jumper cables and a shovel with a short handle. A person could never be too prepared this time of year.

He got into the passenger seat beside Nell. "Okay," he said.

"I'm so excited you're coming up to see the rink this morning." Nell was beaming.

She put the car into gear, and they bumped along the narrow mountain road. She said nothing as she drove, just hummed a fast-temp Christmas tune.

"Are you excited for the show?" he asked, curious about what they were doing, as she turned the wheel and brought them into the rink parking lot.

"Oh, yes. And I've been talking it up when I go into the diner every morning. Everyone is doing their bit to contribute to the success of this venture, Uncle."

"As long as they all show up and spend money in our restaurant now and then," he teased.

"Spoken like a true Scrooge." They both laughed before hopping out.

From Nell's trunk, he grabbed his toolbox. Nell had positioned her car beside his own

Jeep, which earlier Emilie had parked half on the parking lot, half on the frozen ground by the trail to the rink.

His breath forming clouds in the chilled air, he hunched his shoulders in his jacket and followed Nell. Over the short hill that led down to the rink, he heard chattering voices. And instrumental Christmas music—the kind that played in shopping malls.

They walked side by side down the path, him hauling his toolbox and sander.

When they got to the gate, she put her hand on his arm. "Wait here. I want to talk with Emilie first. I'll come back and get you."

"What's going on?"

"Nothing." But it was obvious from Nell's twitching lips she was hiding a smile.

And then she stood on tiptoe and hugged him before she turned and dashed off.

She reminded him so much of his sister.

There were two benches before the gate to the rink. Nathan sat on one and looked around in wonder. Somebody had put Christmas wreaths up on the gates, and the fir trees nearby were decorated with strings of white lights. A song played from the direction of the rink that he recognized. "I'll Be Home for Christmas," a real Christmas oldie that just served to remind

Nathan of his grandfather. The music blared out over speakers that Nathan hadn't even known they'd installed.

He stood and unlatched the gate just as Nell arrived.

"Where did the speakers come from?" he asked.

"They're on loan. Emilie arranged for them from her company. Curtis installed them."

"Is he an electrician?"

"Of course not. Don't be silly." Nell laughed, twin red dots in her cheeks.

"What about the music? Do you have to pay royalty fees to use popular music at public performances?"

Nell laughed harder. "All that is taken care of by the production company. Relax," she chided him. "You're much too uptight."

"You would be, too, if you carried the cares of other people on your back the way that I do."

She took his hand and patted it. "Let's go see Emilie, please."

"Is that where the surprise is?"

Nell put her finger to her lips.

When they came into the clearing, he gaped at everything she'd done. Emilie was in the process of making his ugly, broken-down rink into a work of art. A winter wonderland.

Or maybe the North Pole.

Even more Christmas lights were strung in the spruce trees that bordered the rink. Glistening tinsel hung from the boughs. Around the boards of the rink, garlands of holly and mistletoe were strung.

While Christmas music played around him, he stared out at the ice. Before him, the skaters were practicing one of the numbers in their show, albeit not in costume. Despite standing in the subfreezing weather, he was instantly brought back to days on the ship, below decks in Emilie's ice studio. A lone person sitting up high in the bleachers, just watching her while she practiced.

She was currently spinning at center ice, graceful arms extended even if wrapped up in a red woolen sweater, fingers covered with ivory-colored cashmere gloves. She skated gracefully, exactly as he'd remembered, and he had to admit it was especially nice to watch her on the bigger-size rink, because she could stretch her legs and work up speed as well as perform all kinds of graceful intricacies with her steps and glides.

The turns across the ice had names like mohawk, rocker, twizzle. And the jumps: Flip.

Toe loop. Axel, of course—the one with the forward-facing takeoff.

She skated up to him now, out of breath, her eyes dancing. It must have been a solo she was finishing up, because the song changed, and the five men came out in a group this time.

Nathan turned to Emilie. "This does bring me back," he couldn't help saying.

"We have seven numbers in the first act of our Christmas show." She smiled at him. "I've had to recut the length of the music, because everything needs to fit into a stricter timetable. I've also rechoreographed each number to fit the larger rink. It's been so much fun, though."

"Your solo was beautiful. It's worth the price of admission alone."

"Thank you! Will you be coming for the dress rehearsal? Oh, and before I forget, my boss and *her* boss have both booked reservations for the middle of next week."

That surprised him. "Great. The more, the merrier." But privately, he wondered about facing Lynn and her pressure to sell him more business. He still didn't have clearance for that. And he had no answers for her probing questions.

Emilie squinted at him. "Should I have mentioned this earlier? My boss's name is Lynn

Bladewell, if you want to look up her reservation."

"Yes, I know." He kept his voice as neutral as possible. "She might have arranged for rooms already. I don't look at the reservations individually."

"Right. The front desk staff does that." She glanced down at his toolbox. "Should we get started? I'll give everyone a break for lunch."

"That's fine." Relieved that the topic was over, Nathan put Lynn Bladewell out of his mind. Later he would come up with a plan for dealing with her.

He glanced over at her skaters. The ones who weren't on the ice were all sitting on the first row of the bleachers, unlacing their skating boots. Emilie headed over to talk to them.

He motioned to Nell, who was lingering beside him. "Come with me."

"Okay," Nell said, "What are you going to do?"

"For now, I'm going to walk the property and note spots that have boards that need to be sanded."

"Okay." Nell walked beside him while the skaters gathered their things together on the other side of the rink. Nathan headed down the long side of the bleachers. With a clipboard, he made notes wherever he saw a spot where little kids or big skaters might get a sliver or otherwise get hurt.

"How many guests do you think will fit in the audience, Uncle Nathan?"

"Five hundred," he said without missing a beat. He glanced to the end of the rink, now roped off with black curtains to create a make-shift backstage changing area for the skaters. "No, probably more like four hundred or three hundred due to the blocked-off end."

"Did you ever attend a skating show here?"

"Sure, when I was young." He got out a red marker from his shirt pocket, and made an *x* on a board that needed to be smoothed. "I've skated before an audience here, too." He grinned at her. "My grandfather used to host an ice hockey game every year. Management versus hourly employees."

"I would have liked to have seen that." Nell sighed. "Tell me, did the inn sell tickets?"

"No. What we had—and remember, I was about ten years old back then—was an annual Christmas game, usually on Christmas Eve. My grandfather was a generous man. He roped the place off for employees only, plus who-ever was staying at the inn that wanted to at-tend. We had hot chocolate, and people brought gingerbread and whipped cream, Christmas cookies, things like that. There were carolers. If there was snow, he gave sleigh rides, too."

"It sounds really nice," Nell said wistfully.

It had always been Nathan's intention to do the same thing.

He dared to hope it was still possible. His weekly investors' meeting was coming up in a few days.

A particularly rotted board caught his attention. He could just imagine if Jason had been playing near this one—he could have been seriously injured. Shaking his head, he dropped to his knee. Emilie was right about one thing. Parts of this rink weren't in the best of conditions.

He turned the hammer backward and began to pull out the nails from the rotten board.

He was concentrating so hard, he didn't notice Nell departing. And he almost jumped when Emilie spoke in his ear.

"Did you play the hockey games during the day or at night?"

He leaned back on his heels. "What hockey games?"

"The ones you played when your grandfather owned the inn," Emilie said.

He smiled at her. "You were eavesdropping."

"Not on purpose. I came over to talk with you and Nell. I couldn't help overhearing."

"Where's your troupe?" He glanced over to the benches. The music was still playing, but the skaters had left.

"Nell is ferrying them back to the inn in her car. Frank called to say that more of the costumes came in the mail this morning. I want the troupe to try everything on to be sure that the costumes fit. Besides, I don't want the skaters practicing when you have the saws going."

"Who said anything about saws?"

"You're replacing rotted boards."

"Oh. Yeah." He realized what he'd been doing. "Well, just this one board," he said sheepishly. "I'll have to come back later with the replacement."

Emilie smiled at him. He was growing to love that smile.

"So, what position did you play in the hockey games?" she asked, falling into step beside him.

"I preferred forward line. But the games weren't really all that serious. It was more like…"

"A party?" she asked.

"Yes."

She nodded. "The more I hear of him, the more I wish I had met him."

"Me, too."

"He would be proud of you for doing this," she remarked.

"I hope so."

She smiled at him again. "I'd like to help, too. What else do you need done here?"

"Well. Let's start with the sander."

"I already know how to use an electric sander."

"You do?"

"Yep." Emilie knelt and picked up the battery-operated tool. "My dad had one similar to this. He taught me how to use it. You don't need to show me, Nathan."

Emilie had never talked to him about her dad before. She'd merely told him that her parents had gotten divorced shortly after she was born.

So hearing that she'd spent time with her dad surprised him. He'd had this image of Emilie growing up alone with her mother and her older sister—just the three women together. "What did your dad do?"

"He was a handyman at an apartment complex," she said slowly, as if reluctant to talk about it. "When I was young, I spent Saturdays with him."

"You never mentioned that."

She nodded. "He died when I was eleven." She said it in a low voice, staring at the tool while she spoke.

She turned to Nathan and he smiled at her.

Suddenly she said, "Watch the skills that he taught me." Bending over, she held the tool in firm hands as she addressed a piece of wood that Nathan had flagged.

He watched Emilie's face more than he watched her work, looking for signs of grief. But her eyes were clear, as if she'd resigned herself to her father's death long ago.

"I'm sorry I never asked about your dad, Emilie."

She stopped working and gazed up at him. Wisps of hair blew around her pretty face, framing it.

"I should've asked," he clarified.

He reached over and touched her hand. "Did he ever watch you skate?"

She nodded, brightening. "He was the first person who ever brought me to a skating rink. It was a long time ago, but... Mostly I remember that I loved performing for him that day. I mimicked what I'd seen on television. It made him happy." She smiled sadly.

"I understand," he said. "Watching you skate always makes me happy, too."

Turning her palm over, she squeezed his hand in hers.

He held on to her hand for a moment too long.

"Well." Her face clouded over and she glanced away, swallowing. "Shall we continue with our show preparations?" she asked in a bright voice.

"Right." He pulled his hand from hers. Coughing, he added, "This board right here needs sanding."

She bent her head and set to work. When he was satisfied that she wasn't going to hurt herself, he picked up a manual sander and worked on another board beside her.

"You don't mind doing this with me?" he asked her.

"I think it's fun. I always liked working with you, Nathan."

A lump grew in his throat. He'd grown to like being with her again, too.

She noticed him watching her, and she smiled quickly back.

"I think it might snow today," he remarked.

"Really?" she asked.

"Uh-huh. I know the weather report didn't call for snow, but do you see how the sky is so gray and the air feels colder? That's generally a sign of snow coming."

"But there isn't a roof over the ice rink. What happens with that?"

"I'll send Guy up to tie the tarp overhead, just in case."

"Will that work?"

"If the snow amounts to much, Guy will clear the ice with a snowblower and then prepare the surface again for you. If it's a big storm, we might miss a show or two. It's part of the joy of an outdoor ice rink in New England. We have contingencies for all kinds of weather." He smiled at her.

"Then we should try to finish before the flurries start."

"Yes. Good idea."

She surprised him by saying nothing more to him. She did her work as diligently as he labored over his spreadsheets. As soon as she finished with one board, she consulted with him on another, and then got right back to it.

He fell into a groove of activity himself. The manual labor felt satisfying, which surprised him. He was so often deskbound lately—staring at a screen and worrying about numbers—that he'd forgotten how much he enjoyed being outdoors. And working with his hands.

At last they finished, and there were no more boards marked with red paint. Technically, the whole place could stand to be rebuilt and sanded, but that would take them weeks. They'd just done the bare minimum to get by, but it felt like progress somehow.

Together, they strolled over and sat on the same bench that the skaters had used to change out of their skates.

Emilie unzipped her duffel bag and took out a brown paper bag. She opened it, and from the wrappings inside, he realized it was her lunch.

"Would you like to share my sandwich?" she asked. "It's peanut butter and jelly."

He couldn't help smiling. One of the quirks of Emilie O'Shea. Almost thirty years old, and she still ate peanut butter and jelly for lunch.

The smell of peanut butter made his stomach growl. "If you don't mind, I'd love to share half."

"Okay. I have an extra bottle of water, too." She pulled that out of her bag and handed it to him.

He took a long swig—his throat was parched from the outdoor labor—while she set a napkin in his lap and handed over half of her sandwich.

They ate companionably, side by side, the same as they'd worked. Another thing Nathan had done right—the chef he'd recruited at Prescott Inn was pretty amazing. Even his PB&J was world-class.

"I'll tell you a secret," she said, after she'd finished her first bite. "I organized a surprise for tomorrow afternoon. It's all very last-minute and rushed, so that's why I haven't had a chance to tell you yet."

"What kind of surprise?"

"I haven't met Maria yet—" She paused. "Have you?"

"Jason's mom?" He shook his head. "No. But I left a message for her to call me. Martha said she's just very busy. She works several part-time jobs, evidently."

"That's what I heard, too. Julie—one of my skaters—talked to her in the dining room this morning while I was off ferrying skaters. Anyway, she gleaned a bit more information from Jason's mom. Did you know that tomorrow is Jason's seventh birthday?"

He stopped chewing. "Seriously?"

"I hope it's okay with you that I ordered a birthday cake from Claude."

"It's absolutely okay. No worries there."

She rewarded him with a big smile. "Thank you, Nathan! And you're coming to the party, too, of course."

"Right." He wouldn't miss it for anything. He would have to squeeze it around his meeting with Rob, but…

"Well…" He glanced at his watch and stood. As much he'd enjoyed her company, he had to get back to the office and prepare the reports for tomorrow's investor meeting. "I have to get going."

"So soon?"

"I'm sorry. Yes." He brushed off his hands, and then he realized that Nell still hadn't returned.

"I wonder where Nell is?" He patted his back pocket, but his phone wasn't there, either. "My phone is in Nell's car, or I would call her. Would you mind giving me a ride back to the inn in my Jeep?"

"It would be my pleasure," Emilie said.

WHAT EMILIE HAD seen today from Nathan were appealing glimpses of the man she'd fallen in love with. And all it had taken was her being her honest self and telling him the truth about how she felt… Suddenly, cracks were appearing in Nathan's tough outer shell.

She still felt as if she had a ways to go in order to understand exactly what drove him—indeed, she was making new discoveries about him with each encounter, it seemed—but for the first time since she'd arrived at Prescott Inn, it seemed she was really making headway with Operation: Mr. Nathan Scrooge. Understanding Nathan's heart wasn't as impossible as she'd once thought.

Side by side, the two of them walked up the path toward the parking lot, swirls of snowflakes landing on their clothing like tiny stars.

Yes, it was finally snowing!

"I can't wait for my first white Christmas," she told him.

"Have you ever experienced snow before?"

"Just on television."

"That isn't the same thing at all."

"I know." She grinned at him and then stuck out her tongue to catch a flake so she could taste it. "So bland," she said, disappointed.

He laughed. She loved the sound of his laughter. "It's not even sticking on the ground yet," he teased. "This is a small flurry, and it will probably go away without amounting to much."

"Then tomorrow there will be snow, yes?"

He chuckled. "You're always so optimistic. That's what I remember most about you." They were approaching his Jeep now, so he held out his hand. "May I have the key?"

"Certainly. It's your vehicle, after all." She pressed the key into his hand. He held his toolbox in the other hand, and he stepped around the car, to the trunk.

"Oh, no," he muttered.

"What?" She stepped over beside him and followed his gaze downward.

The right rear tire was flat.

He opened the trunk. "Where's the spare tire?" he asked, staring at the gap where the tire belonged. Emilie had taken it out to make more room to transport their costumes.

"Oh, sorry. The spare tire is down in Frank's valet parking booth. He's holding it for me."

"Do you have a phone so I can call him?" Nathan asked.

She patted her jacket pocket, but it was empty. Then she checked the duffel bag she'd carried over her shoulder. Where was her phone? She hadn't seen it since this morning. "I must have left it back in my room."

"Well, we'll just have to walk back to the

inn together." Nathan seemed happy, strangely enough.

"Through the snow flurries?"

He smiled. "Yes."

She knew the journey wasn't that far. It wasn't even *that* cold outside. And today she was finding that she could bear the northern weather.

Whistling, Nathan put his tools into the back of the Jeep.

"I'll bring those up to your office later," she said.

"No need to carry them upstairs. Just drop them at my house sometime, when you have a few minutes. Call me first, though, to make sure I'm at home."

"Okay." So he wanted her to visit him at his house. That made her smile.

As they set off down the hill, it began to snow even harder. She glanced down at the ground and noticed the flakes were starting to stick.

"When will there be enough to make a snowman, Nathan?"

He smiled. "It will be a while yet."

"I was thinking of Jason," she said sheepishly. "I really am a novice at this. It's certainly different from Florida."

A cold breeze seemed to penetrate her jacket just then, and she shivered.

Nathan stopped and took off his coat and gave it to her. Then he unwrapped his scarf and gave her that, too.

"I don't want to take your coat and scarf," she protested. "How will you keep warm?"

"Please, I want you to have them. Besides, I'm wearing a much heavier sweater than you are."

"Thank you," she murmured, wrapping his oversize jacket around her short, thin one that was really more suited to a Florida ice-skating rink than a New England December. His jacket was much better.

Especially because his coat was still warm with his body heat. And it smelled like him.

"Tell me about your other skaters," Nathan suddenly said.

She was glad that he was interested. "Well, Katya and Sergei are our star pairs skaters."

"The big guy and the petite blonde. I saw them on Janet's TV special. Who else is on your team?" he asked. Nathan had always liked to hear her tell stories about her coworkers.

"Well, there's Gary. He's my right-hand man. He's the oldest, besides me, so I sort of treat him as an assistant ice captain."

"Very wise. A leader always needs a trusted assistant."

"Nell is *your* trusted assistant, right?"

"Yep, she is." Nathan reached for Emilie's arm. "Watch the pothole."

"Oh, thank you." Emilie sidestepped it. She'd been so enthusiastic, talking with Nathan, that she'd been watching him, marveling at the snowflakes in his hair, rather than paying attention to the road.

"There's always a skater hanging around my chef. What's her name?" Nathan asked, getting Emilie back on track.

"Julie. She has a flirtation going with Claude, but lately he seems to have eyes for Rosie, so I am kind of worried about that."

"Uh-oh." He smiled so hard that the small lines around his eyes crinkled adorably. "There's always drama in the skating troupe. I remember that part."

"I've been keeping Julie close—she's always coming in and out of my room, and I haven't discouraged it. I think it's best to keep a close eye on the situation."

"Probably wise, so long as you get your sleep."

"I have to admit, it's nice not to have bunk

beds. And to have a bigger bed than those tiny cots we had on the ship."

Nathan laughed aloud. "Wow, I forgot about those. Yeah, you're right, those were pretty bad."

They rounded the corner to the inn parking lot. The time had passed so pleasantly, it had almost felt like the old days.

Emilie clutched Nathan's arm and squeezed it. "Thank you," she said honestly. "I'll give you your coat back once we're inside."

"It's no problem at all, Emilie." His eyes were shining brightly at her, and he was smiling more than she'd seen him smile in a long while.

"Mr. Prescott! Emilie!" Frank came over to greet them.

Emilie sighed inwardly. Her short interlude with Nathan appeared to be at an end.

"Yes, Frank?" Nathan asked patiently.

"Did you walk all the way down from the rink together?" Frank glanced at each of them in turn. He seemed discomfited by this fact.

Nathan kept his composure. "Frank," he said, in his polite, managerial tone, "please retrieve the spare tire for the Jeep, and then head up to the ice rink and change out the flat, please."

"Of course, sir. Right away." As Frank hastened toward the inn, he gave one backward glance at Emilie.

"It appears you have a fan," Nathan remarked.

"Frank has been kind to us, yes," she murmured.

"Because he likes you." Nathan said it in a matter-of-fact tone, as if it didn't bother him in the least. He stopped before the door of the inn and said, "Goodbye, Emilie. If you need anything else, then please come and see me."

"Yes." She smiled inwardly, knowing that he was suddenly being so formal only because other people were watching them.

She still wore his coat. She dipped her nose to the collar and inhaled the scent of him.

She decided that she liked it.

She really liked it.

CHAPTER ELEVEN

THE NEXT DAY, Nathan sat in his office, trying to concentrate for his meeting later in the afternoon. But he was still thinking about how close he and Emilie had been together at the ice rink. The way that they'd gotten along so well—like before, only better—continued to make him smile, but even more broadly now, because he'd just finished putting together his weekly numbers report.

It was *fantastic*. Better than he had ever dreamed. Their room bookings were way, way up. Their efforts at promotion were certainly paying off.

His cell phone beeped. A text message from his major investor, Rob. Call me soon.

Nathan texted him back.

Reservations are up sharply. Looking great! Will gather more info and see you at the meeting.

"Uncle!" Nell knocked once on the door and

then barged inside without waiting for an invitation.

He lifted his head and swiveled in his chair. Her grin went from ear to ear. "You look like you saw the good news," he said.

"I did! And we're getting *a lot* of calls asking if people can buy tickets for one of Emilie's performances. We'll have to add that as an option instead of just booking rooms."

"Excellent idea. After the birthday party, why don't you figure out how many empty seats are available at the rink each day? I'm preparing for the investors' meeting. I'll check with them how they want to set up for this."

"Actually, Uncle, I was thinking of adding more bleachers. I know of this company who rents out seats and—"

"Numbers, Nell," he said, smiling at her. "You need to think of numbers, always. How much does it cost?"

She scowled at him, her enthusiasm dampened. "If I wanted to crunch numbers, I'd have been an accountant like you. I went into marketing because it's creative. And collaborative. Look at all the attention we're getting!"

"Yes, and *I* get the attention of my investors by showing them numbers." He got up and headed for the door, opening it. "And by the way, Nell, every profession has to deal with numbers. So get used to that."

"What a wet blanket you are." Nell exhaled as she headed for the door. Then she crossed her arms and looked slyly at him. "Emilie doesn't deal with numbers."

"Sure she does. Just yesterday she told me she notes the length of each program in her show in order to keep the performance within a certain time frame." He couldn't help smiling at the memory of his afternoon with Emilie.

Nell's eyes widened. "You *like* her, Uncle."

Yes, he did. He'd liked her two years ago, and he liked her again now. There was no denying that fact.

He gazed out the window that overlooked the lobby. Maybe Emilie would walk past on the way to the birthday party.

"Are you watching for her?"

"Yes," he admitted.

Nell clucked beside him.

He took a breath. He'd kept this from Nell for far too long. It was time to go public. More and more it seemed possible that he and Emilie had a chance again.

"I was in love with her once." He gazed down at the fireplace, now dancing with flames.

"You...?" Nell seemed gobsmacked.

"We worked together on the *Empress Caribbean*."

Nell's mouth remained open.

"I'm sorry I didn't tell you the truth before. I guess I just wasn't ready."

Maybe it didn't really matter why he was confessing, just that believing in a bright future made him feel better in his own skin. In turn, he supposed that would help him interact better with others.

"You've been a good helper to me, Nell. The success we're having is largely due to your talents in connecting with people." Like Emilie's knack for looking out for others.

"Wow, I'm... Thank you, Uncle." Nell blinked. Then she threw her arms around him, hugging him tight.

He gingerly patted her shoulder. "You're welcome." He stepped back. "Ah...Jason's party should be starting soon. Want to head downstairs?"

"Right." Nell wiped her eyes. "Oh. You should probably know that Emilie was going to escort you downstairs herself—she's already figured out that you tend to get caught up in your reports. But she asked me to do it because she said she's busy dealing with 'skater drama.' And yes, I really like Emilie, too, by the way."

He nodded, biting his lip to keep from smiling. *Skater drama.* He knew that well.

"I'm glad you and Emilie are getting along, Nell. But remember, nothing is set in stone yet. She and the other skaters are only here for a short while." And just because he and Emilie were getting along well again didn't mean that all had been mended between them. He still hadn't—and couldn't—share with her or her boss that the inn's future had been on shaky legs. He was waiting for the final okay from his investors. It would come, he hoped…

And he did have hope. Hope for a successful investors' meeting, and hope for a future relationship with Emilie. Yes, he'd caught her infectious enthusiasm—that was the important thing. Maybe they really could pull this off, and in the process, maybe he could reconnect with Emilie again.

"Don't worry, I promise to be discreet about you and Emilie." Nell tugged on his arm. "Come on. Let's go to the party."

"Yes. Of course. Just let me save my data and shut down the laptop."

"I'll wait." Nell sighed, fiddling with a package on his desk that he'd received in the mail but hadn't opened. *Jason's Christmas stocking.*

"Did you know, Uncle, that Jason's mother took some time off from work for the party?"

"Yes, Emilie told me." And he hadn't even asked how much this party was costing. Nope, he hadn't asked, and that made him proud.

"And that reminds me of another thing." Nell pressed a slip of note paper into his hand. "Martha asked me to give this to you. The women's shelter in town called just before you got in. Martha said they asked if you have any more vacant rooms to house another family for Christmas? They have an emergency with a mom with three little kids. She's in a homeless facility at the moment, but they want to move her to a place with a private room for the family."

Those poor kids. "I'll have to take it up with my investors," Nathan said softly.

His numbers were so fantastic—he was sure he could convince Rob and the other investors to expand the program. "Don't worry, Nell. I'll handle it."

He shut the cover of his laptop and then stood. "But I should probably return the shelter's call now, before their office closes. I want to include their numbers in the report."

"Will you come down to the party first?" Nell asked.

"No, it'll take just a moment. You go on down. I'll join you when I'm finished with the call. Tell Emilie I'll be along in a few minutes."

"Okay. I know those kids are important to you." Nell waved. "Don't be too long, though." She opened the door and left him to his call.

But just as the door closed, his phone rang. Nathan saw that it wasn't the homeless shelter, but Rob. Jumping the gun on their meeting, Nathan supposed.

Still, he needed to take the call.

Nathan sat in his leather desk chair. He turned to face the back wall as he picked up the phone. "Rob, did you get my text about the increased bookings due to our publicity?"

"Did I?" Rob chortled aloud. "I didn't need to—everybody knows. This skating project of yours has been boon for us. A real godsend."

"Yes," Nathan agreed, relaxing into the chair. "Then, while I have you in a good mood, let me make my pitch to house more local families in the west wing this Christmas."

"What? Oh, no," Rob replied. "We can't do that. Certainly not."

"Sure we can," Nathan said. "At the meeting later, I'll show you how well the numbers work. It'll be easy to absorb the additional costs and we can—"

"Slow down," Rob interrupted. He made a clucking noise. Nathan could well imagine his principal investor sitting at his own desk in his bank downtown, one hand raking through his shock of white hair, the other hand tapping his desktop with nervous energy as he spoke. "I called to tell you *my* good news, Nathan. First, the meeting to review expenses is cancelled. There's no need for it. Not only do I have a buyer interested in Prescott Inn—I've got *two* buyers interested, and they're both bidding against each other, driving the price up every time I turn around." He cackled again.

Nathan's blood ran cold.

Buyers? "What do you mean? You said if we improved profits, then we would keep the inn open. Why is it even on the market?"

"It wasn't. But you did such a bang-up job bringing in money and attention due to the skaters that word went out in the industry. I've been swamped with calls from out-of-state big investment groups and hotel chains interested in hearing about the property."

"So tell them no," Nathan snapped.

"Nathan, by selling, the investors could make a nice amount of money. It makes business sense to say yes. And the price they're offering is too darn good to turn down. I've already spoken to the other three stakeholders, and they've all agreed. It's a clear majority vote. The sale will go through, and we're shutting Prescott Inn down the day after Christmas. I called to tell you to cease all spending and start wrapping things up."

"Wrapping things up?" Nathan repeated incredulously. He couldn't comprehend what he was hearing. "What's the benefit of shutting down immediately? Let's slow down and think this out."

"Nathan, the buyers are anxious for a locked-in agreement. This sale will happen fast. They're planning a rebranding, which means a shutdown for renovations."

A shutdown. He and Emilie and Nell and everyone else on the team had partnered so well together that they'd unintentionally hurt themselves in the process?

Nathan stood, the blow hitting him as if

physical. "Rob...we've made commitments to people. I *can't* renege on them now."

"We're well aware of your commitments. We've reviewed the agreements, and we won't be in breach of contract. We've voted, Nathan. It's done. Prepare to shut it all down or we'll have someone do it for you."

Nathan paced before the window, running his hands through his hair. This was impossible. "You can't just do that!"

"Contractually, we can. It's business, Nathan. Nothing personal. Again, no additional expenditures beginning today."

"And the kids who are already here? Where do they go?"

"It's up to the new owners whether they stay on or not."

"Who *are* the new owners?"

"I can't say yet." Rob coughed. "The negotiations are delicate, and it's moving fast, but at this time, it's still confidential. You'll know who the owners are as soon as the deal is closed."

"And the skaters?" he demanded. "What are they supposed to do?"

"As I said, I've reviewed the contracts," Rob said. "We don't owe them anything—we can cut bait whenever we wish."

"So, they just skate their shows as we're shutting everything down? I don't understand."

"That's not our problem."

"Sure, it is. And we have guests coming, expecting them to perform! What about our responsibility to the guests?"

"As long as you make sure the skaters perform and the production company doesn't pull the plug, all will be well. I really don't see the problem. Publicity-wise, we've promised them a place until Christmas, and we've delivered. We're still willing to cover their room and board until Christmas—that's fine. And the cruise line covers the salaries. If Lynn Bladewell balks about anything, just tell her it's in her best interest to keep the skaters here and performing until the close date. Whatever you have to say to her, just do it—but don't mention anything about the sale until I give you the go-ahead that it's finalized. You're part of this community. You're loyal to us. You know what you're supposed to do."

"But…what about my job at Prescott Inn?"

"The hope is that the inn will reopen eventually under the new owners and keep some people employed. We'll just have to wait and see what the new buyers want to do with the property. I can't read the tea leaves for you on that one. But rest assured, as a minor investor, you'll get a return for your investment on the sale."

Nathan's mind just went blank. He couldn't think of a counterargument to make. Ironically, it wasn't *his* job he was worried about. It was the homeless kids. And…Emilie. He knew that Rob, from a business perspective, was right—they had no obligation to the skaters. But he wasn't sure that Emilie would understand that.

She'll never forgive me if I make her look bad in front of Lynn, and set her skaters out on the street. She needs this opportunity in so many ways. It's her dream to be a choreographer.

And things had been going well between them! He'd been so hopeful for him and Emilie getting back together.

"Rob, let me head over to your office now," Nathan pleaded, trying to buy time. "We'll sit and talk about this."

"I'm sorry, Nathan. The plans are set. As I said, the vote has been taken."

"Please just take the option on the skaters' contract and sign them up for a few weeks salary in January. Throw them a bone. It's their influence that's gotten us this far."

"Nathan—"

"As a friend, as a member of this community, I'm asking you for this one favor."

"I'm sorry, Nathan." There was genuine regret in Rob's voice.

The line clicked off.

CHAPTER TWELVE

AT THREE O'CLOCK, Emilie faced the table full of beaming people and finally felt that things were going to work out.

It was too bad that Nathan wasn't here yet. Nell had assured her he would be down soon, just after he phoned the homeless shelter to fulfill more requests for kids to move in for Christmas.

Emilie smiled as she thought how kind Nathan truly was. She would have postponed the cake-cutting, waiting for him, but Jason's mom was on a tight schedule and couldn't delay any longer. Nathan would surely understand.

Emilie picked up the birthday cake she'd ordered from the kitchen, its seven birthday candles already set ablaze, and then turned and pushed through the door with her shoulder.

"Happy birthday to you!" Nine of her skaters, with the exception of Sergei, who was mysteriously missing—a big part of the drama she'd been dealing with earlier—sang aloud to Jason. His little face beaming, he blew out the candles. He still hadn't said much, though. Prescott sat in the chair beside him. Somebody had gotten Prescott a plastic dish filled with tuna water, and the cat was slurping to his heart's content, his pink tongue darting in and out.

"It *must* be against all the rules to have a cat in a public dining room," Rosie whispered beside Emilie.

"It is." How changed Nathan seemed. Lately he'd been giving and generous. Emilie went over to Jason's mom, who was hugging her son.

"Hello, I'm Emilie. It's good to finally meet you." Jason's mom was short and plump, with kind, pretty eyes and a shy manner.

"I'm Maria. Thank you for making my son happy." Maria was so soft-spoken that Emilie had to lean closer to hear her. She touched Maria's sleeve, a uniform for a cleaning service, its company logo on the back.

"It's my pleasure. And if there's any help I can give you and Jason, don't hesitate to ask."

"He loves watching you skate after school," Maria said.

"We love having him with us. We watch out for him, too—we make sure he's bundled up in warm clothing. Gary has lent him his hat and a long scarf."

"Thank you so much." Maria's eyes grew wet. "I would be with my son more if I could."

"I know." Emilie's heart was breaking for her. She could only imagine just how sad and desperate Maria must feel.

"May I ask you how long you've been staying at Prescott Inn?" Emilie asked, settling into a chair beside her.

"We've been here just for the last month," Maria said in a hesitant voice. "Before that, we were in a shelter." Maria blushed. "We will be okay," she said firmly. "Mr. Prescott has been generous to house us here." She pressed Jason closer to her breast. "And the reason we don't have so many warm clothes is because we're not used to cold weather. We're from Florida."

That surprised Emilie. But it explained what she'd observed. "I'm from Florida, as well. I can relate to having issues with the cold. I've been a bit homesick for the Florida sun, myself."

"My sister lives up here," Maria confided. "She found me work nearby. We stayed with her family for a time, but it got to be too much. Her husband asked us to leave. And Jason wasn't doing well. I'd like us to get a place of our own, but rents are so high… The county homeless shelter helped for a time, but they're crowded and we couldn't stay long. Mr. Prescott has been a savior."

Nathan. After his revelations yesterday, she was no longer surprised.

"He is a wonderful man. And I help him as I can. I keep the room clean myself," Maria said with pride. "Our room has a microwave and a small refrigerator. I cook our meals."

"How did you end up at Prescott Inn?" Emilie asked, curious.

"We were sleeping in my car in a parking lot when the lady from the county found us one day. I was so frightened at first, especially when the police came, but…they gave us a room at Prescott Inn. I'm not sure, but I believe Mr. Prescott arranged it."

Emilie bit her lip and nodded. Each day revealed more of Nathan's good character.

Jason tugged on his mother's sleeve. Maria bent her ear to listen to him. She nodded and then smiled at Emilie. "If you will excuse me, I'm going to get my son another piece of his birthday cake, and then I have to leave to get back to work. Thank you again, Emilie."

"It was our pleasure." Emilie watched the mother and son walk hesitantly to the table where Claude presided over the cake, serving utensil in hand, and Rosie flirted outrageously at Claude's whispered attentions.

Uh-oh. As she'd noted earlier, trouble was brewing there. But Emilie was monitoring it and Julie hadn't seemed to notice what was going on. Instead, Sergei was the one Emilie was worried about at present. He was the only one who hadn't come out of his room, and usually Sergei was all about the sweets.

Strange there were so many sweets tonight—more than usual. She'd only ordered a single birthday cake from Claude!

Emilie went over to Katya, who, as she so often did, was bent over, petting Prescott the cat and crooning softly to him in Russian. It was actually strange, but Emilie got the feeling that the cat really was bilingual.

Emilie whispered in Katya's ear. "Is everything all right with Sergei?"

"Am I his keeper?" Katya answered tartly.

Guess not. "Well…aren't we all keepers for each other? We're a team, are we not?"

Katya straightened. "Please. You should worry about Lynette and Curtis, not Sergei."

"Why?"

"They are in a fight."

"Since when?"

"Yesterday, during practice. Did you not notice?"

Emilie's heart sank. No, she hadn't noticed. But she'd been distracted at practice yesterday, what with Nathan being present. Before that, there had been the emergency clinic trip with Gary, and before that...

Emilie lifted her hands in bewilderment. "Help me out, please, Katya. What exactly is going on?"

"They are breaking up."

"I didn't know they were together." When had that happened?

"It was only for a very short time." Katya bent to pick up Prescott and then curled the striped-gray tabby cat expertly inside the crook of her arm. "They are so young."

Yes. Lynette was just eighteen. Curtis was nineteen, and they were both away from home for the first time. Emilie felt guilty that she hadn't been paying better attention to them.

Emilie scoured the room until she found Lynette sitting behind a couch, hidden from the world. The young woman was crying silently, her eyes red, her lips trembling. Curtis was suddenly nowhere to be found.

Emilie sat down beside her. "What happened?"

"Can you please not partner me with Curtis in the sleigh bells number?" Lynette burst into fresh tears.

Emilie took her hand. "We're professionals," she said gently.

"You are. And I am. But he's not!"

"What happened?"

"I thought he liked me," she wailed, "but now he won't talk to me."

Emilie drew the young woman close. "I know it hurts." Breakups were horrible.

"How would you know? You're never with anyone, Emilie!"

Emilie just shook her head. If only she could describe to the young skater how hard it had been for Emilie at first, here again with Nathan. Her ex. How confusing it had been.

"You don't see my pain because…well, when I said to be a professional, Lynette, what I meant is that you have to always behave in your role as an entertainer. That means you smile even if you feel like crying, and you do so because people count on you."

Lynette looked downcast. "Maybe we're not all as perfect as you," she muttered.

"I'm not perfect, and I'm not counseling you

to be that way. Far from it. I just think it's best to…cry when the children aren't around to see you."

"Seriously?" Lynette sniffled. "That's your advice? To *fake* it? Is that who you are, Ice Mom? A faker?"

Her words took Emilie aback. She'd never thought of it that way.

"But our job is to help people like Jason— to lift their spirits," Emilie pressed, diverting the subject. "He's so sad, he doesn't talk very much. Anyone can see that. Can you imagine being him? Seven years old. Not even showing excitement that Christmas is coming…?"

"If I lose Curtis, then I don't care if Christmas is coming, either!"

Emilie held Lynette's hand. That was all she could do. She could feel the pain in Lynette's heart as if it were her own, and right now, Lynette didn't want to talk or to reason about other ways of looking at her breakup. Lynette just wanted comfort and agreement. Emilie could give that, too. "Room with me tonight, Lynette. All right?"

"But what about Julie?" Lynette said. "She said she was moving in with you tonight because she was sick of Katya's drama."

Yes, Emilie should check on Julie, too. And

Julie was headed for heartbreak, too. "We'll all three room together. We'll have a girls' night. Popcorn and pedicures. I'll go find her, okay?" Emilie rose from her position behind the couch.

But Nathan had arrived. Emilie saw him standing at the edge of the party. He looked downcast. She wondered what had changed his mood, and tried to see the scene from his perspective—a table bursting with foods and dishes. Claude's under-chef, Pierre, was attempting to woo Katya with treats on a special platter. Katya—who was surprisingly amenable to his flattery—was tasting a chocolate éclair. Suddenly Emilie realized why there were so many treats, and also why Katya's costumes were fitting snugly.

That's why she'd been gaining weight— because of Pierre's pastries.

Emilie knelt to Lynnette again. "Is Katya interested in Claude's assistant?"

Lynette wiped her eyes. "I heard him offer to marry her if she stays here with him."

"Okay…if they're in love…"

Lynette shrugged. "Maybe not. Maybe it will be easier for her to send money home to her family that way."

Emilie groaned and held her head in her hands. Was Katya setting herself up for more heartache? Suddenly it seemed like everything was falling apart. Emilie had to figure out how to solve this problem now, too.

She stood again. Nathan caught her eye across the busy dining room. He was staring straight at her. She smiled at him, but he just stared dully back.

I'm sorry! she telegraphed. Was he upset by all the sumptuous tables of treats that the kitchen staff had made to fulfill Emilie's simple request for a birthday party? He was surely angry that he was spending so much money on the event.

Despair filled her. The stress was more than she could bear. *I'm trying so hard to hold everything together.* It wasn't her fault that Nathan's under-chef had a thing for tiny Katya.

Emilie walked over to Nathan. She could almost feel herself putting on her happy, diplomatic Ice Mom mask. *Was* Lynette right about her? Was she a "faker"?

A "pleaser," Nathan had called her. But maybe the pressure of the skater drama had gotten to her. And, truth be told, maybe it was seeing Lynette express the pain she was going through.

Emilie was tired of being the one with unrequited love. She had *loved* Nathan. And it hadn't been enough for him. Would he always love his inn more than he'd loved her?

She stood before the table with the cake, hands shaking, unable to fake that all was well anymore, and not sure what to do about it.

Somber, Nathan just gazed at her. "How is Jason?" he asked, shocking her. "Am I too late to watch him blow out his candles and make a birthday wish?"

"Yes. I'm sorry we couldn't wait for you, Nathan. His mom had to go back to work, so we did it earlier while she was here."

Nathan nodded, resigned. "I've been on a phone call. It…couldn't be helped."

"Yes. I know." The call must not have gone well, judging by his mood.

Hands at his sides, Nathan stoically took a step back. "Thank you for arranging to make him happy," he said in his formal voice. "You've been good to him and I appreciate that."

"Why are you saying this to me?" she asked.

"Because no one else would have thought to do this but you. Look how happy he is." He glanced to Jason. The boy seemed to have come alive with the attention. He and Katya were sharing a bowl of ice cream and playing with Prescott.

Nathan turned back to Emilie. "I won't keep you from the party. We'll…talk later."

"About what?" she asked.

He gave her the briefest of smiles. "I honestly appreciate you, Emilie." Nathan dipped his head and then left her.

Her mouth hung open. *What* was happening? Was she missing something with Nathan just as she'd missed what was going on between Curtis and Lynette?

Emilie balled her hands into fists and stalked after Nathan to catch up with him.

But before she could reach him, Gary caught her sleeve. "Ice Mom, Sergei is here. And he looks ticked off at Pierre."

Emilie diverted her path to attempt to avert a disaster in the making. Sergei stepped in front of his romantic rival and plucked up a packet of tea, Katya's favorite. He tore out the tea bag and put it in a mug. Then he poured hot water inside. He brought it over to Katya and placed it before her.

From her position on the floor beside Jason's cat, Katya smiled feebly up at Sergei.

"He is just not giving up, is he?" Gary breathed to Emilie.

"Sergei," Emilie called, getting to the end of her rope, "*what* are you doing?"

"He can't answer you." Katya gazed at her with wide eyes.

Emilie went over and knelt beside her. "Then please help us translate."

"Sergei will be fine." Katya dipped her bag in her hot tea and looked away. Jason had already trotted off after Prescott.

Emilie leaned close to Katya's ear. Pierre was far enough away that he wouldn't be able to hear, but Sergei wasn't. "Please help me talk to him so I can keep us all together and happy for the show's sake."

But Katya just stared at her.

She *had* to connect with her. "Please, aren't I helping you with your money and with your future with the company?"

"Please do not speak to me of money and future. I am tired of thinking of money and future," Katya said, tight-lipped. She stood and whirled on her toes, leaving Emilie kneeling in her wake. Emilie felt as if she could do nothing to please the people she needed to please most.

How had everything fallen apart so quickly?

NATHAN STOOD IN the lobby, his heart heavy. He'd gone downstairs to the dining room, intending to tell Emilie about his phone call with Rob so she could prepare for any consequences.

But the moment had been wrong. She'd been fighting to keep her troupe together. She was also busy giving a little boy the birthday party he deserved. Nathan had been too ashamed to tear her away and ruin that for her and the others just then. How could he *ever* hurt her with the news?

He had out-and-out lied to her, and he needed to make that up to her. She'd been beautiful to him, as always. How would she ever forgive him for this?

Martha waved to him from the front desk. It occurred to him that he would have to let everybody go, and on the day after Christmas.

The burden of that responsibility was crushing. But he went over and met Martha's gaze with a steadying look. "What is it, Martha?"

"Um, you had a call come in just now. She said it's important. Very important."

"Who is it?"

Martha handed him a slip. The call was from Lynn Bladewell. Had she heard the news about the inn being sold somehow? Would she threaten to pull the skaters out, which Rob had specifically instructed him to prevent?

Nathan groaned inwardly, though he kept

his face schooled. "Thank you." Nathan nodded at Martha and then headed for the stairs to his office.

Seated at his desk, he inhaled deeply. He thought briefly of pulling Emilie from her party and conferring with her, but no, his responsibility to the inn came first.

Nathan smoothed out the wrinkled slip of paper. Then he bit the bullet and dialed up Lynn Bladewell's number. He would do everything he could to make the situation easier for Emilie.

Lynn answered quickly. "Hello, Mr. Prescott." She obviously had his phone number plugged into the contact list on her phone.

"Hello."

"I'm glad we've finally gotten a chance to speak. Your associate and I discussed the details of the earlier contract, and I haven't managed to catch you about extending it. How are you today?"

So this was it, then—a standard sales call, pressuring him to act on the option in the contract and to purchase more performances from the skaters. *She doesn't know about the sale yet.*

"I'm fine," he said cautiously. *Could be a lot better, actually.*

"So, I'm just calling to see if you received my packet with news about our option opportunity," she said.

"Right." Nathan leaned back, his chair squeaking at the shoulders. He decided to deflect, to buy himself some time to figure out how he would approach this. "I did receive it. What do you want to know about where we are in the decision process, specifically?"

"Well, are you personally satisfied with our skating cast? I understand that the first official show is set for this weekend. I'll be present next week, of course."

"Yes," Nathan said, as blandly as he could. "I did see your name on our booking list."

"Great! Well, I'm calling mainly because I want to know if we can count on you to order up another month of shows, at least through January? Perhaps we could meet and talk next week?"

He steeled himself to do what needed to be done.

"Well, Lynn, thank you for calling. Believe me, if we could, we would take you up on the contract option to extend the shows. As it is, I'm afraid we'll have to pass on it."

There was silence on Lynn's end. Nathan said nothing, waiting for her to respond.

"That's shutting it down earlier than we'd hoped." There was a distinct note of disappointment to Lynn's tone. Nothing compared to how Emilie would feel, however. "May I ask why?" she said with an edge.

"I assure you the troupe has been fantastic. In fact, you could probably book an arena for them and sell it out. Emilie is doing a first-rate job managing the show. She's a real pro at what she does. I give her my highest recommendation."

"Then *why*?"

He cleared his throat. "I'm sorry, Lynn. I wish I had better news for you."

"I saw the television publicity," she insisted. "And the print commercials. Emilie has sent me copies and forwarded news about everything completed so far. Tell me, haven't you been getting calls for show tickets?"

"Yes, we have. But there are other factors. And I'm sorry, but my hands are tied. I'm not at liberty to pick up the option."

"Well…what if we were able to help with those other factors?" Lynn asked.

"I'm sorry. It just isn't possible."

"Let me speak with my boss about what we can do for you. Will you hold back on your decision until I talk with you again?"

"Unfortunately, I can't," he said politely.

"We can commit to booking a block of rooms." Lynn just wasn't giving up. "Would that help influence the factors you mentioned?"

Nathan closed his eyes. How he would love to say *yes* to Lynn's offer. If he owned Prescott Inn outright, he would do it in a heartbeat.

"I'm sorry, no," he said to Lynn. "The skaters will have to leave once this particular contract is satisfied."

"You want the skaters to leave the inn?"

"No, it's not what I want, at all. I just can't expand the scope of the project. I'm sorry about this."

There was a short silence. Nathan knew he really was giving her nothing to work with.

That was his intent. He just couldn't give false hope.

"Well. I'll phone Emilie and break the news," Lynn said finally.

"Thank you for calling," he murmured.

As Lynn hung up the phone, Nathan knew exactly how it would look to Emilie.

That he'd lied to her. That he'd chosen the inn over her. That he was betraying her and blindsiding her—just like he had done before.

Nathan grabbed his coat and headed down to speak with her before Lynn did.

And then the call he'd been waiting for came in.

It was the homeless shelter.

CHAPTER THIRTEEN

EMILIE WAS STILL downstairs in the dining room lounge, but now she was knee-deep in letting out a seam on Katya's costume. Jason had gone upstairs with one of the other families, and only her troupe remained. She was concentrating on ripping out a row of stitches when her cell phone rang.

She decided to let the call go to voice mail. Tomorrow was their first dress rehearsal, and she was crunched for time.

"Katya," Emilie murmured, picking at the tightly sewn threads, "You spent six months at sea with all those huge buffets and you didn't gain an ounce. We're here two weeks and you've changed a dress size."

"It's Pierre's hot chocolates," Katya said.

"They're that good?"

"It's not *that*. I have to drink them. It makes him happy."

"Katya, can we talk about your situation?

Are you sure you want to do this? Are you sure you're okay?"

Katya took the opportunity to snatch up Emilie's still-ringing phone. "Oh, look." She held out the screen. "It's Lynn at the production company."

"Lynn?!" Emilie did need to take that call. She took the phone from Katya and ditched her sewing supplies. She hustled out to the hallway for privacy.

"Lynn, I'll be with you in a moment," Emilie said into the phone. Rosie popped her head out of the room to observe her, so Emilie turned and strode away, phone still to her ear, and hurried upstairs.

In the lobby, the huge Christmas tree was all lit up and twinkling with multicolored lights. Emilie settled into a couch and curled up her legs. She stared at her own expression, reflected off the bright red tinsel of a round red Christmas tree ornament, and took a deep breath.

Fake it, yet again. Act like the troupe isn't falling apart, and that you have it all under control.

"I'm here," she told Lynn in her most confident tone. "We're getting ready for the dress rehearsal tomorrow. Everything is going well on our end. The inn is showing increased receipts, and Mr. Prescott is happy with us. What's up with you?"

There was a slight hesitation and Emilie got a queasy feeling in her stomach.

"Emilie… I have news for you."

She tightened the phone in her grip. What news…? What could possibly be wrong?

"Are you still flying out to see us this week?" Emilie asked. She'd really wanted Lynn and Donnie to watch one of their shows in order to see what a great job they all had been doing.

There was an awkward silence, and then Lynn coughed slightly. "You should know that I talked with Nathan Prescott just now."

Emilie sat up. "How long ago was this?"

"A few minutes," Lynn said reluctantly.

Emilie thought back. At the party, he'd acted awkwardly toward her. She'd thought it was because he was simply busy, but obviously something was going on.

"So…what did he say?"

"Well, he informed me that Prescott Inn has decided not to pick up the option for any post-Christmas show dates. Donnie isn't happy about it. As a result, I'm afraid I'm going to have to ask you to wrap things up there now and disband your team."

Disband? Emilie put a hand to her mouth.

"Emilie? Hello?"

"Did he say why he's ditching us?" she asked Lynn in a small voice.

Lynn sighed audibly. "No. I have no idea. He wouldn't say."

Emilie clutched her phone. Tears were filling her eyes, and she didn't trust her throat to speak.

So many people were looking forward to the show. And it was going to be a great show! She was proud of what she'd accomplished. She'd done everything that Lynn had required of her, and she'd done it well.

"Where...did I go wrong?"

"I'm sorry, Emilie," Lynn murmured. "It happens sometimes. Consider it a business idea that didn't pan out."

"But..." So many people relied upon her. Her team members. Jason. She'd *promised* them she would take care of them all!

And what of her own dreams? This had been her chance to prove herself worthy of one of the few choreography jobs. And now that seemed further and further out of reach.

Emilie suddenly glanced up, realizing that there were people—customers—in the lobby, gazing at her curiously. She simply couldn't cry in front of them. She tried to paste on a smile, but for the first time in her life, she couldn't do that, either.

Hurriedly wiping her eyes, she scrambled up, phone still to her ear, and strode for the hallway that led to her room.

Thankfully, she passed no one on her way. She spoke into the phone as she rounded the last corner to the west wing corridor. "Please, let me talk to Nathan and get back to you. I have some influence with him."

But as soon as Emilie said it, plugging her key into her hotel room door, she realized how ridiculous that sounded. And untrue. If she honestly had influence with Nathan, then he would have trusted her enough to tell her what was going on.

"Emilie, customers sometimes don't come through," Lynn said sympathetically. "You can't beat yourself up. It happens."

"Not to me." Emilie tossed her room key on the table and slumped onto the bed. "I've been working my butt off, Lynn. I did interviews and organized parades. I've fought to create the best shows possible, like you asked me to, and out of very little to start with."

Indeed, she'd gone head-to-head with Nathan about the rink almost daily since she'd arrived, even though she was uncomfortable being so adversarial. "I rechoreographed the show to fit the outdoor conditions and the larger-size rink. In addition, I came up with a new, original show geared for the facility. I've been looking forward to its debut next week."

The theme of the show was personal to Nathan and she'd planned to surprise him with it—to show her respect and goodwill for him and his inn. "Lynn, this is the best show I've ever been involved with. I wish you could see it. I know you would change your mind and find something for our troupe if you could just see what we've done—"

"Emilie, all of these things sound intriguing to me. You were on the right track, it's true. But the most important thing for Donnie was for the option to be picked up, and it wasn't," Lynn said patiently. "That doesn't help our business. We're not going to be sticking with this project after all."

So…they were all out of work. And at Christmas.

Gaping in shock, she found it difficult to breathe. What about Katya? And Rosie and Gary and all the others?

And Jason… She'd promised Jason he could be in their Christmas show!

Tears prickled Emilie's eyes.

"What will become of us?" she whispered.

Lynn's voice was gentle. "We've talked about this, Emilie."

Emilie's gut clenched. They *had* talked about this.

"At the moment, I don't have anything to give you. There simply isn't another opening. Our ships' casts are full."

"That…goes for the rest of the cast, too?"

"It does," Lynn said reluctantly. "And the *Empress Caribbean* isn't scheduled to go back into service this season."

"But…what about all the publicity we've generated? Won't it look bad for the company if we're left out in the cold?"

"Donnie has decided the termination won't reflect poorly on us now—we tried in good faith to have your contract extended. Frankly, it's on Prescott Inn now. They're the ones turning you out in the cold."

Nathan. Nathan had done this.

But why?

"What if…what if we did everything in our power—absolutely everything we could think of—to change Nathan's mind? Please, Lynn, could we reverse this decision?"

"Emilie, I'm sorry." Lynn sounded genuinely sad for her. "You and the troupe will be going home."

She let that sink in for a moment. Home, to Florida. Home, to start all over again.

She felt desolate. And powerless. Everyone would be upset because she hadn't been able to convince Nathan to take a chance on them.

"When does he want us to leave?" she asked miserably.

"He wants you to stay and fulfill the contract. But we don't see any need for you to stay. The cruise line is paying your salaries until Christmas as a form of goodwill, whether you perform at the inn or not."

Lynn sighed. "Regardless, I'll leave the decision to you, Emilie. If you want to pack things up and cut ties after the dress rehearsal tomorrow, then do it. There's nothing in the contract that obligates you to the inn. In fact, I would strongly suggest leaving. If you depart now, then you'll have more time to work on finding yourself a new assignment."

A new assignment? But where? And what about everybody else?

"However," Lynn continued, "if you want to stay and perform your shows until Christmas Eve, I'd understand. And that would let Nathan off the hook, that's for certain. I imagine he's booked quite a few customers expecting a skating show. Just know that you and your team are under no obligation to help him."

"I...don't understand." She'd hit rock bottom. "Was this worth anything for us, Lynn? Because I feel as though I gave it my heart for nothing."

"Emilie, it's show business. It happens."

Not to her, it didn't. Emilie never failed. She brought happiness to people. She didn't let them down.

"The kids are coming to the dress rehearsal tomorrow," she remembered.

"Record it for us, will you? I'll keep the file with your portfolio. It will be helpful to refer to if we have jobs in the future."

Emilie just felt like crying. Tomorrow was supposed to be the dress rehearsal for the standard show—the same one they'd performed on the ship. The other program, the new one she'd designed for Donnie's visit and for Christmas Eve especially, the one she'd hoped to give Nathan as a gift—that one wasn't ready yet. And now might never be performed.

Why, Nathan? she thought. *Why was I not enough for you?*

But it didn't matter why. Nathan had held

himself back from her. She'd believed in him again, enough to trust him, but he'd pulled the rug out from beneath her once more.

Her choice was obvious. She should be loyal to her troupe and let them go home to find work, disbanding them after tomorrow's dress rehearsal performance.

How? she thought. *I can't do this!*

Her job as ice captain was to be responsible for them. She'd always felt that if she just stayed upbeat, if she kept positive and kept people happy, then she would succeed.

But she'd done all that, and in the end, she'd still failed. She really was a faker.

So how was she supposed to operate now?

"Goodbye, Emilie," Lynn said. "Take care with the dress rehearsal. We'll keep the video on file to show Donnie what you and your skaters can do, in the event that something comes up."

"Yes," Emilie murmured. But she no longer believed that any of it would make a difference.

She hung up with Lynn and turned off her phone. Then she climbed into bed and pulled the covers over her eyes. She honestly had no idea what to do.

And what most frightened her was that she found she didn't really care.

WHERE IS EMILIE?

Nathan stood in the lounge, where the skaters were still mingling from the party that had taken place earlier.

Everybody seemed to be in a festive mood—Emilie's work. The Christmas decorations in particular had perked the whole place up. Two of the skaters were kissing beneath the hanging sprig of mistletoe. Jason's mom had returned and was hugging him, and the little boy, wearing his birthday hat, looked happier than Nathan had ever seen him.

Nathan had to turn away. Little did they all know, but their Christmases were about to be ruined.

Gary walked past Nathan, chatting on his cell phone.

Nathan touched his shoulder. When Gary faced him, Nathan asked, "Where is Emilie?"

"Excuse me," Gary said into his phone, and then covered the receiver. "I don't know, Nathan. Did you call her?"

"She's not picking up her phone."

"Did you try her room?"

He hadn't. Not yet. He'd tried the gym, the lobby and the dining room, but not her room. "When was the last time you saw her?"

"About a half hour ago," Gary said. "She

was altering Katya's costume for the dress rehearsal tomorrow."

"Okay. Thank you." With any luck, Emilie hadn't received Lynn's call yet. Maybe Nathan still had time to ease her into the news. It wasn't lost on him that a big part of his worry was the fact that he hadn't been totally honest with Emilie—he'd been keeping the financial reality about the inn all to himself.

That was the way he dealt with keeping them all safe—by shouldering the burden so they didn't have to. He envisioned himself as a rock wall, because that's what he'd thought he was supposed to be.

Emilie was upbeat and enthusiastic and caring with others. He stayed grounded and contained. That was how he operated.

But his methods hadn't worked. After all he'd done to save the inn, its inhabitants and its workers, it was still being sold. He'd even made it worse, because if Emilie had received Lynn's call by now, then she would think he'd betrayed her again. In fact, if he remembered rightly, he'd specifically reassured her that the inn was "financially viable."

Nathan groaned aloud. Just great. She would certainly think he'd made the decision personally. He wouldn't blame her.

She would be devastated. Nathan couldn't bear to see her that way. He didn't want her to believe that he could betray her again.

But looking at it from her point of view, what else would she think?

She'd tried to open him up, to get him to talk about the truth and what was really going on, the feelings that bothered him, and he'd refused. His philosophy had been to hide any unpleasantness and act like a stoic rock.

He had to show her he was willing to make some changes. If he ever hoped to convince her to stay with him, he had to show her how he really felt about her, and how positively she affected him.

Nathan double-checked that his Jeep was in the lot. It was. Only then did he beeline to her hotel room.

CHAPTER FOURTEEN

"EMILIE?" NATHAN KNOCKED on her door. Not a peep came from inside her room. All around him the corridor was quiet.

"Emilie?" He knocked louder. "If you're inside, please open up." He paused, waiting.

The door slowly opened from the inside. Emilie's tearstained face peered out at him. "It's not a good time for me right now," she said in a choked voice.

"Emilie…" He wanted to crush her to his chest and comfort her. From the wounded look in her eyes, his worst fears were realized. Lynn had already called her, and he'd hurt her deeply. He had a hard, rocky trail to bring her back to him. "Please let me in. I really need to talk to you."

"Why?" she whispered. "You're sending us away. You're putting me and my troupe out in the cold."

"I don't want to. Believe me when I tell you

that it's the last thing I want." He put his hand on the doorjamb. "May I come in? *Please*."

She seemed to waver for a moment. Then she stepped back. "It's your inn. You can do what you want with it."

That wasn't the reaction he'd been hoping for, but he took advantage anyway. He stepped inside the darkened room. Cold, because he hadn't let the inn temperatures be turned up too high.

He suddenly felt ashamed. Emilie was shivering, wrapped in a blanket. The covers on her bed were rumpled, and he could tell she'd been huddled beneath the layers of wool and cotton coverings. Crying. In the dark.

She wouldn't accept comfort from him—he'd been the one who'd hurt her—but maybe he could provide comfort another way. He remembered how she'd been talking about missing the Florida weather.

"May I take you someplace warm, Emilie? It's cold in here, and that's my fault. I've been a Scrooge for far too long. A Grinch who should know better."

"Can you bring our jobs back, Nathan?"

He couldn't. He shook his head sadly. "It wasn't supposed to end like this. I've been keeping things from you because I wasn't supposed to tell anyone, but now, I'm going to lay everything on the table for you. My investors are selling the inn. I received the news just before Lynn called. Emilie, it's not just your troupe. The kids are being displaced, as well. I talked with the shelter right after I hung up with Lynn. It's why I couldn't talk to you first. I'm in agony over this."

Her hand went to her mouth. "The kids are leaving, too?" She looked at him with stricken eyes. "When?"

"The day after Christmas."

"Poor Jason!"

"I know."

"Poor Maria." Emilie slumped on the bed, her head in her hands. Then she looked up at him. "Did you have any idea this could happen?"

He couldn't lie to her again. He couldn't pretend any longer that everything was all right and nothing was wrong. That he was a rock who could protect people from disaster.

"The inn has been in financial trouble," he admitted, sitting facing her on the other bed. "And it was always unlikely we'd be able to stay open past Christmas unless I was able to perform a miracle. I'm sorry I lied about the financial viability of the hotel when you asked me. My investors made it clear that I was not to let on to anyone about the money problems."

She slumped further. Emotional pain radiated from her body.

It scared him, because he'd never seen her this way. Not even when her ship had sunk.

She looked as if she'd completely lost faith in him and the world.

"Emilie, please don't give up on me. I want to make things right for you."

MAKE THINGS RIGHT? At each step of the way, he'd chosen his inn over her, and she'd been oblivious. Until now…when the worst had happened. When everything had fallen apart, and her troupe was on the street.

So, yes, she had lost hope this Christmas.

"Please come out to the Jeep with me," Nathan pleaded. "I have someplace I want to bring you."

"Why? It doesn't matter anymore. I won't fight your decision. We'll leave tomorrow after the dress-rehearsal show for the kids."

She would soldier on for that much. But that was all.

"Don't make a decision just yet." Nathan stood. "And please don't judge me until you hear what I have to say."

He placed her jacket over her shoulders and set out her boots for her to slip into. She felt so tired and defeated, she just didn't have the energy to argue with him.

And she wasn't the least bit curious where he wanted to go. What difference did it make where he took her, anyway? If the inn was closing, then the inn was closing. She would never see Nathan again after tomorrow, and he knew it, too.

It's futile. But she was too beaten to fight, so she let him guide her down the hallway. His fingertips were lightly on her elbow, but she didn't let that fool her. Their story together was almost finished.

Outside, the weather was as harsh and cold as she felt inside. A biting wind whipped across her cheeks.

Tears leaked from her eyes. The parking lot was gritty with winter salt crunching beneath her boots, and she was suddenly homesick for her familiar tropical home.

At least, she would soon be back in Florida. Even if that meant moving into her mom's spare bedroom until she got herself on her feet again.

Nathan unlocked the passenger door for her. Then he climbed into the driver's side, turned on the engine and cranked the heater to full blast.

She got inside the familiar Jeep, too. Shivering, she put both hands against the heating vents.

From Nathan's expression, she could see he was sorry they'd ended up this way. Well, she was, too.

"Lynn blindsided me today," he said. "She called me before I had the chance to talk to you. She gave me a sales pitch to extend the contract, and I answered her the only way I could."

"Are you unhappy with the work I've been doing?" She found that she had to know the answer.

"No, on the contrary, I…" He sighed. "I haven't given up on us, and I don't want you to, either."

She felt tears leaking from her eyes as she shivered in her seat. Even the heating vent was still blowing cold air. "I just w-wish I was warm."

Nathan put the Jeep into gear. "Put your seat belt on, Emilie."

"Where are you taking me?"

"Someplace where you'll be warm." He set

his chin. "Or, as close to warm as you can be here in the north."

She didn't understand him. All she could think was that she'd been so intent that everyone else should feel happy this Christmas, that she had lost her way. He was right about one thing—she'd never expected that she would be the one to lose heart.

NATHAN WAS SERIOUSLY worried about Emilie. He'd never seen her so despondent. Through all the trials and obstacles she'd encountered, she'd always kept her optimism. She plugged onward. She never gave up, not even when she'd lost everything.

He had to do something to convince her that there was still hope. This was his last-ditch effort to beg her not to give up on him. Or on *them*.

She leaned her head against the window, and though he couldn't see her face, she seemed to be dully watching the road fly by.

He drove out to the state road, and he pegged the accelerator so they were whisking along at fifty miles per hour. Green pine trees flanked them on either side, their branches gilded with the light dusting of snow from the day before.

She didn't seem too excited about the prospect of snow anymore. He hated that she'd seemed to lose her natural enthusiasm.

"We're almost there, Emilie."

She glanced at him, and her eyes were red and bloodshot.

She was on the verge of tears. His heart cracked open in his chest.

"Emilie, it's not personal to you that we didn't extend the option. It's just business. It happens."

"But that's where you're wrong. It *is* personal. It was personal when you left me on the ship, and it's personal that Lynn's asking me to leave now because I gave her bad information."

"My partners didn't give me a choice. I was asked to keep the situation quiet."

"That's an excuse. If that were true, then you would have told me everything up front when we became partners in this project. But you didn't. You wouldn't let me in. You kept me separated from who you are and what's really important to you, and just expected me to go along because I'm eager to please."

"Yes. Yes to all of it. You're right."

Her mouth dropped open.

He pulled into the parking lot of the place he'd wanted to bring her. "Let's go inside."

She looked at the large, glass-enclosed structure and its sign that read L'Orangery, and gazed at him questioningly.

He unbuckled his seat belt. "This is the largest greenhouse for miles around. There are orange trees inside, a whole grove of them. It's the one local place that reminds me of Florida. And you."

"Why me?"

"You used to wear an orange-infused scent. I used to come here and sit for a while when missing you became too unbearable."

"*You* missed *me*?"

"I did. But my pride wouldn't let me admit it to anybody."

She stared at him, mouth open.

He kept talking, ushering her forward. "I give this place a lot of business during the year, so the owners won't mind if we take some time inside. It's warm and sunny and there are benches to sit on."

He took a breath. "You accused me of keeping myself separate from you, and you were right. Today I want to change that. I should have done it long ago, but I avoided the pain of my past and even hid it from you. I was afraid it would make me look bad to you. But I've been too much about pride. I need to show you why so you'll understand."

"Understand what?" she asked.

"Understand *me*. Understand that I love you. I've always really loved you." He swallowed, wanting so badly to touch her, to convince her. She was biting her lip, gazing at her hands, frozen before the heater.

"Emilie, please come inside."

He didn't want to lose her.

He couldn't lose her.

"What could you possibly want or see in me?" she asked.

"Are you kidding? You're the sunshine that everyone wants to bask in. I would love to have your ability to connect with people," he told her. "You help people. I know you don't believe it now, but it's true."

Something in her eyes seemed to spark, and she finally straightened her back, opening the Jeep door.

He got out, too, hopeful.

Inside the greenhouse, the owner nodded to Nathan, and Nathan returned his greeting. "Hello," Nathan said. "We're going to sit inside your greenhouse for a few minutes, if you don't mind."

"Sure, Nathan. Let me know if I can help with anything."

"Will do."

The owner nodded and went back to stocking plant food on the shelf. The store was empty of people other than them. He and Emilie had privacy.

He directed her toward the back, to the entrance of the greenhouse.

"You really come here often?"

"I honestly do."

Inside the glass structure, the atmosphere immediately changed. Warm, humid air enveloped them. Sunshine streamed in from the glass ceiling and walls. Emilie's eyes widened. Then she sighed and leaned her head back, arms open to the heat. "I feel like I'm home."

Watching her, Nathan derived more pleasure from her enjoyment than he felt from the warmth itself.

He led her to a group of orange trees planted in ten-gallon pots and forming a mini orange grove in the corner. She gravitated toward it, inhaling the aroma. The citrus air smelled delicious to him.

Just like Florida. Just like Emilie. As always, his memories transported him to their past, to simpler and happier times. He hoped it did the same for her.

They could have that same happiness again.

He believed it. That was the point he wanted to make to her. The reason for her to have hope.

Emilie sat on a nearby love seat–size bench and squeezed into one corner, giving him room. He sat beside her, his thigh just touching hers. He was gratified that she didn't flinch from him. And it did feel heartening to be close to her again.

He leaned forward and put his elbows on his knees. "I know you don't think so right now, but I was gutted when we broke up. It took me a long time to get over you. Maybe I never did."

From the corner of his eyes, he watched her. She gazed down at her hands, saying nothing. She was listening to him and concentrating.

"I know we're very different people, Em," he said softly. "You're bubbly and outgoing and expressive. I'm quiet and I tend to keep things bottled up. You're optimistic, and I'm…well, pessimistic."

Here, she smiled. He smiled back at her. But he had a lot more to say. He didn't want her to misunderstand him, not anymore. The last thing he'd wanted to do was to hurt her with the phone conversation he'd had with her boss.

"I don't talk about it much, and I know you've been frustrated with me because I never spoke to you about it, but I had a pretty lonely childhood, sort of like Jason's in a lot of ways." He took a breath. "Some of that might come out in how I treat him, and maybe some of it slipped out during the television interview you saw with Janet. And I realize I should have talked with you about it when you asked me. Maybe…maybe if I could've been more open two years ago, it even could've helped prevent our breakup down in Florida. I can't say."

It was his turn to stare at his hands. This was excruciating for him. What he had to say was intensely personal—too personal—and this was why business was so much easier for him to focus on than private feelings.

"Em, my parents pretty much dumped my sister and me with my father's parents. We were abandoned as kids—there was no doubt about that. My sister—Nell's mother—is older than me, and she had a tough time of it emotionally, too. Our grandparents were…well, I think you have an idea by now that we considered them the best people we knew. They were saviors to us, and to many people in the community. They loomed large in our little town, and people respected them."

He gazed at Emilie. She was nodding. Emboldened, he continued. "You asked me once about my grandfather—Philip Prescott. He was this tough old Yankee gentleman." Nathan smiled at the memory. "I wish you'd met him. He taught me and my sister that the way to survive hard times was with stoicism and practicality. Always practicality. We had chores. We were expected to work. We didn't talk about our feelings—we just moved forward. Whatever issues we had, we kept them private, and we were expected to carry ourselves with dignity. His philosophy was that busy hands quieted the mind. In time, he believed, issues resolved themselves. In any event, it was more important that we think about how we could help everybody together, as a community, rather than focusing on our own individual problems."

He paused. She was intensely interested in what he was saying. It was the most he'd ever revealed about himself to anyone, by far. But now that he'd started talking, he couldn't seem to keep it bottled up inside any longer. The words just seemed to flow.

"I know I never told you too much about my background, or what I was brought up to believe in. Maybe I just expected that things would work out between us—a kind of warped version of my grandfather's philosophy." He smiled at her, hoping she understood.

"Emilie, when I first met you, I thought you were so different, so exotic, and I was drawn to you. You fascinated me. You were so enthusiastic—you performed and made everybody smile, and you always saw the potential in life if we just believed hard enough." He watched her as she bit her lip, frowning a bit at him.

"Em, don't misunderstand, please. In time, I realized that you and I both actually share a lot of values in common—the best values, to me. We both care about helping other people, maybe too much. We both want to save our teams, our communities. The people who are important to us—and right now, I'm thinking especially of little Jason, who lives across the hall from you."

She nodded at that.

"Maybe I don't always seem caring to you. Maybe I seem cautious. I don't see the hope of Christmas spirit that you do, maybe because I've been too often disappointed in life, and you haven't."

"You think I haven't been disappointed?" She stared at him.

He shook his head. "Not really. Not in a major way. Or else how could you be so positive? And I'm glad for it. You should keep your upbeat personality. Your love for Christmas spirit. The kids need it." He stared at his hands again. "Jason needs it, for one. I don't know how I'm ever going to let that little kid and his mother go the day after Christmas…"

He let his voice trail off. He wished he could have showed Emilie these things when they'd been on the ship together, but their relationship seemed very different now. Even though they weren't together, the feelings were deeper and more honest, at least on his part.

"When I first met Jason, seeing him so frightened and sad in the corner, wondering whether Santa Claus was going to find him—it reminded me of my first days at the inn, too. I wanted to be a rescuer to him, like my grandfather was to me. I wanted that pride of helping him. I wanted to be worth something, especially in comparison with my father, who'd just abandoned me and the community." He made Nathan feel shame.

"Nathan, I asked you to tell me about him, but you refused. You said your parents were show people. Tell me now."

Nathan was well aware that he had deflected Emilie before when she'd asked about his parents. He swallowed. He'd gone down this path of opening himself up to her. He had to keep going.

"They…left us here because they were on the road together. They were in a band." He swallowed again. "It's not…a bad thing they were musicians away from home, but they just… weren't interested in us. At all. I know that's not usual for parents, and it made me feel…" Like something had been wrong with him. But he didn't say that aloud. He just shrugged. "They didn't come back until I was fifteen, when my grandfather died. To my father, the inn was a windfall."

Nathan paused, still feeling the old bitterness. "My parents squandered it all. My father took every nickel out of the inn that he could, and he spent it on himself. He didn't care what was happening around him—the fact that people were being laid off, that hardship was coming to the townspeople who depended on Prescott Inn. It was as if he wanted to destroy everything about my grandfather's legacy. Or maybe he only cared about his own pleasure. I don't know. Emilie, it's not a happy subject with me. It's probably why I've been trying extra hard to bring back Prescott Inn to what it once was."

"Why were you ever in Florida if your heart

is here?" she asked him. "Did you want to get away from what you considered his failure?"

"Yeah. I think you're right about that." Part of it, anyway. "My sister went away to college in California. I went down to Florida." The best thing that he'd ever done. "I learned accounting—I thought it would be useful—and I took practical jobs, saving up my money. Working for the cruise line seemed ideal because of the room-and-board situation. It saved even more money."

"And you met me," she said flatly.

"To my great happiness," he answered honestly.

She stood. "Maybe if you'd included me emotionally in your decisions, then things would have worked out differently between us."

He winced. "I know. You're right."

She stared at him for a long time and then shook her head. "That's not fair of me to say, Nathan. I didn't show you my true self, either."

"What do you mean?" he asked.

"I'm not truly hopeful about Christmas or any of it. I fake it."

He blinked at her. He'd never seen her like this, agitated and angry. It wasn't in character for her. "You're just upset right now about the contract ending. What you're saying is not true."

"It is." She began to pace, eyes on the floor. "It's more than that. I didn't piece it all together until I was sitting here just now, listening to you."

"What do you mean?"

She stared at him. "Nathan, you weren't the only one with a difficult childhood."

Was she talking about her father? "I'd like to hear about it."

She crossed her arms. "I'm the youngest in my family, too. My sister is older. You've met her."

He had. Twice, he and Emilie had journeyed up to Fort Myers to her mom's condo for a home-cooked Sunday dinner. Her sister had been there with her then-infant daughter. The visits had been pleasant and upbeat.

"I liked her very much," he said. "Your mom, too. They were always kind to me."

"My mom worked really hard when my sister and I were growing up. Maria—Jason's mom—reminds me of her. My mom always had two or three jobs. It's only in recent years that she's been able to let up a bit." Emilie's mouth twisted. "But that wasn't the bad thing. The bad thing... It came when I was younger than Jason... I wasn't even school-age yet." She rubbed her arms, as if shivering. "My mom's mother lived with us." Her voice cracked. "She was so depressed, all the time. I never knew why—I was too little to understand—but she didn't leave the house. Her job was to care for me while my mom worked and my sister was in school. But really..." Emilie swallowed. Nathan waited, sensing just how much what she was about to say hurt Emilie.

Emilie took a breath. "*I* was the one who took care of her. It sounds weird to say, I know, but it was my job to keep her happy." She glanced at Nathan. "I always knew this— I guess I never really thought much about the consequences of that time until..." She sighed. "Until dealing with all this hardship. It's coming out now. It's making sense to me suddenly. Listening to you."

They both affected one another. He'd always known that. He reached out and touched her hand. "I see you going overboard to care for your skaters. Is that because you fear any sign of depression or unhappiness in them?"

"Probably. Yes." She nodded. "I hadn't realized." She closed her eyes. "The day that my grandmother passed, I was the one who found her. She was in her bedroom, and she wouldn't wake up. I ran next door in my bare feet and told a neighbor, who called my mom at work. I was so scared. I listened, and I heard my mom talking with the EMTs who responded to our neighbor's call. She'd taken pills, is what I heard them saying. My mom never talks about that day." Emilie smiled sadly at Nathan, whose heart was breaking for her. "My mom is even more of an optimist than I am. She likes to look forward."

Emilie touched one of the ripe oranges, idly rubbing its skin. "I love my family. They're good people. But when my grandmother died, I felt it was my fault. I was supposed to keep her happy, and I didn't. So after she was gone, I tried doubly hard with the others around me. To perform for people, stay upbeat. Never, never show sadness, and certainly not anger."

"So that's why you perform. Why you make it your career. You're comfortable pleasing an audience."

She nodded slowly, her face flushing. Then she released the orange, looking downcast. "I was angry the evening before my grandma passed," she murmured. "I'd sassed her, and she'd seemed even more sad than usual. And of course, I know now as an adult that that wasn't the reason she…well, that she made the choice to take her life. I'm not going to speculate on her reasons. But maybe a part of me felt…guilt. Or blame. Or whatever."

She turned to Nathan and took in a breath. "I'm not ashamed for being a performer, not in the least. I still think it's my calling, but maybe for different reasons than when I originally pursued my career. Yes, my skating made my dad happy. It made everybody come together and feel proud when I made the final ten finishers at Nationals during my high school years. And when I discovered the joy of skating before a show audience on the cruise ship—well, I thought I'd found heaven."

"And you still do believe that, that it's your calling," he said, realizing what this meant for the two of them, his heart sinking.

"Yes, I still do."

Then nothing has changed for our future together, he thought bleakly.

"Nathan, you were right about one thing. This making-people-happy philosophy might be part of me, but it isn't smart for business. I failed at keeping our troupe employed. I thought I was doing everything right, making people happy, keeping myself positive, but in the end, here we are, on the street. Putting a smile on my face isn't going to change the mind of a suit. People are going to do what people are going to do. I have no influence over that."

She stared at him, her eyes sad. "The troupe—everybody—can decide what they want to do tomorrow. I'll soldier on and finish my commitment to Lynn for the dress rehearsal, but honestly, my heart isn't in it."

"Emilie, you can't mean that."

"I do. I need to think practically and detach myself emotionally from the outcome, like you did. Let's go back to the inn, please."

"Emilie, no."

But she wasn't listening to him. She was already walking toward the car.

What had he done? He'd wanted to show her that she wasn't wrong to believe in other people. That he believed in her. And that he recognized why it was so important to her to make tomorrow's show a great one.

He'd never thought she'd lose her upbeat spirit completely.

It was his fault she'd lost heart and detached herself from caring.

He stared at her, realizing that Emilie without Christmas hope was the saddest, most demoralizing thing he'd ever seen.

That's what shocked and chastened him most. He *loved* this woman. And yet, it was his terrible influence that had turned her as hard and as pessimistic as he was.

But he wouldn't give up. He would turn to Nell for help. And the kids. And her skaters.

Together, they would find a way to bring Emilie back to herself again.

CHAPTER FIFTEEN

WHEN NATHAN DROPPED Emilie off at the inn, she knew what she had to do. Her heart wasn't in it, but her purpose was so much clearer now.

She wasn't responsible for everybody's happiness. She *was* responsible for figuring out her own life. Whatever that would be.

She left Nathan at the Jeep and trudged down to her own room, alone. Julie and Lynette would probably be by later for the girls' night, but she would tell them to cancel. And she would not feel badly about that.

Fifteen minutes later, there was a knock on the door, followed by Nell's voice. "Emilie?"

"Come in." Really, what difference did it make?

Nell came inside and shut the door behind her. Her phone was in her hand. "Uncle Nathan just told me that the inn is being sold, and that you might be leaving after tomorrow."

Emilie wrapped a blanket around herself.

"Yes." It occurred to her that Nell was losing her job, too. "I'm sorry, Nell," she said.

Nell's entire body drooped. "He tried so hard to keep the business going. I don't know what we're going to do now."

Emilie, for once, had nothing reassuring to say. Life was hard. Dreams didn't always come true.

And hope didn't always work. Nathan was right about one thing: practicality was the way forward.

"I'm tired," Emilie said. "We have a dress rehearsal in the morning."

"And now it might be your only show!"

Emilie didn't say anything. She would call the team together later and let them vote. Honestly, she was finding it hard to care one way or the other what they decided. She glanced at Nell. "Would you mind videotaping the show for us tomorrow? My boss wants a copy. It's the only thing she really asked me to do."

"Of course I will!" Nell paused. "Isn't that good news that she wants a copy?"

"I'm not getting my hopes up."

"Think about it. If you impress her, then maybe she'll step in and do something for you."

Emilie shook her head. "I'm being practical."

"Still…" Nell grabbed another blanket as she

sat on the bed. "Will you be performing your new show, the one you've been working on?"

Emilie snorted. "The soundtrack isn't narrated. The props aren't painted. There still are costumes to adjust."

"I could rally everyone to help."

Nell just wasn't letting this go.

"To what end?" Emilie shook her head. "No. I don't see how it will do any good."

"You worked so hard on it. And it's a special show, using your special talents. I think you should perform it just to please yourself."

Emilie stopped. *Just to please herself?*

"Admit it," Nell said. "Don't you want to see it performed? I mean, I know you were choreographing that show for…well, you had your list of reasons."

Pleasing Nathan, impressing Donnie, keeping her team employed. Yes, Emilie remembered those reasons.

"What if…you just did it?" Nell pressed. "For the joy of it."

Emilie sat on her bed, chewing on that. It was true that designing the special show had excited her. It had been a challenge. A pleasurable challenge.

"Am I right, Emilie? Can't we just have fun?"

Fun. A refreshing word.

Like she and Nathan had done back on the ship, when they'd lived just to enjoy the days.

Emilie found herself nodding.

Nell clapped her hands. "Let's get started! We have so much to do. Oh, how I love a show! Especially a Christmas show!"

ANOTHER TEN MINUTES LATER, and Emilie was dressed in her rehearsal clothes—comfortable yoga pants and a warm, long sweater that tied around her waist. She'd pulled her hair back into a ponytail and she carried a clipboard.

"Come on, Nell. We have a long night ahead of us."

Nell grinned at her and gave her a thumbs-up. Emilie opened the door to the corridor and headed outside, with Nell close behind.

They stared down the length of the west wing hallway. Emilie's team was in party mode. Pop music blared from someone's open door. Laughter echoed, followed by the pounding of someone running down the hallway adjacent to theirs.

Emilie tucked her clipboard under her arm, put two fingers to her mouth and let go an ear-piercing whistle.

Dead silence greeted her. Everyone seemed frozen in place.

Emilie knew she'd shocked them because she'd never acted like this before.

They all faced her, mouths closed and ears open.

"That's better," Emilie said to them all. And then she began to issue orders. "Everyone into my room, please. There will be no exceptions. No absences will be tolerated. Leave your drama at the threshold, because I will no longer permit it."

Every single person gaped at her.

"Who are you and where have you left Ice Mom?" somebody whispered.

"Enough!" Emilie said. She pointed her finger. "I am not your mother—I am a professional. We're all professionals. It's time to act like it."

Gary turned to the others. "Come on. Let's do as she says."

Nell went inside Emilie's room first. She was followed by Gary, Curtis, Lars, Drew, Katya, Sergei, Rosie, Julie and Lynette—the whole team. When they were all present and accounted for, seated on the two beds and the desk chairs, Gary nodded at her.

No one said a word. They all waited for her lead.

Emilie stood before them. "Gary, please shut

the door. I don't want the children across the hall to overhear our meeting."

Gary did as she asked. Emilie waited until he was seated again before speaking. "I received bad news today," she announced. "Due to circumstances beyond our control, the inn has decided not to extend our performances past Christmas, and the production company has given us the option of pulling the plug early in order to give us more time to look for other work. We will still be paid our salaries until Christmas either way, whichever option we choose. I'd like to put it to a vote after the dress rehearsal tomorrow—we can either perform all the shows we'd originally agreed to, or the dress rehearsal tomorrow will be our last show performed together."

A collective gasp went up. They all looked at each other.

But Emilie squared her shoulders.

"So let's consider this dress rehearsal tomorrow as a real show—the most important show of our continued careers." She looked at each skater in turn. "We will all skate our hearts out, because Lynn has requested a recording of the show. She may use it for reference if other jobs come up. Consider it an audition tape for each of you for your next assignment."

Emilie gazed from face to face, reading the unasked question in their eyes. "No," she answered, "the *Empress Caribbean* will not be put into service again, at least not this season. But there could be other openings. So I suggest that if you want to keep skating professionally with the company, then you use this opportunity to showcase your skills to the fullest. Are there any questions?"

No one dared to speak. Emilie again looked from face to face, but she'd done the impossible, she'd stunned them all into silence.

No skater drama. They would keep the drama strictly on the ice for the audience's pleasure.

And for their own.

"Great. I realize we've been focusing on the Christmas show from the ship, but I'd like to suggest we switch gears and do the new one. So now I'm going to pass out assignments, and we're going to pull together as a team. We all need each other to do our jobs. Gary, you and I will have to work late to finish the narration for the soundtrack. Lynnette and Julie, we'll have to reschedule our girls' night. Then tomorrow morning, we'll all meet at eight o'clock in the yoga room outside the gym. We'll walk through the show then, so you're all familiar with the added narration.

"Rosie, Julie and Katya…" Emilie glanced at each of them in turn. "I'm relying on you to finish sewing your own costumes—all of them." She didn't give them time to protest or groan; she just kept moving on. "Drew, Lars and Sergei—you'll be finishing painting the props."

Who had she left out? Lynette. Lynette looked forlornly at her.

"Lynette," Emilie decreed, "you will have the most important job of all. You're to talk to the families of each child who lives in this hallway. I'll need you to invite them all to the dress rehearsal. It's extremely important that they're present, since I'm hoping that they'll be part of the show, too. In fact, I'm going to choreograph a special part for each of them. Can we trust you to do this?"

Lynette nodded. Her eyes had seemed to spark at "the most important job of all." Lynette, the youngest, was usually a sidekick to the others. Emilie had a hunch she'd wanted a more powerful role, and now Emilie was giving it to her.

"Okay." Emilie nodded to each of them. "We're all counting on each other to do our parts. That means we need to pull together and move forward as a team. Am I understood?"

They each nodded.

Good. She wanted this show to be as beautiful as they could make it. The rest of the shows…well, she was personally willing to let them go.

This show was for *them*.

Her heart pounding, she nodded to Gary. "Let's get to it, then. We have a narration to record."

THE NEXT DAY, at a quarter to three, Nathan sat in the spot Nell had directed him to take in the stands above the outdoor skating rink in the clearing of the woods.

The mood in the air was electric. Fifteen minutes until showtime, and the bleachers surrounding the rink were filled with excited people.

"How did you pull this off? How did you manage all these details?" he asked Nell, who was seated beside him. She was in charge of operating the spotlight and a receiver that she said was for special effects. Nathan and Nell were seated at center ice in a special roped-off box created just for them.

"We've been working together all night," Nell said softly.

He wasn't surprised. Nell had also set up a video camera in front of him, one she'd borrowed from somewhere he wasn't certain, the base screwed into a tripod for steadiness. His job was to man it. She'd just finished giving Nathan a quick tutorial.

"Please do a good job with the recording, Uncle Nathan. I'd like us to give Emilie a decent audition tape so she can secure another job."

"You bet," he said. It saddened him that he couldn't offer her a longer-term position. But that wasn't within his power. What could he personally do? He might be out of a job himself. He would probably be able to find another accounting position.

But an "accounting position" couldn't hire Emilie. Neither could it hire back his old employees. Or give the kids at the homeless shelter more permanent homes.

"When are you going to tell everyone the news about the inn being sold?" Nell asked.

"I don't know," he admitted. "I've been asked not to say anything until the deal is finalized. So please, keep the news to yourself."

"All these people will be so sad when they

find out." Nell gestured toward the audience. Besides the hotel guests in the stands, he spotted many familiar faces. These were his colleagues, neighbors and friends.

"Look," Nell said, pointing her finger. "The fire chief is here. And he brought his family and the fire department."

Indeed. Four roaring campfires, each situated in a pit dug at either end of both long bleachers, were being tended by a member of the local fire department.

"And look—Nancy, the school nurse, came, too." Nell pointed to a spot near the fire chief. Sure enough, Nancy sat on the edge of a bleacher, next to the long curtain that separated the skaters' "backstage" area from the rest of the ice.

"I recognize a lot of townies here today." Nathan squinted. Was that one of his investors—B.G. Richards?

It was. B.G. sat with his wife and two young daughters. They were nibbling from a bag of popcorn.

"Is Frank making popcorn back at the inn?" Nathan asked.

Nell shook her head. "Claude made it. We carted that big machine into the lobby—you know, the one that's just been sitting in the back storeroom?"

Nathan did. They'd originally used the machine to make popcorn in the lobby for the guests in the afternoons. But it had seemed an extravagance to him, so he'd stopped the practice. One of his early cost-cutting measures, implemented some months ago.

"Claude said there was a huge package of popcorn left that was still good, so I told him to just go ahead and make it. The waitstaff on duty are down in the inn parking lot, passing out the popcorn to kids. Then Frank is driving everybody up the hill. Actually, Uncle, some people are walking. The mood is quite festive."

Yes, everyone was getting into the Christmas spirit. Jingle bells had been attached to Nathan's Jeep. Boughs of holly and swags of pine decorated the rink and the railings that led to the stands. A huge spruce tree at the end of the edge of the clearing had been decorated with white lights and a glowing star on top.

"It's almost showtime." Nell checked her watch. She reached over and pressed a button. Yuletide, family-friendly rock music filtered over the speakers, increasing the anticipation that something big was about to happen.

Nathan perched on the edge of his seat. He'd

always loved watching Emilie skate on the ship, but the rink in the woods at Christmastime was even more special. There was an old-fashioned, community feel due to the rustic surroundings. The cool, clear mountain air was refreshing— Nathan smelled a hint of snow on the way. Indeed, a few sparse flurries filtered down from the heavens.

A true White Christmas, just like his childhood with his grandparents. And as in those old days, the body heat of so many audience members seated closely together made the viewing stands feel cozy. The laughter of children, the deep voices from the men, the soft chatter of the women, gave the ambiance a family feel. Nathan recalled the yearning he'd experienced as a child to really belong. *This* was what he'd really wanted. Not the pride of inn ownership. But the sense that people were together, and that he was an important part of it.

Marveling at this realization, he took a moment to study all the faces in the crowd. Nell must have emptied out the diner, the barbershop, the drycleaners, the crafts fair market, the police station, the tiny movie theater. Every corner of the rink's seats were filled. Everyone in town seemed to be present.

Most conspicuous, at center ice, on the opposite side from him, sat the kids who lived in his hotel.

The knot rose in Nathan's throat again. He'd been agonizing over them. What to do with them. How to help them now.

He still had no good solution.

His gaze fell to the one-page show program that Nell had whipped up with Emilie just this morning. He'd seen the two conferring over coffee during a break in the skaters' final "walk-through," as Emilie had called it, down in the conference room of his gym.

Curious, Nathan picked up the flyleaf. "Christmas at Prescott Inn," was the title.

Nice, he automatically thought. *An advertisement.* But then he also felt a twinge of sadness in his heart. All the advertisements in the world couldn't make his vision for the kids come true. But yet, the sentiment was there on Emilie's part.

Nell must have noticed his expression. "Here," she said, pointing to the program. "While you're waiting for the show to start, check out the cast bios. I never realized how impressive they all were."

She read aloud. "Julie Johnston is a former US Nationals ladies' freestyle champion. She represented the US at the World Championships, where she placed fourth."

"That's a pewter medalist."

"I know. And read Katya's bio."

"Two-time Russian champion pairs skater, with two different partners. An Olympic medalist with a third partner." He whistled.

"She's had quite a life. Many tragic losses and disappointments, from what Emilie has told me."

"And yet, here she is."

"That's right." Nell pointed. "Look at Curtis and Lynette, too."

"Canadian ice dance champions." He put down the program. "I had no idea. Why didn't this come out in the interview with that television reporter?"

"Because we were focusing on the inn," Nell said softly. "That was our plan."

He nodded. Emilie had emphasized the fact that the team was a homeless, shipwrecked show-cast rescued by Prescott Inn, a family establishment in the mountains of New Hampshire, as far away from the sunny Caribbean as one could be.

"Almost time." Nell nudged him to gaze toward the black curtain. Emilie had poked her face out and was signaling to Nell.

"That's the one-minute mark. They're ready." Nell stood up and craned her neck to better see the front entrance. "No more stragglers. There's Frank coming in to sit down." Nell waved at him and then sat again. "Before I start the soundtrack, do you remember what to do with the camera, Uncle?"

"Yes," he said patiently. "I press this button, and the red light goes on. I look through the viewfinder and I keep the whole ice in frame. When there's a spotlight soloist, I zoom in to get the close-up, but always keep their skates in view."

"Right. Never, never cut off the skate blades." Nell nodded. "Emilie said her boss will want to see all the intricate footwork in her chore-ography."

"And for group numbers, I pull back and get everyone in the frame."

"Correct. You'll do great." Nell flashed him a genuine smile.

He almost laughed aloud at the change in their roles. Now the tables were turned, and she was the teacher and he was the student. It was refreshing. He felt younger, with the weight of the world lifted off his shoulders, even if for the moment. He was glad to be able to do something that would help Emilie out, even if it was small.

"Now, Uncle, I need to warn you. The show is quite different from what you're expecting. Emilie has kept pieces of previous routines, but she made a whole new storyline as the focus. The audio for the show is substantially changed, so don't be confused by the speaking voice in the beginning."

"Got it. I hope this show helps her."

"Well, I'm just saying—don't expect to see Emilie skating much. She said that, mostly, she'll be backstage, helping the cast meet their entrance cues with the new marks. They only laid out the final show just this morning."

"So Emilie's not skating?" he asked, disappointed.

"She has a small, ongoing role in the show, but I think she only skates in one solo and then the ending number."

"Oh." It was strange how saddened he was by Nell's explanation. He'd really wanted to watch Emilie skate again.

"Are you ready, Uncle? I'm going to start the audio now."

"Yes." He sat up and pushed aside his thoughts. He had to concentrate on his camera work.

"It's showtime." Nell grinned wickedly and pressed the button for the audio to begin.

CHAPTER SIXTEEN

"Go," EMILIE MURMURED, and she opened the curtain for Gary so he could skate onto the stage. Nell had started the theatrical fog machine, and a hazy smoke clung low to the ice, giving the nostalgic mood that Emilie had hoped to achieve.

Gary made a moody and dramatic line of gliding loop steps down one side of the rink. Nell kept the spotlight on him as he moved through the mist. Emilie had meant for her set design to feel like the forest in winter. A gasp went up from the audience members as Gary skated past.

Emilie breathed a sigh of pleasure. From the murmuring she heard, it appeared that they recognized the character Gary played. He wore a groomed but bushy beard, meant to mimic the look that Philip Prescott sported in his large portrait, which was located both in the lobby of the inn and also up in Nathan's office, over his desk.

Emilie glanced toward the box where she knew Nathan was seated. He was working behind the video camera, following Gary as the other man skated intricate steps meant to mimic meandering through the New Hampshire woods.

And then over the music, the narration sounded. Gary's voice, meant to represent that of Philip Prescott himself, explaining how he'd come to New Hampshire.

Nathan's lips parted in surprise. The audience clapped and then cheered. A few people whistled.

Yes, Emilie had created this show specially to represent the dramatization of the founding of Prescott Inn. She was taking a risk performing it today. Everyone had been expecting to see her company's generic Christmas program, with songs and skating routines that represented a child's view of Christmas.

That was not this show. Originally, Emilie had hoped that Lynn and Donnie would appreciate how she'd created a program specially tailored to the regional venue and its audience. She'd also chosen routines that showcased her team's technical and interpretive talents. Lynn and Donnie weren't in the audience, and neither one of them might ever watch this recording, but if they did, she hoped they'd see that the audience at Prescott Inn understood and enjoyed the theme. From the clapping and cheering, it appeared that they did.

In the next number, Katya and Sergei skated an adagio piece that was meant to represent Philip's courting and marriage to Ava, Nathan's grandmother. This time, Sergei wore Philip Prescott's bushy beard and his costume had been altered to resemble a distinctive midcentury suit. Katya wore a beautiful white wedding dress, with a lace veil.

Katya was exquisite in her representation of Ava doing the wedding waltz. Katya was an Olympian with great skill. Not only was the local audience viewing a story catered to them, which they knew well, but they were also viewing world-class skating from a former champion who was at the top of her game.

Sergei, too, was skating more passionately with Katya than Emilie had ever seen him skate. He picked Katya up easily, with little apparent effort, and together they executed a flawless triple twist. They had the space of the large rink to execute the daring and breathtaking moves, so Emilie had asked them to put in all of their most difficult elements.

Sergei launched Katya expertly into an awe-inspiring throw triple loop jump. Katya landed perfectly on one blade, her arms extended in a gorgeous dancer's pose. Even the skaters behind the curtain with Emilie were peering through the cracks, sighing at the beauty of the program. When Katya landed her jump, Emilie heard more than a few squeals and the muted slap of high fives being exchanged between the backstage skaters.

This was the most technically and artistically difficult show Emilie's cast had ever produced. It was daring for them.

She felt ecstatic at the effect.

The voice-over next described the war years and the expansion of Prescott Inn. It was time for the rest of the cast to cue up backstage for the first big group number. The remaining seven members of the troupe skated onto the ice, representing the workers at Prescott Inn: waiters, chambermaids, desk clerks—and even Frank's grandfather, the original valet at the inn.

Emilie hung behind, waiting until Katya and Sergei were safely behind the curtain again. Emilie assisted Katya as she changed into her next costume. A red velvet dress, meant to represent Ava as a young mother and Christmas hostess.

"You did beautifully," Emilie breathed into Katya's ear. "I'm going to send you a copy of the tape so you can watch it, too."

"I landed the throw triple loop!" Katya whispered excitedly. "Did you see it!"

"Yes, we all did."

Katya was excited because she hadn't performed the difficult move before an audience since her competitive days.

"Help me with my prop," Emilie whispered to Katya. She needed to attach a large harness to her waist, which would have a particular effect on her skirt as she executed her spins.

"I have it," Katya said, snapping a series of large gossamer handkerchiefs into place. She glanced around. "Where are the children?"

"They have their cues," Emilie murmured. She only hoped they remembered. They were little kids, after all. But they would all do their best.

The soundtrack changed to a quirkier, more humorous tune. "That's my cue," Emilie whispered, as Katya held open the curtain for her. Emilie skated onto the ice, still in the shadows. She waited until the seven other members finished their number.

Hugging herself, Emilie focused on Drew. The young champion stepped into a back crossover, and then executed an entrance of six or seven more gliding steps with deeply bent knees, building up a tremendous amount of speed, the fastest that any of her troupe skated by far. He started down the end of the rink closest to the curtain and then headed directly toward Frank, who was standing beside one of the firepits. Halfway across the rink, he stepped into a shallow forward-inside three turn, and then launched himself into the hugest quadruple toe-loop that Emilie had ever seen in person.

The audience gasped. Drew seemed to be flying.

After what seemed like an especially long time, he finally landed cleanly. The place broke out into cheers. Even Sergei jumped up and punched his fist beside Emilie.

It was the most difficult move any of them would perform. This was not a kiddie carnival show. This was world-class skating, and it was exactly what Emilie had set out to achieve.

Now it was her turn. The pacing of the music changed. She was meant to bring down the emotion from excitement—representing the energy of building a new, successful business, where patrons came from all over the country—to the gentle genesis of the young couple's family.

Emilie skated gracefully to center ice. She felt gratified when she was recognized and cheered roundly. But she went ahead with her dance, finally stepping into a strong forward outside edge to begin her combination spin finale. Spinning was Emilie's forte—what she'd been known for her in her younger, competitive days. But years of working with professionals on the ship had helped her mature her style to that of exquisite grace and beauty. The delicate ribbons on the skirt of her dress enhanced the vision. The spotlight caught the metallic sheen of the costuming. The audience sighed and gasped.

She moved from a camel spin to a layback with many changes of arm position. She slowed the spin down and then sped it up again. She changed feet and did it all once more, ending with the most dramatic, fastest blur of a backspin that she could manage. She kept the spin centered and tightly rotated. Not having to worry about the stage dipping and jerking as it had on the ship was wonderful. Prescott Inn now had a superbly smooth ice surface, and being outside, in the open air, was exhilarating.

But her number wasn't finished yet. The theatrical fog machine started up again. Dramatically, Emilie skated to the open door near the firepit, where Frank had been stationed.

There they were, Emilie's cuties. Jason was the littlest, so she held out her hand and led him forward. He ran and then glided like a wobbly colt on his new hockey skates. Gary had bought them for him. The cast had been taking turns enthusiastically teaching the kids a few beginner moves whenever they had the chance. All six kids skated eagerly out to center ice, and joined hands as Emilie had coached them. Gliding on two feet, they twisted their hips so they were first skating forward, and then when she called out, they switched so they were going in reverse. They looked so adorable. The crowd cheered them on.

And always, Gary's narration sounded over the music. Now he was telling the story of Ava Prescott, the lady of the inn, who so loved to skate that her husband had built her a rink in the mountain clearing. There she'd given lessons to local children. They had Friday night dance parties and Saturday afternoon hockey games. Ava Prescott had skated to her heart's content.

The song came to an end, and Emilie lined up the children to take their bows and curtsies, first to one side of the audience, and then to the other side, just as she'd taught them. Emilie herself dipped into a curtsy. She rose and saw Nathan staring directly at her, a smile on his lips.

She caught her breath. Her blood was already pumping with the adrenaline and intensity of performing for a live audience, but when she caught his admiring look, it felt as if two years and a lot of recent emotional conflict fell away, as if they'd never been separated by anything. Emilie blushed and then couldn't help but give him a little wave.

The impulsive gesture made her late for her cue. It was time for the ice dance number—the Friday-night dance parties recreated. Sheepishly, Emilie skated as quickly and unobtrusively as she could to the back curtain.

Even if her gambit to impress Lynn with this show so her boss would consider her for a choreographer job was no longer relevant, for this one moment, it didn't matter to her. They'd all been having so much fun, Emilie wouldn't take back the experience for the world.

But it was all for just this moment. She was *practical*. Tomorrow, she'd leave Prescott Inn. And Nathan. After what he'd told her about his parents, she now knew he could never be with a traveling show person. Not given the way his parents had abandoned him when he was a child.

As she'd said to him, she still wanted to be involved in performance, whether as a skater or as a choreographer. And to truly be with Nathan, she would have to give up the flexibility she'd need in order to travel to be a creative choreographer.

She now knew what she wanted. So why did the idea of leaving fill her with so much pain?

NATHAN'S HEART WAS beating so loudly, it was a wonder that Nell couldn't hear it, even over the pulsing music on the soundtrack and the audience's enthusiastic cheers.

The show was utterly fantastic! Emilie had put together an amazing, entertaining performance, and the fact that she'd organized the theme around Nathan's grandfather…it honestly brought tears to his eyes. He'd been shocked at first to discover that the show's theme was his grandparents' story. Then when he realized just how much Emilie understood how Nathan cared about his family's past, he'd been utterly humbled.

She'd gotten every detail of the inn's history right. He wasn't sure where she'd gotten all of her information from, but it didn't matter, because she'd managed to capture the great love Nathan felt for his amazing grandparents. And people in the audience appreciated that the show was tailor-made for their community and this setting.

Not to mention the talent that this young cast displayed—he'd never seen anything like it in person. Not even on the cruise ships had the skating been this excellent. Locals would have to go into the city to catch a traveling skating show of this caliber, and even then they would be seated in a massive arena, far above the ice. The rink in the woods at Prescott Inn had low and intimate seating. When a skater jumped on the ice, it seemed possible he might actually land in Nathan's lap.

Smiling to himself, he concentrated on the video recorder, making sure to follow the action so he could get the skaters' every step and move clearly recorded. He did this for Emilie mainly, but an idea was fast taking shape in his mind, as well.

By the time the skaters had performed the finale, the crowd was on their feet, wildly cheering. Nathan kept the camera trained on all eight skaters at center ice, planning to hold it there until the final strain of music faded away into the afternoon air. The snow flurries were coming down a bit harder now, which added to the festive excitement. When the melody abruptly ended, the kids sitting in the front row were so excited, they hopped over the barrier, sliding across the ice, toward the skaters.

Chuckling softly, Nathan kept the video running. By now, a great throng was dancing and partying at center ice. The kids were having so much fun, and anyway, Emilie could always cut the tape later.

"Can you believe this?" Nell asked, laughing beside Nathan. "Should I turn on the fog machine again, Uncle?"

"No," he said, laughing despite himself. "I don't want anyone to get hurt."

"You have to admit, it would be really fun for everyone to skate through."

"Yeah." And he also had to admit that he was itching to hop the railing and join the dancing. Nell rewound the final song to play it again. "We Are Family" by Sister Sledge started up once more.

"All we need is a disco ball," Nathan said with a laugh. He finally stopped the recording and stood. The scene was getting too crazy, and he'd lost sight of Emilie. All he wanted to do right now was see her.

She emerged from the crowd at last. She wore a green dress and glitter in her flowing hair, and she was heading his way.

He stepped down from the bleacher seats to greet her, never losing sight of her face. Her cheeks were rosy with joy and her eyes flashed brightly. It felt just like it used to be between them, after he'd been to one of her shows on the ship—only better. A lot better.

Nathan reached forward and lifted Emilie up from the crowd to the first set of benches. He twirled her around and then set her down beside him. It was as if they were in their own protected bubble and nobody else was part of their world.

"I got the whole show for you," he said, indicating the tripod three rows above them. His voice felt husky. "All of it."

He gazed deeply into her eyes, and he seemed to get lost there. She licked her lips and tilted her head back. He was acutely aware of the heat of her body so close to his.

He bent and kissed her. She kissed him back, gladdening his heart. Her arms went up, around his neck, and he kissed her more deeply as he drew her closer to him.

He loved her. He'd never stopped loving her, but now, after this journey they'd been through together, he much better appreciated what she meant to him. He would never forget this moment. Would never take her presence for granted again.

Shyly, she drew away from him, blushing a bit, softly laughing. "I didn't mean to do that," she murmured into his ear. "I really didn't."

"Well, I did," he said. He kissed her cheek. "You were amazing, Emilie. You're always amazing, but choreographing this show was the best thing you've ever done for me."

Her cheeks flushed redder. "Is that what you think I did, Nathan?"

"Well, you did it for all of us, of course. For everybody. You know what I meant," he said, flustered. This wasn't coming out right.

"I have to go," she said, pointing to her skaters and laughing in delight. Everybody was hugging and kissing and jumping up and down for joy. "Isn't this incredible? I never thought I'd be part of such a fun show. This day was magical." As Emilie hopped back down to the ice, she blew a kiss at Nathan, performer-style, and Nathan couldn't help smiling even though she was leaving him.

And maybe the separation was only temporary. A plan was unfolding in his mind. A plan that would enable them to be together. A plan to keep his kids—and he thought of them as his kids—with a roof over their heads. A plan with Nell working beside them. And Martha and Frank and Claude…everyone would be employed.

Nathan stepped down to the path that separated the ice rink from the bleachers. Bounding past townspeople, shaking hands, nodding at old friends, he completed nearly a full lap around the rink before he found the one person he'd been looking for.

B.G. Richards, his minor investor. B.G. was standing with his wife beside the firepit, gazing thoughtfully at the ice as he listened to one of the firefighters.

Nathan greeted B.G's wife with a half hug and a "Hello." He caught B.G.'s eyes. B.G. clapped the firefighter on the back, and then headed over to Nathan's side.

"That was some performance," B.G. said. With his chin, he pointed toward the mass of humanity still mingling on the ice surface. "My kids are out there, playing."

"Did they enjoy the show?"

"Are you kidding? I'll be hearing about this for days. My daughter already told my wife that she wants skating lessons." He glanced at Nathan. "Too bad we couldn't set up a hockey league here for the kids who want to hockey skate, too."

Nathan stared hard at him. "You want to keep the inn open as is, don't you? Well, consider what a risk it might be to sell to out-of-towners, at any price. Who knows what they'd really do to the property? The locals would have no say. Am I right?"

B.G. averted his eyes. "It's not my decision," he said softly. "I'm not the majority investor."

"How come Rob didn't come out today? Nell said she invited everybody in town."

B.G. shrugged. "Probably didn't want to see it."

"Well, I know what will excite him."

"Ah…10 percent interest rates again?" B.G. cracked.

Nathan laughed. "Sorry, I'm not Santa Claus," he teased. Sobering, he added, "We've got two more weeks until Christmas. If I can convince Emilie to stay for the duration, she has two choreographed shows teed up and ready to go—this one and their traditional Christmas-themed show. What if we asked her to schedule one show per day, alternating shows, from now until Christmas Eve?"

"You think you can do that?"

"Yes, I believe I can." One thing that Emilie and Nell and the skating troupe had shown him was that, with enough belief, anything was possible.

"Well…" B.G. said cautiously. "I don't see why she would want to do it."

"I'll start by sweetening the pot for her skaters. They're taking a vote tonight about whether or not to stay—I have an idea for how to convince them. Several of them came to me asking for comped rooms for their families so they could be together for the holiday. That's what I'm going to give them."

"Rob won't be happy about that."

"That's too bad. I'm not happy with Rob, either."

A smile twitched on B.G.'s lips.

"In the meantime, I need you to find out who the potential buyers for the inn are," Nathan said. "That's critical to the plan."

"Are you going to try and buy them out?"

"No. On the contrary." Nathan realized now that his dream had to change and grow. Philip Prescott's legacy wasn't just this inn; it was the love he'd given Nathan and his sister. And honoring that love meant trying to do what he could to make sure Emilie's dream came true. So he had a plan to get Donnie and Lynn here for Christmas Eve. Nathan might not be able to save Prescott Inn, but Emilie could achieve her choreography dream.

She was great at it. Anyone could see that. And if he could engineer the meeting between her management team and a new potential owner of an ice rink...well, he was counting on good things happening for her.

"What are you going to do Nathan, if you don't have your grandfather's inn?"

"Well, the world needs itinerant accountants, too."

B.G.'s eyes bugged out. "Seriously?"

"Yeah." And Nathan felt perfectly content with this choice. His grandfather's dream didn't necessarily have to be his dream. It was time to make his own.

Emilie needed to travel in order to be a choreographer. Perhaps he could travel with her...

"Sounds like you've come full circle."

Maybe he had.

"Let's get started," he said to Rob.

Time to win back Emilie.

CHAPTER SEVENTEEN

AN HOUR LATER, the post-show cast party had moved to the downstairs lounge at Prescott Inn.

Nell arranged for a roaring fire to be laid in the fireplace. Julie—who knew how to operate most everything in the inn by now—set up a Christmas pop rock soundtrack from an internet streaming service. Music poured over the overhead stereo speakers.

The cast had unpacked the red-and-green boas from the prop bag for the Christmas show, and the three young women—minus Emilie and Katya—danced in unison to "Jingle Bell Rock." The shelter kids joined in, too. Katya and Sergei were sitting on the couch in the alcove—Katya with Jason's cat in her lap—and were speaking earnestly to each other as they drank spiked cranberry punch.

Nathan surveyed the scene, surprised to find he was enjoying himself. He'd grown to love being part of their revelry. He wasn't sure where Emilie was, but she had already taken the video card from the camera, and since Gary was missing, too, Nathan suspected they were reviewing the footage on Gary's laptop.

Good for her, he thought. He would do all he could to help Emilie achieve her dream.

Nathan beckoned Nell over to him. She stepped down from mischievously fastening a sprig of mistletoe over the doorway.

"I saw you kissing Emilie this afternoon," she said.

"And?" He grinned at his niece. He wasn't embarrassed at being caught. In fact, he wanted to keep the momentum going. "Look, Nell, I need you to help me." He hadn't been paying much attention to the skaters in Emilie's troupe, but that was going to change. "You and I are going to meet with Emilie's skaters. I want to influence them into voting to stay and perform until Christmas."

"How are you going to do that?"

"Bribery." He grinned wickedly at her. "We still have some rooms that haven't been booked from now until Christmas. I know some of the skaters had arranged for their families to meet them here for the holidays. I'm going to offer to comp these rooms for the skaters' families. It's the least we can do."

Nell's eyes widened. "You mean you're not giving up?"

"Nope."

"What about your investors group? What will they say?"

"I'll deal with them." Nathan gestured toward the door. "Shall we begin?"

"Yes!"

They both trotted up the stairs, toward his office.

"I'm sorry I didn't think of something like this earlier," he confided to her. "I was so hung up on cutting expenses, I missed the forest for the trees."

"I have an idea, too, Uncle!" Nell gave him a brilliant grin. "If we get the skaters to stay, then we should double down to make sure and pack the stands with people at *every* performance. Our whole focus will now be on selling tickets rather than booking rooms. Packed stands will make Emilie look even better to her bosses."

"I like it," he mused.

"There have to be day trippers within driving range that we can target. Let's get the skaters to help get the word out. Did you know some of them have blogs and mailing lists? And they *all* have social media. And..." She clapped her hand to her mouth. "What if they make cold calls with us, too? To past customers who've indicated that they like skating—remember those marketing cards I kept last year?—well, those people who indicated they were interested in skating might really get a kick out of talking to real, live champion ice-skaters. Especially if they've got kids who are fans." But Nell wasn't finished. "Uncle, we could organize special meet-and-greets, too! For the skaters who are willing, of course." She smiled apologetically. "But you know what I mean. It's like when you go to a live concert, there's an option to buy special VIP passes."

"You're amazing, Nell," he said to her. "Have I told you that lately?"

"Not nearly enough," Nell said.

"Well, that's gonna change." He opened the door to his office and gestured for her to lead the way to the computer. "You *are* amazing."

"And you, Uncle, have found Christmas spirit! At last!"

Nathan guffawed at that one. But maybe Nell was right. And Emilie had a whole lot to do with that. Maybe everything.

"In any event," he said to Nell, "bring the skaters to my office. We'll talk to them up here.

Try to make their absence inconspicuous with Emilie, okay?"

"Oh," Nell said, understanding. "This is going to be a surprise!"

"Yes, for Emilie." He nodded. "I want Emilie to get the Christmas present that she deserves."

EMILIE STOOD IN her bathroom, the door closed. She felt like knocking her head against the mirror.

What had she done, kissing Nathan like that?

The hardest part was that it had felt right at the time. Maybe it was the excitement of the afternoon—the after-performance glow—but when she'd seen him smiling for her, loving her, she just couldn't resist expressing the love in her own heart. The barrier between them had faded. His pure heart was all she'd seen.

Now, under the cold fluorescent lighting in the hotel bathroom, she cleaned her stage makeup off her face and combed the glitter from her hair. This was reality again. She was a skater and hopefully someday a choreographer, and as such, she needed to travel. Nathan would never leave his inn, his town, his community. He was the kind of guy who wanted roots, not moving from place to place.

Nathan had said he loved her, and she believed him. She loved him, too. His strength. His caring. His humility.

But with the parents he'd had, he could never go on the road, or be with someone who was constantly traveling.

Viciously, she scrubbed at the heavy rouge on her cheeks, willing it to come off. It wasn't fair—she really did love him. She loved his funny ways, his loyalty to what he believed in, his kindness toward Nell and the kids who lived in the inn.

She and Nathan did share a lot of values in common. But ultimately, they wanted different things.

She changed out of her skating dress and hung it on the shower rod, probably for the last time. Sadness permeated her.

She put on a pair of soft cotton yoga pants, the warm red sweater she wore far too often these days and a fluffy pair of wool socks.

Gary was waiting for her in the main part of the room. He sat at the desk with his laptop turned on. "I've already started reviewing the footage. Whoever recorded our show did a good job."

"That would be Nathan." Emilie dragged over a chair and sat beside Gary. "Let's check the footage before we send it on to Lynn's email account."

"Already did that while you were getting changed," Gary said. He'd taken off the "Philip Prescott" beard, but he still wore his skating pants and shirt. "It looks good, except…you might want to cut this part."

Emilie swallowed. Was her kiss with Nathan on tape?

Gary stopped the footage, pressed a button and let it run.

"Oh," she said, relieved to see the moments after the show. "This is when the kids mobbed the ice after the music stopped."

"Technically, it's not part of the performance."

"Leave it," she said. "Let Lynn and Donnie see how the audience enjoyed themselves."

"And it was only a dress rehearsal," Gary marveled.

"It was more than that." To Emilie, it was proof that she could enjoy herself and do what she loved.

She got out her phone and dialed up Lynn.

Her boss answered right away. "How did it go?"

"Great. Better than great. We're sending you the footage now."

"Thanks." Lynn cleared her throat, and then paused. "Emilie, I'll do what I can, but…"

But she wasn't optimistic.

"You should prepare yourself for…whatever comes next," Lynn said.

"I know." Emilie felt as if she'd climbed the heights and then plumbed the depths, all in one afternoon. She didn't have the heart to talk about her future anymore.

"I've decided to give the cast the option to vote on whether we stay through Christmas. Gary will call you later with the decision on whether we're staying or not, once he meets with the cast to take their vote."

"Fine," Lynn said. "I'll be waiting to hear."

Emilie hung up the phone. As she did, she felt deflated. She had absolutely no hope left.

Gary was staring at her, thoughtful.

"Is the tape uploaded to Lynn's email?" she asked him.

"Yes."

"Then please, I'd like you to be in charge of the vote. You know what mine is—I want to go home. I'm going to stay here and sleep."

Gary stood. "Okay…"

She went over and peeled back her bed covers as he opened the door and left. But before the door could close, there was another soft knock.

"Emilie?" It was Nell's voice.

Emilie rolled over. "If you need something, please see Gary."

"I want to see you."

"Why?"

Nell tentatively came over to her bedside. "Are you feeling okay?"

"Not really."

Nell touched her wrist to Emilie's forehead. Emilie couldn't remember the last time somebody had worried about *her*.

"You don't seem feverish. Is something else the matter?"

When Emilie didn't answer—what could she say?—Nell added, "There's a party going on in the lounge. Everybody's dancing. When I saw you weren't there, I was worried about you."

"I'm just not in the spirit for a party."

"Wow," Nell said. "You and my uncle have really switched places." She smiled wryly.

"Is Nathan dancing?" She found herself hoping that he was. *Nathan deserves enjoyment in his life*, she thought sadly.

"Oh, no." Nell laughed. "No, Nathan is up

in his office. He's bound and determined to work miracles for you, Emilie."

"Right. Let me know how that goes."

"I spotted you guys kissing," Nell said shyly. "Nathan is pretty happy about that."

"Nell, I'm sorry," Emilie murmured.

"Yes." Nell finally got the hint, and stood. "I understand. You're tired from the show."

"I'll see you tomorrow."

"Right. You have another show at three o'clock."

"Very funny," Emilie said.

"You really do. Your troupe voted to stay until Christmas."

"But the vote hasn't even been taken yet. Gary just left…"

"We've been talking to the skaters over the last hour or so, and the majority want to stay. Your and Gary's votes won't change the result. So I'll let you rest. You're going to need it!"

Nell departed and Emilie lay in bed, blinking. It *was* a miracle. And Nell had said *we*. What could have changed Nathan's mind?

THE NEXT AFTERNOON, Emilie spotted Nathan in the stands beside Nell again. Nell was once more in charge of special effects.

Each time Emilie had a moment during the

show—and sometimes even when she didn't have a moment—she looked through the crack in the curtain at Nathan.

He was so handsome, it made her heart hurt. His boyish hair was tangled by the wind, and he always seemed to be smiling. And when she skated, she felt only his eyes on her.

The next afternoon, when they skated the "Prescott Inn" show again, as they called it, Nathan was in the seat next to Nell again. This time, he wasn't taping them. He just watched.

For the past two days, he hadn't dressed in his business suit and tie. He'd been in casual clothes—corduroy pants and a rugged coat, the one that he'd let her wear that day when they'd walked home from the rink together.

After the show, he mingled with people by the sides of the boards. The stands were even more packed than they had been the day of the dress rehearsal, but Emilie had the sense that many of the audience members weren't local but were guests staying in the inn.

And the inn was *busy*. It certainly seemed to be more bustling these days. But Emilie, in her quest to avoid Nathan—and therefore the ache of eventual separation—went directly from show to her hotel room, each day.

By the week after the dress rehearsal, it was

an entrenched habit. Fewer and fewer problems were brought to her by her troupe members. Gary was the de facto ice captain. They even called him Ice Dad.

Emilie just felt relief. She wasn't responsible for anyone else any longer. Their drama didn't bother or affect her.

Every evening, after the show was over and she'd returned to her hotel room and taken off her makeup and her costume, Nell knocked on the door.

Two days before Christmas, Nell came in again. "Hello, Emilie," she said cheerfully.

She brought Emilie a tray with tea and sandwiches, the little, fancy kind that Emilie had grown to love.

Nell sat with Emilie while she ate, and Emilie didn't mind, because Nell never expected her to say much, just listen. And that was fine with Emilie.

Amid Nell's chatty news—and it was never news about the skaters, which Emilie appreciated—she always dropped a tidbit or two about what Nathan was up to.

"So, today he asked me to visit each of the children across the hall and ask them what they wanted from Santa. Jason still doesn't think that Santa will find him, which just makes Nathan more determined to surprise him."

Emilie put down her fancy teacup. "Nathan is playing Santa?"

"Oh, yes, Emilie." Nell nodded, wide-eyed. "He's such a different person—you can't imagine."

"But isn't he going to lose the inn?"

"Well, maybe, but is that a good reason to skip Christmas?"

"I should say so," Emilie murmured, sipping her tea. Each day was a different blend. Today was herbal—spicy cinnamon, in honor of the coming holiday.

"Christmas should never be skipped." Nell shook her head vehemently. "I'm surprised at you," she chided.

"I'm just tired. I'm telling you honestly how I feel." Emilie warmed her hand over the teapot. "How is Nathan?"

"He made the tea for you. Would you like to see him?"

A lump grew in Emilie's throat. Nathan always had gone up on deck for tea with her on the ship, after her shows at the ice studio.

"Has he been making the tea for me *every* night?"

"Yes. But I wasn't supposed to tell you that."

"*Why* is he being so good to me when I'm not being good to anybody right now?"

"He loves you," Nell said simply. "And who says you always have to be the one who takes care of everybody else? Maybe it's okay sometimes for people to take care of you. And, maybe it's okay to take care of *yourself* when you need to, don't you think?"

"Is that what Nathan says?"

But Nell just smiled and stood. "I'll see you tomorrow, after the show?"

"Tomorrow is Christmas Eve. The last performance." They were performing the traditional show.

"Yes, I know that. Will you be there?"

"I have to. I'm in it."

"Be on your best game," Nell said.

"What does that mean?"

"Nothing." Nell smiled mysteriously.

"What have you done?"

"Me?" Nell gave Emilie an innocent look. "It's not me who's taking care of you. I told you, it's Nathan."

NATHAN STOOD AT center ice on Christmas Eve. It was the last show that the *Empress Caribbean* ice-skaters were performing at Prescott Inn. The stands were completely full. The *inn* was completely full. And he had invited a stable of VIPs and sat them at a bench at mid-ice for the best view. But right now, he was trying not to think about them.

Instead, Nathan roared out his best Santa Claus imitation. "Ho! Ho! Ho!" he called. Nathan was dressed in a rented red Santa suit, complete with white beard, hat and a belly stuffed with two small pillows, which he thought looked silly but Nell assured him was absolutely necessary for the costume. On his feet, Nathan wore hockey skates.

Gary and Curtis pushed out a small sleigh on runners that Guy had found in the back shed. The sleigh was piled high with presents. Nathan had done his best to make sure that each child staying at the inn—whether guest or resident—had a present with his or her name on it.

Julie and Rosie had wrapped everything. They'd resolved their differences in the spirit of Christmas, as had Katya and Sergei, and Curtis and Lynette.

"Ho! Ho! Ho!" Nathan called the kids forward. One by one, they leaned over the rail and Nathan—with assistance from the skater elves—passed them their presents. Nathan found that he loved playing Santa. He'd financed it all himself, and it was giving him great joy.

The last child that Nathan called up was Jason. Nathan was a bit nervous that Jason would recognize him—the boy believed in Santa Claus, after all—but Jason was so starstruck with his wrapped present that he didn't notice. There were more presents for the little boy back in Maria's room, too. Nathan had gone a bit overboard with his generosity for all the "shelter" kids, coordinating sponsors and purchasing bags of clothing and shoes and outerwear.

"You found me, Santa," Jason whispered before leaving the ice. Of Nathan's journey during the past year, this child's happiness was one of the things Nathan most dearly treasured.

"And now for the skaters," Nathan announced. This was a surprise for them. Nell had helped him out by doing the shopping. He'd assisted by attempting to wrap the packages, even though he was a terrible giftwrapper. But he'd tried.

Nell had assured him that the skaters would most love to receive gift certificates so they could choose personal items to replace what they'd lost in the sinking. Nathan called each skater's name, one by one, and they stepped forward to receive a cheer from the audience *and* a gift from Santa.

Emilie's present was last of all. Nathan had planned it that way. She hung back from the rest of the troupe, quiet, but he'd known where she was. He always knew where she was. It saddened him that she wasn't feeling herself these days—she'd been shy and withdrawn— but he wasn't going to give up on her. Nell assured Nathan that she needed the time to regenerate.

"Emilie O'Shea," Nathan called out. She skated over to him. She was wearing her skater elf costume, which just made the audience cheer all that much harder. Emilie blushed when she approached him.

They hadn't really spoken much since the afternoon they'd kissed.

He spoke low, so only she could hear him. "There are two people sitting in the audience for you today."

Her brow furrowed. "My mom and sister just talked to me before the show. They both said they're in Florida."

True. Emilie's mom hadn't wanted to fly this year. Nathan had offered her a room, but she'd declined.

Many of the skaters had parents and family

in the audience. Emilie hadn't yet put two-and-two together as to why this was so—Nathan was arranging it—but Nathan didn't mind. She also hadn't yet realized who *her* two guests might be.

"I was speaking of Lynn Bladewell and Donnie Ryan," Nathan said. The presence of Emilie's bosses was what she'd most wanted. He understood that.

Emilie's face drained of blood. Her hand went to her lips. "They're here for me?"

"Yes. I invited them to come and they accepted. Donnie is here for the holiday with his family, but Lynn is flying home tonight. I told your skaters—so they would be sure to perform extra-well for them, but I wanted to surprise you." He peered at her, trying to gauge her expression. "Did I make a mistake? Should I have told you about this earlier?"

Her eyes seemed to be tearing up. She blinked rapidly. "No, Nathan. You didn't make a mistake." She placed her hand to her heart.

Relieved, he gave her the gift he'd picked out for her. "Merry Christmas, Emilie," he murmured into her ear. Not even Nell knew what was inside the small box he pressed into her hands.

EMILIE CLASPED THE red foil-wrapped box with trembling fingers. Nathan had touched her heart with his love and kindness. Lynn and Donnie, *here*? He'd actually gotten them to agree to come—this could only be good for her! Surely they would want to speak to her about her future now!

And though Emilie had initially been sad that her mom didn't want to fly, this made her feel better. Nathan was going out of his way to understand her and to show her she was important to him.

And the gift, too, was a surprise. The package was bigger than a ring box—it certainly wasn't *that*—but whatever it was, the present wasn't a boxed gift certificate, either.

Emilie stepped back into line, clutching her gift to her chest. Nathan picked up the microphone and invited everyone back to the inn for a Christmas Eve ball in the evening.

Tomorrow, Christmas Day, the restaurant was open. Through Gary, Emilie had learned that Nathan and Nell were hosting a Christmas dinner for all of the workers at the inn, their families, and the skaters and their family members on hand in the restaurant's private dining room.

The dinner was scheduled for one o'clock

and would be cooked and served by a contracted catering firm. Emilie hadn't been sure whether she was going to attend or not.

But since Nathan had invited Lynn and Donnie, that meant they were invited to the dinner, too. That still shocked her.

She didn't have time to think more about it. After "Santa's" announcement, the audience filled the ice surface. They'd all been told to bring their skates to the performance so they could go around the rink with the cast after the show. There were quite a few kids, and her troupe was kept busy.

Taking advantage of the hubbub behind her, Emilie slipped around the stage curtain. In a place of privacy, she opened the gift Nathan had given her.

On a delicate gold chain was a tiny golden figure skate, and in the center, a great big ruby.

Tears sprang to her eyes and rolled down her cheeks. The pendant was beautiful. Nathan was replacing the special gift he'd given her on their two-month anniversary—the necklace that had gone down with the ship.

Emilie took the delicate chain and clasped it around her neck. With her hand to her throat, she knew at last, to the core of her heart, what it was that she wanted, and what would make her happy.

It was time to let go permanently of her need to take care of her troupe.

She didn't need another troupe, or even an audience.

She wanted Nathan, who'd given her space enough to learn just how she wanted to choreograph her own life. He respected her dream.

She wanted to go with Nathan, wherever he landed. If he managed to win back his inn, then she would be the Ava to his Philip, if he would have her.

If he didn't end up with Prescott Inn, she would go where he went. There were all kinds of ice rinks in the world. The world needed self-determined skaters who stayed put, too.

Then she noticed the note in the bottom of the box.

Dear Emilie,

I hope that all you desire becomes yours.

Best,
Nathan

She found a tissue and blotted the tears from her eyes—thankful she was wearing waterproof mascara—and got herself together. She still had to meet with Lynn and Donnie.

NATHAN WAS DISAPPOINTED that he didn't see Emilie later that evening.

Nell went on a reconnaissance mission looking for Emilie, and returned to inform Nathan that she was dining privately with her boss, Lynn.

He'd realized this might happen. He'd flown Lynn in as part of Emilie's Christmas gift, after all.

"Thanks, Nell," he said quietly. "I forgot to ask what you'll do if it turns out the inn can't be saved." They still hadn't heard from B.G. as to whom the inn's buyers might be.

"I'm a marketing manager," Nell said. "What did you think I would do?"

"Sorry." He smiled at her. "You've been a fantastic marketing manager for me. I should have known better than to ask."

"Well, I might need a glowing recommendation letter from you, and soon, so don't go too far," she joked.

He laughed. "I almost forgot. Here's your

Christmas present." He passed Nell a box he'd wrapped himself. "As you can see, I couldn't figure out how to put a ribbon on it properly."

His niece laughed adoringly. "May I open it?"

"Please."

She ripped it open like a little kid and then lifted the lid on the antique velvet jewelry box.

"Ooh, this is so beautiful! You shouldn't have, Uncle Nathan." With awe, she lifted one of the jeweled earrings from the box. "I swear, no one can ever call you Scrooge again."

He laughed good-naturedly. "Actually, Nell, those belonged to your grandmother. I found them when I was cleaning out a dresser in the attic. Maybe Ava set them aside for repair and then forgot about them. In any event, I had some missing stones replaced and the earrings cleaned and polished."

Nell fastened them in her ears and then ran to a mirror to admire them. "They're stunning!"

"I wish you'd met her."

"I feel like I have met Ava, thanks to Emilie's ice show."

Emilie. Nathan's smile faltered. He had to wait for her to come to him. If there was one lesson he'd learned, it was to give her time to decide what she wanted.

In the meantime, there was a ball to attend. "Nell, will you host the Prescott Inn Christmas ball with me tonight?"

"Of course I will, Uncle. And Christmas dinner tomorrow?"

"Actually, I'm serving as a waiter tomorrow. The caterer needed help, and I feel it's the least I can do."

"A waiter?" Nell blinked at him, but Nathan just shrugged.

"It's part of owning an inn. Besides, this will be our last official day open for business as Prescott Inn. I may as well savor every moment of it before it's gone."

"Are you *sure* it's not going to work out with the inn?"

"I still don't know who the buyers are. If you can think of a way to make *that* work, then please, by all means, let me know."

But it was Rob himself—Nathan's major investor—who stopped by the Christmas ball to let Nathan know.

Nathan saw Rob in the vestibule shaking snowflakes from his cap.

"You came," Nathan said, approaching the

bank president and escorting him into the lobby.

"You invited me," Rob replied in a low voice.

"Yes, and it's my personal money I'm spending for the night's entertainment," Nathan informed him.

"Yes, I understand." Rob bent his head. "I wanted you to know that the deal to sell Prescott Inn has been finalized. The new owner represents a large chain of hotels. They plan to change the name of the inn and rebrand the public rooms."

Nathan sucked in his breath. He shouldn't have been surprised by the news, but still, it hurt. Try as he might, it was difficult to see how he could continue to influence or advocate for the good of the townspeople with this decision.

"So, the facility will definitely be kept open as a business?" he finally asked.

"Yes, Nathan." Rob cleared his throat. "B.G. Richards will be working with the new CEO on the transition process. You'll hear more about it in the coming days."

Nathan relaxed somewhat. It was best to remain optimistic and trust that B.G. would keep his eye out for the community's and the kids' best interests.

Still, Nathan wondered what would happen to him and Emilie now? Was this really the end?

CHAPTER EIGHTEEN

Christmas Day at Prescott Inn

EMILIE READ THE title of the dinner menu that the waitress had passed her. She was a temp waitress, hired for the day, and Nell had whispered to Emilie in greeting earlier that this was the last day the inn would remain open "as it was," at least for the foreseeable future.

Emilie felt choked up. It was a sad day for Nathan and also for Nell, the staff and the shelter families. Prescott Inn would be no more.

From her position at a dining table with Donnie, his wife and two well-behaved preteens, Emilie had the perfect view across the dining room. A large group of twelve had just vacated, and Nathan—Nathan!—was bent over, clearing the dirty dishes from the table into a plastic dishwasher's bucket.

Donnie caught her gazing at Nathan. "Who is he?"

"Nathan Prescott," she murmured.

"Did you know, he wrote you the most glowing review I've ever had a client give an employee?"

"Did he?" Emilie asked, surprised.

"He convinced me."

"Convinced you of what?"

Donnie patted her shoulder. "Today is Christmas. It's not the time or place to talk about job offers for top-shelf choreographers." But he gave her a wink as he picked up his fork and knife and tucked into his turkey dinner.

Emilie could only stare at him. He was offering her a choreographer's job? Two weeks ago, she would have done anything to have heard those words. And Nathan had helped make it happen.

Emilie dabbed her lips with her napkin and nodded to Donnie as she stood. "Excuse me," she said, reaching for her small purse and tucking it beneath her arm.

She'd waited too long to go to Nathan. But now it was time.

"Shall we order you anything else?" Donnie's wife asked her.

"No, thank you."

"How about coffee?"

"No, I'll just finish my water when I return." She smiled gratefully at them—how could she not? They'd just given her a generous offer. Her dream had come true, actually.

But her mind was on Nathan. She made her way over to the table where he worked.

She placed her purse down and began to help him, picking up a dirty water glass and placing it in the bucket.

He saw her and blinked. Emilie caught a wave of hope that passed over his handsome features.

"Merry Christmas, Emilie," he said warmly.

"Merry Christmas, Nathan." Her voice caught, and she touched her fingers to her lips. "I'm sorry." She waved her hand. "It's just emotional to me that your family inn is closing."

He smiled sadly, but resumed clearing the water glasses. "I had a last-ditch plan, and we did our best, but it didn't quite work out the way I'd hoped. Still, all might not be lost."

"What about the kids?" she asked.

"They had a nice Christmas. Go upstairs after dinner and look at all the stockings hanging by the fireplace."

"Jason's, too?"

"Jason's, too." Nathan smiled. "The boy is in heaven. It was worth it."

He pointed to a table in the corner. Jason sat

with his mom, and the boy had a smile that went from ear to ear as he played with a Lego set. Prescott sat at Jason's feet and was lapping at a bowl of milk.

Emilie's voice caught in a sob.

"Hey!" Nathan reached over and touched her hand. "Buck up! We haven't given up hope that the new owners will work with the homeless shelter to give the families a place."

"You…completely surprise me, Nathan."

"Because I've decided to embrace optimism?" He smiled at her. "I find I rather like it."

She swallowed. "I'm sorry I've been holed up in my hotel room for the past two weeks."

"You have nothing to apologize for."

"I needed the time to think about what was important to me."

Nathan's hand stilled. "And what did you decide, Emilie?"

She wiped her eyes with a tissue. "May we go upstairs, please? I'd like to see the Christmas stockings by the fireplace."

He grinned at her. "Of course."

He took her hand and they went together upstairs.

There, in the lobby of what would always be Prescott Inn to her, by the great stone fireplace beside the trimmed Christmas tree sparkling with lights, were a row of Christmas stockings tacked up along the mantel.

Emilie saw Jason's stocking, plus five other stockings with different children's names. She also saw a battered old stocking that read "Nathan," and a newer one for Nell. And at the end was a stocking that read "Emilie."

"You put one up for me!" she said.

"Of course we did. You're part of our family."

Crying, she took it down and saw that inside were candy canes and a chocolate Santa, along with some colorfully wrapped packages that were a total surprise.

She went to Nathan and let him enclose her in his arms. "I love you, Nathan," she said, snuggling against his broad chest and inhaling the scent of his soap.

"Wait a minute." He gazed into her eyes. "Did you just say you love me?"

"I certainly did." She reached up and touched his slightly scratchy cheek. "These past weeks, I've thought a lot about myself and where my home is and what I want in my life. It's not my job to make everyone happy. I've realized that. I need to make myself happy first before I can begin to help anyone else. And being with you, Nathan, makes me happy."

"It does?"

She nodded. "I'm turning down the job that Donnie's offering. Or will offer. He technically hasn't even discussed it with me."

"But...I don't have anything for you. I don't even own an outdoor rink anymore."

"That's not what's important to me. We'll make a place together. That's what's important."

He drew her into his arms and kissed her.

Clapping and cheers rang out around them, and she realized they had an audience.

"Nathan!" A man interrupted them. "There you are."

"Emilie," Nathan said, "let me introduce you to B.G. Richards, a member of the former ownership team at Prescott Inn."

"I'm pleased to meet you," Emilie said.

"Hello, Emilie. I've heard a lot about you. Merry Christmas!" Then B.G. turned to Nathan, excited. "The new owners want to hire you as general manager! Joel is in the private dining room with us, and he's ready to talk. He's asked for you to be there for the discussions."

"Wow," Nathan murmured. "Joel Desroches

is CEO for the international chain that's buying Prescott Inn. They own convention centers and business retreats around the world."

"So…he would sell business meetings for his clients at Prescott Inn?" Emilie asked.

"Yep," Nathan said. "We're close to golf courses in summer and skiing in winter."

"And the popular ice shows," B.G. interjected. "That's what really attracted him to the property in the first place—the venue is unique. He wants to upgrade it and make it even more luxurious and intimate. His family has been with him at your last two shows." He guffawed. To Emilie he explained, "We were ragging on Nathan for insisting on busing tables today. Turns out that's what most impressed Joel Desroches about Nathan—that he's the kind of manager who'll do whatever it takes to get the job done."

B.G. looked at Emilie. "Joel might also need a skating director."

"Yes, I believe he will," Nathan realized.

"Hmm," Emilie teased. "I'll have to think about it."

Then she turned to Nathan and wrapped her arms around his neck, rising on tiptoe to kiss him.

"I still have your engagement ring in my

safe upstairs, if you want it," Nathan whispered into her ear.

"You kept it?"

"Of course."

Emilie chuckled low in her throat. But he saw the tears of happiness in her eyes. "You're going to have to give me a better proposal than that, Nathan Prescott."

"Shall I go on my knees here, in the lobby?"

"That would be a nice start."

Nathan obliged. It was Christmas after all, and Emilie deserved a perfect one.

* * * * *

Get 4 FREE REWARDS!

We'll send you 2 FREE Books plus 2 FREE Mystery Gifts.

Love Inspired® books feature contemporary inspirational romances with Christian characters facing the challenges of life and love.

FREE Value Over **$20**

Get 4 FREE REWARDS!

We'll send you 2 FREE Books plus 2 FREE Mystery Gifts.

Love Inspired® Suspense books feature Christian characters facing challenges to their faith... and lives.

FREE Value Over $20

2018 CHRISTMAS ROMANCE COLLECTION!

You'll get TWO FREE GIFTS & TWO FREE BOOKS in your first shipment, plus a trade paperback by *New York Times* bestselling author RaeAnne Thayne!

This collection is packed with holiday romances by internationally famous *USA TODAY* and *New York Times* bestselling authors!

Get 4 FREE REWARDS!

We'll send you 2 FREE Books plus 2 FREE Mystery Gifts.

FREE Value Over **$20**

Both the **Romance** and **Suspense** collections feature compelling novels written by many of today's best-selling authors.

YES! Please send me 2 FREE novels from the Essential Romance or Essential Suspense Collection and my 2 FREE gifts (gifts are worth about $10 retail). After receiving them, if I don't wish to receive any more books, I can return the shipping statement marked "cancel." If I don't cancel, I will receive 4 brand-new novels every month and be billed just $6.74 each in the U.S. or $7.24 each in Canada. That's a savings of at least 16% off the cover price. It's quite a bargain! Shipping and handling is just 50¢ per book in the U.S. and 75¢ per book in Canada.* I understand that accepting the 2 free books and gifts places me under no obligation to buy anything. I can always return a shipment and cancel at any time. The free books and gifts are mine to keep no matter what I decide.

Choose one: ☐ **Essential Romance**
(194/394 MDN GMY7)

☐ **Essential Suspense**
(191/391 MDN GMY7)

Name (please print)

Address   Apt. #

City   State/Province   Zip/Postal Code

Mail to the **Reader Service:**
IN U.S.A.: P.O. Box 1341, Buffalo, NY 14240-8531
IN CANADA: P.O. Box 603, Fort Erie, Ontario L2A 5X3

Want to try 2 free books from another series? Call 1-800-873-8635 or visit www.ReaderService.com.

*Terms and prices subject to change without notice. Prices do not include sales taxes, which will be charged (if applicable) based on your state or country of residence. Canadian residents will be charged applicable taxes. Offer not valid in Quebec. This offer is limited to one order per household. Books received may not be as shown. Not valid for current subscribers to the Essential Romance or Essential Suspense Collection. All orders subject to approval. Credit or debit balances in a customer's account(s) may be offset by any other outstanding balance owed by or to the customer. Please allow 4 to 6 weeks for delivery. Offer available while quantities last.

Your Privacy—The Reader Service is committed to protecting your privacy. Our Privacy Policy is available online at www.ReaderService.com or upon request from the Reader Service. We make a portion of our mailing list available to reputable third parties that offer products we believe may interest you. If you prefer that we not exchange your name with third parties, or if you wish to clarify or modify your communication preferences, please visit us at www.ReaderService.com/consumerschoice or write to us at Reader Service Preference Service, P.O. Box 9062, Buffalo, NY 14240-9062. Include your complete name and address.

STRS19R

READERSERVICE.COM

Manage your account online!

- Review your order history
- Manage your payments
- Update your address

*We've designed the
Reader Service website
just for you.*

Enjoy all the features!

- Discover new series available to you, and read excerpts from any series.
- Respond to mailings and special monthly offers.
- Browse the Bonus Bucks catalog and online-only exclusives.
- Share your feedback.

Visit us at:
ReaderService.com